Interview with a Jewish Vampire

A Novel

Erica Manfred

Published by Fredonia Communications
19 Mosher Place
West Hurley, NY 12491

ISBN-13: 978-0-9710968-1-3

This is a work of fiction.
All characters and incidents are imaginary,
and any resemblance to any real person,
living or dead, is entirely coincidental.

To my late mom, Freda, and the "goils."

Acknowledgments

I am eternally grateful to my writers' critique group: Rachel Pollack, Carla Reuben, Cynthia Sinharoy, Linda Gravenson Geuthe, Jillen Lowe, and Sharon Doane, without whose appreciation, laughter and incisive editorial suggestions this book would never have been conceived or written. I also want to acknowledge my editor, Chris Noel, who "got" what I was doing (despite being a goy) and helped me turn this book into a fully realized novel.

Preface

I've always been a vampire fan. I remember the delicious terror of watching Bela Lugosi and Christopher Lee movies on late night TV in the 1950s, when I was babysitting—alone—curled up on a couch in the basement of a suburban ranch after putting the kids to bed. The movies were usually hosted by the wonderfully campy Vampira or Zacherly.

My favorite vampire novel was *Dracula* by Bram Stoker, because that's the only vampire novel there was, until Anne Rice's *Interview with a Vampire* came along. No one before or since has ever imagined such an intricate, brilliant vampire world or written such gorgeous gothic prose. Anne Rice's fabulous undead creatures with their tortured souls and intense relationships mesmerized me. I fell for vampires and fell hard; a love affair that never ended.

Then vampires became a craze, and I became a fan of *Buffy* and *Twilight*. But as I got older I noticed that vampires kept getting younger. Most were in high school. Why would a vampire want to go to high school, I wondered? Most of us can't wait until we get out of that hell. Rice's vampires were adults, some of them even middle-aged when they were turned. I started wondering why vampires had to be young. I know teenagers are a lot prettier than geezers, and if you're going to live forever you want to look good, but kids don't fantasize about living forever. They think they're going to live forever anyway. It's us old folks who know we're not immortal, and as death approaches maybe we'd like a second chance.

It occurred to my twisted brain that turning the genre on its head, with old vampires preying on the young, would be fun. The idea for *Interview with a Jewish Vampire* came from a fantasy of saving my mother from dying in her eighties, and still having her and her friends around to schmooze with. I wanted to pay homage to Anne Rice in a way that she might appreciate if she had a Jewish sense of humor (which, who knows, she might, even though she's Catholic). I imagined what would happen if Anne Rice and Mel Brooks had gotten drunk one night at Grossingers and collaborated on a vampire novel. *Interview with a Jewish Vampire* is the result.

Chapter One

"So nu?" asked the vampire thoughtfully, as he sat down next to me at the Mitzvah bar on Orchard Street. "You must be Rhoda?" He'd picked me out of a line-up of twenty-somethings. I didn't know whether to be flattered or insulted.

We had met through JDate. I was a Jewish divorcee of forty-one who claimed to be thirty-five and might be considered zaftig if you defined that liberally. He had been dead for a long time but I didn't know that right away. I just thought he was pale. An undead double for Jeff Goldblum, he was tall, slender, with a mischievous smile, flashing green eyes and long black hair. His incisors were kind of pointy when he smiled and his skin was pasty white, but that didn't put me off. Everyone looked pretty sallow in the dead of winter in New York City. I immediately wondered if I could drag him off to my lair later that night.

Despite the fact that I had a pretty face, I didn't get a lot of action on JDate because I had checked "a few extra pounds" in the body-size box. "A few" was an understatement, which is why I always met dates at night in bars. I wore black and got there first so they would see me sitting down. My face was a lot slimmer than the rest of me. Jewish guys were the worst when it came to weight— and everything else. Only a Jewish supermodel who ran a law firm was good enough for the Jewish princes I met on JDate.

I was perched on a barstool too teeny to accommodate my rear end, which spilled over the edges. I peered at everyone else's barstools and felt worse seeing all those visible edges. I decided that from now on my goal in life would be to sit on a barstool and be able to see the edges. I tugged on my low-cut tunic top trying in vain to hide the bulges between chest and crotch which seemed to have a mind of their own, ballooning out despite my best efforts. At least I was showing some cleavage, my best physical attribute. He rescued me from what was rapidly becoming a severe fat attack.

"So, you're a journalist..." he said, putting his elbow on the bar and turning towards me. I had listed that profession on my profile. "Do you have a tape recorder with you?" he asked, not realizing I suppose that tape was so last century and reporters now carried digital recorders.

"Why do you ask?" Men had asked me a lot of strange opening questions on first dates but whether I had a tape recorder was not one of them.

"I would like to tell the story of my life." He leaned forward and gave me such an intense look I had to turn away. "Would you be willing to interview me?"

No, I wasn't interested in the story of his life. I was interested in getting to know him in a more biblical sense. I figured he was just another narcissistic celebrity wannabe. As a writer, I was constantly getting hit on--not by attractive men--but by people who thought their lives were so fascinating they would make surefire bestseller material. All they thought they needed was a writer to tell their story which, of course, I would be thrilled to do on spec because they didn't have any money. None of them realized that writers are not charitable institutions.

"You will want to write my story," he said urgently, "You've never heard anything like it before. It will make you rich and famous."

"Sure, sure. So what's so special about your story?" I asked wearily, disappointed that he was only interested in my writing skills, not my body.

"I'm a vampire," he said matter-of-factly.

"Sure, and I'm the Queen of the Damned."

"What will convince you?" he asked.

"Hmm. Hold on a minute," I said, playing along. I dragged a cross out of my purse, which I happened to have because I'd visited St. Patrick's Cathedral with my niece earlier that day and got one for free. I held it up in front of him.

"I'm a Jewish vampire. Doesn't do a thing for me."

"How about a Jewish star?"

"Don't be silly, only Christians are afraid of the devil."

I dragged out a mirror and held it in front of his face. No reflection. He said '*Ah*' and the mirror didn't fog up. When he opened his mouth, I saw that his long incisors were, in fact, fangs. I shrank back, not thrilled about the notion of becoming dinner. I looked more closely at him, noting that like Anne Rice's Louis, he was utterly white and smooth, as if he were sculpted from bleached bone, with brilliant green eyes that looked like flames in a skull. Unlike Louis, however, he was not wearing a finely tailored black coat but an overly long shlumpy one that looked like it came from the nineteenth century without a stop at the cleaners along the way. His full black hair, with waves combed over the tips of the ears and curls that barely touched the edge of his white collar, made me long to touch it. He was one handsome dude although his wardrobe could use some help.

"So," he said, "ask me some questions."

He certainly had piqued my curiosity, so I decided to go ahead and interview him. If he really was a vampire, I'd have the scoop of the century, if anyone believed me. If not, at least I'd have the opportunity to flirt with a good-looking guy. Maybe I should have been more frightened, but I'd interviewed many dangerous types, including serial killers, so I was pretty nonchalant about the risk involved.

Plus my life had been seriously lacking in drama lately and here was an opportunity for a little excitement.

I pulled out my pen and started making notes.

"Wait a minute," he said, sounding upset. "I thought you were going to record this"

"I am recording it. This pen is a digital recorder." I showed him my latest reporter's gadget. "As I write, it records, so I can play back any part I want."

"That would have come in handy in Hebrew class when I was a kid. I was always getting lost during the rabbi's Talmud commentary. Too bad I had to use a quill pen."

He wanted me to give him a pseudonym so I'm calling him "Sheldon" after my ex-husband, who was a bloodsucker if ever there was one.

"I didn't know there were any Jewish vampires." Actually, I didn't know there were any vampires at all, but I was suspending disbelief for the moment.

"Vy not a vampire? Vy a duck? Just kidding. I miss Groucho. We used to hang out at Grossingers in the heyday of the Borscht Belt."

I laughed. In addition to being a hottie, he was a regular vampire comedian. You never know what will turn up on JDate.

Then he reached out over the bar towards me. I automatically recoiled. He clamped an icy hand on my shoulder and said, "Believe me, I won't hurt you."

"I'm not worried," I said, wishing he did want to hurt me—just a little bit, not fatally of course. "I've interviewed worse than you. I once interviewed John Gotti. Now *he* was scary."

"I met Meyer Lansky once. He didn't scare me a bit."

I shook my head in bewilderment. I couldn't imagine why anyone would scare him, but then maybe he was a wussy vampire.

4

"How did you become a vampire?" I asked, playing along, while I made notes.

"I was a rabbi who was killed by the original Count Dracula, Vlad the Impaler. You didn't know Dracula was an anti-Semite, did you? He thought it would be amusing to turn a Jewish rabbi into a vampire. I mean we Jews have the strictest rules about what's kosher and forcing a rabbi to drink blood, well, that was his idea of a joke. He didn't laugh for long. Little did he know that I'd still be around a hundred years later and he'd be staked in his coffin by rampaging villagers. Dracula was just too obvious, what with that cape and that nasty-looking *punim.*"

"So how did *you* get away with living as a vampire? Didn't people notice?"

"I had a big advantage as a Jewish vampire. I was a Hasidic Jew at the time I became a vampire and so naturally blended in. The last thing I wanted was anyone knowing the truth about me. Once people start being afraid of you, you're at the mercy of hordes of villagers wielding wooden stakes and opening coffins. We Hassidim already are very pale; we turn mirrors to the wall, don't wield crosses and wear black. As for garlic, I was so used to it in Jewish cooking it didn't bother me at all. Jewish services begin at sunset so that's convenient. You can be a teenager forever in eighteenth-century black hats and black clothes--you always look old. You can drink blood instead of wine and no one will notice that you don't eat. You can refuse food on the grounds that it's not kosher enough. No one will argue. It's a great cover."

"Didn't you feel guilty about killing people and draining their blood?" I hoped he had some restraint. I might have been sexually starved but I wasn't suicidal.

"Did they feel guilty about killing us all these years? I don't think so. I preyed on the anti-Semites and let me tell you, I never ran out of blood--until recently. It's not so fashionable to kill Jews these days. Actually I don't kill people anymore," he sighed. "I stick to animal blood these days. It doesn't taste so good but at least I don't hate myself in the morning. If I were going to suck human blood today I'd stick to the goyim or Republicans. I wanted to hunt some of George W.'s born again buddies, especially the ones waiting for the Rapture. They think they're going to be transported right up to heaven. Hah! They'll be in for a big surprise when they find the big guy in the sky is a rabbi, just like me. Why do you think he has a long gray beard? In fact, just wait till Mel Gibson gets there. Actually, he might get there sooner than he thinks if I have anything to do with it. *Passion of the Christ*, what a *shanda*. That movie was the work of a man obsessed with blood and he's not even a vampire, and he never will be or we'd all be in trouble."

"I voted for Obama myself," I told him reassuringly. "Did you vote for him?"

"No, I'm an illegal alien. I can't even get a Green Card, much less become a citizen. The immigration office is closed at night."

"If you're a Hasid where is your beard?" He was clean-shaven, without a trace of five o'clock shadow.

"I shaved it, of course. Do you think I'd show up for a date looking like Charlton Heston in *The Ten Commandments*? Luckily, like anything else I cut off, it will grow back by tomorrow after my night in the coffin. You didn't think I'd spend a hundred years in a black hat and *payess*? I wanted to have some fun."

"Actually, you are very nice looking, but I suppose you're aware of that."

I was surprised to see his huge grin, fangs flashing. Those green eyes fastened on me with a look of hunger, which I hoped was of the carnal, not carnivore variety.

"No I'm not aware of it. Thank you."

6

"What have you done to make your life, or rather undeath, easier?" I changed the subject, feeling a bit embarrassed by his intense gaze.

"I created a golem, a creature of mud that comes to life. Jews have believed in golem for centuries and will accept golem where they will not accept vampires. Golem don't eat so they don't have to be kosher. My golem, named Goldie, cleans, guards my coffin and goes out during the daylight to get what I need. She's good company. I've taught her to read Yiddish so she keeps me from being bored when I'm stuck in that coffin during the day. You think we vampires sleep all day. Well I suffer from insomnia and I get really tired of lying in that *farshtunken* coffin for twelve hours at a time. It's the rule that we have to stay in the coffin during daylight or who knows what might happen. I don't want to find out. I can't watch TV in a coffin so Goldie reads, mostly Isaac Bashevis Singer. He knew from the undead. The only problem is that she's jealous when I talk to any woman but her. She thinks she knows what's best for me. She reminds me of my mother. Don't ask! I used to use Goldie to do all my shopping since stores closed at sunset, but now, with Wal-Mart open twenty-four seven, I can do a lot of my own shopping. I just adore Wal-Mart."

"What could a vampire want at Wal-Mart? Especially a kosher vampire?"

"I like auto parts and hardware. And electronics of course. I once had an all-night electronics store in Times Square but that's another story. I would be in undead heaven at Home Depot but it's not open late enough. I get great deals on EBay, though."

"You shop on EBay?"

"I get the best buys there because no one else is up at 4am. I wait till the last second when an auction closes and then go for the jugular. Metaphorically speaking, of course." He gave me a mischievous grin, which I found charming.

"Why do you have to shop for bargains? After centuries you should have multiplied your investments?"

"Ever heard of Bernie Madoff? I got talked into investing my lifetimes of savings with that *goniff.* I've got nothing on him in the blood-sucking department. I'm thinking of making him my first Jewish victim. If you hear about him dying in jail from unknown causes with mysterious puncture wounds in his neck you'll know who did it. Now my circumstances are reduced. I work in the diamond district at night since I was trained as a diamond cutter in the nineteenth century. It doesn't pay great but hey, it's a living. Luckily I'm very entrepreneurial. I'm thinking of creating a vampire video game since we're so popular with kids these days, if I can find a computer maven to program it. I like modern technology but I'm still using a pen and parchment to write my memoirs. IMHO computers are the work of *dybbuks.* Mine is always giving me the blue screen of death. That thing knows who I am."

"If you're writing your own memoirs why talk to me?"

"You think I know how to write in English? I only write Yiddish and who's going to translate? If I try to get one of those Hasids, they'll probably start *davvening* over me. Plus who would believe me? You're a journalist. You've got clips."

As Sheldon spoke, I became mesmerized by his voice, which was soft, with an adorable Yiddish accent. Or maybe he was doing his vampire hypnotic thing on me. Whatever it was, I found him irresistible. I had no idea if he was attracted to me.

I hated having to date again in my forties. I thought marriage meant I was through with all that adolescent angst, but ever since I'd been dumped for a younger, thinner, blonder, dumber *shiksa,* my self-confidence was at an all-time low. I'd prayed that tonight's date would at least find me attractive. I'd had a long string of JDates who had made it painfully clear that I didn't pass their hotness test. My standards had plummeted so far that just about any high school graduate taller than five feet two who had all his teeth passed my hotness test these days, no matter how inappropriate he was, which explains why I didn't run screaming out of the bar when Sheldon introduced himself as a vampire.

I should have been ashamed of myself for lusting after every man I saw, but I was going through post-divorce pent up demand. After ten years of spending all my sexual energy avoiding sex with my husband, I was insatiable. Not coincidentally, my husband had also been avoiding sex with me—but then he was getting it elsewhere.

I'd always had terrible taste in men. I tended to go for the bad boys, who were dangerous biker types when I was a teenager, and then dangerous hedge fund manager types when I got older and decided to marry money. Of course, my ex-husband was the baddest boy of all. After fifteen years of promising that one day he'd take me on a vacation, he took the *shiksa* at the next desk instead. They headed for the Bahamas where he'd stashed a lot of cash, but not before cleaning out our joint bank account and canceling my credit cards. His finances were so tangled that I would have had to hire a team of accountants full time for a year to sort them out, and by that time, I'd be broke. He was kind enough to give me the house in Scarsdale with the huge mortgage I couldn't pay. That's how I wound up in a tiny Manhattan studio apartment on the Upper East Side with a rent I struggled to meet every month.

Maybe Sheldon still had some money? I doubted that Madoff could have taken it all. After a hundred years he must have a few nest eggs stashed here and there. He didn't have a family to support after all, only Goldie, and how much could a golem cost these days. But by the time he finished talking I really didn't care how much money he had, I was a goner, but in a good way. Ironically, considering he was a fearsome creature, he had a sweet smile, an adorable dimple in his chin, an old world courtliness and charm.

"Why don't we finish the interview at my place?" I'd had too many drinks, it was very late, and he was the most attractive guy I'd met so far on JDate.

"You want me to come up to your place?" he asked, all of a sudden looking at me appraisingly. "Did you have maybe a nightcap in mind? You have any blood in the fridge?" He chuckled. "You're not afraid of me?"

"You told me yourself you only feed on animals."

"I did say that, but why should you believe me? I'm a vampire, not a boy scout."

"I'm not interested in boy scouts," I breathed heavily. I didn't want to ask him directly what his sexual proclivities were. Or if he had any. Was there sex after death? Didn't Woody Allen ask that question? I couldn't remember what the answer was. I vaguely remembered Anne Rice's vampires. They didn't seem to have actual sex, but got off on the act of sucking human blood. However, Stephanie Meyer's vampires loved sex, but only with other vampires because they got pretty rough during the act. There were as many myths about vampire sex as there were vampire novels. I wondered what vampire series Sheldon had read. I hoped it was *Twilight* and, like Edward, that he would fall totally and madly in love with me.

"Why don't you hail us a cab?" I suggested.

"Cabbies never pick me up. Blacks and vampires, it's prejudice pure and simple."

I hailed one. As we smooched in the back seat I found out Sheldon knew how to use his tongue as well as his teeth.

Chapter Two

I was breathing heavily in the cab, but by the time I got to my apartment, I was gasping for breath. I lived in a third floor walkup and I was out of shape. Sheldon seemed to float effortlessly up the stairs because vampires probably didn't have to go the gym to stay in shape. Wouldn't that be great? As soon as I walked in the phone rang. I didn't have to look at the Caller ID to know who it was.

I picked it up, put my hand over the receiver and said to Sheldon, "It's my mom, I'll be off soon, make yourself a drink." It occurred to me he might not drink but at least I was being a good host.

"Hi, Mom, it's midnight, why are you still up?"

It was a rhetorical question, I knew she'd stay up so she could call and ask about my date. If I looked at my Caller ID I knew I'd see that she'd called at least five times and hung up before my voice mail picked up. She didn't want to seem like the nuisance she was.

"C'mon, Rhoda, this is your mother here. You know I don't have a life. I'll never have another date—not that I'd want one of course. Forty years with your father was more than enough. I have to live vicariously. And of course you're my only child and I want you to be happy."

I worried about Mom these days more than she worried about me. She'd already had a quadruple bypass but she refused to stop eating fatty foods and start exercising. She lived in Century Village in Florida, and her life consisted of sitting by the pool, hanging out with her girlfriends, going to early bird specials that were laden with greasy food that old Jewish ladies love. Yes, she did go

12

shopping, which was a pretty strenuous form of exercise considering that she hunted bargains with the zeal of a lion stalking its prey, but she refused to take the stairs like I told her to. She was still a kid who loved escalators.

"Mom, my date happens to be here as we speak, and he doesn't look happy. Can I call you back later?"

"Have a good time, darling. Don't rush on account of me."

"I have no intention of rushing. I'll talk to you in the morning." I hung up.

Sheldon actually didn't look impatient, even though he didn't have all that much time until dawn. I assumed he had to be back in his coffin, or at least in his neighborhood, by then, but what did I know? I hadn't really inquired. I sat down next to him on the couch, looked into his eyes and said, "How about if we finish the interview some other time? I'm really too tired to keep asking questions."

"I'm tired of answering them. I 'd rather get to know you better." Then he did the whole sweeping me into his arms and kissing me passionately thing and I swooned. I swear I actually swooned. That had never happened to me before.

"You are such a succulent morsel, Rhoda. Most women these days are so skinny it's disgusting. Where, or actually when, I come from, only the peasants were skinny. Jewish women from good families were plump and voluptuous, like you." He pressed his lips together and voiced a hum of approval. His hands ran over my body, stroking me very slowly, working up to my naughty bits. I could tell he wasn't rushing to get foreplay over with so he could put it in like a lot of guys—he liked to take his time.

Then Sheldon lifted me up to carry me to the bed as if I weighed almost nothing. No man had ever lifted me up before, much less carried me anywhere. It was thrilling. Why did it take a vampire to make me feel like a real

13

woman? I will not go into detail about everything that happened after that because I do have some discretion, despite the opinion of my mother who thinks that whatever goes through my head comes out my mouth, but suffice it to say that Sheldon was terrific in bed. OK, I'll go into some detail. I will dispel the myth right now that vampires are cold to the touch. When they get excited they heat up quite nicely. There's no worry about bad breath, since they don't breathe. It is uncomfortable though to be huffing and puffing while your lover is deathly quiet.

"Do you think you could breathe a little for me honey?" I asked in my sweetest tone of voice. I didn't want to insult him. "You're making me nervous. I keep wondering if you've had a heart attack."

"Sorry," Sheldon smiled. "I can breathe but I don't have to so I forget. I'll try to remember while we're making love."

Another interesting fact, vampires can keep it up forever. They can have multiple orgasms without losing their erections. They never need Viagra. If they have an erection lasting over four hours they don't have to call a doctor—they could actually have one for all eternity without any ill effects.

Sheldon was a regular tantric vampire…he just wanted to please me. And he did, oh yes he did. His fangs did descend a bit during the act because he was excited, just like you'd expect, and he did give me a teeny hickey, but he refrained from sinking his teeth in, saying, "Don't worry, I had dinner already…don't ask!" I didn't.

After about two hours, a few orgasms and many positions, including some I'd never experienced, I begged for mercy. We even had sex standing up while Sheldon easily lifted me so my legs could wrap around his back, a position I'd seen in the movies and always wanted to try. I'd never found anyone near strong enough.

14

"Sheldon, I think you better let me down before I pass out. I'm exhausted."

He gently brought me back to the bed, laid me softly as if I were breakable and leaned over me stroking my hair and gazing into my eyes. I felt like letting go and weeping from an excess of emotion, which I sometimes did after great sex, to the consternation of my partners, but I didn't want to freak him out. I broke the spell instead by asking him more questions, though the recorder was long forgotten.

"You know, I never asked you what your love life was like. Did you have girlfriends? Who were they?" I wanted to know everything about him.

"Yes, I did have some vampire girlfriends who were made around the same time as me by Count Dracula. He liked to prey on Jewish women. It was easier for him to get away with it. Then, once there was a group of us, we drifted off into our own community in Transylvania separate from the shtetl. Eventually we went to America. We actually rented a boat just for Jewish vampires where we could all bring our coffins and dirt from the old country. Most of the vampire girls were nice Jewish girls from the shtetl, except for being vampires. Think your grandmother at nineteen but with fangs. They weren't liberated like you. I had a couple of vampire girlfriends but it didn't go anywhere—where could it go? We couldn't get married and have kids. I haven't been with a woman since then. It's been almost a century. I've been so lonely, I thought I might go crazy—or kill myself. If I hadn't met you, I don't know what would have happened. You saved my life."

I was totally stunned. I couldn't imagine that I'd really saved his life? Maybe he was just saying that to flatter me. No femme fatale, I wasn't used to having that kind of effect on men. I was more the "he's just not into you" type. How did a vampire commit suicide anyway? I decided not to ask that question. He was virtually a vampire virgin.

"Why haven't you had any girlfriends? What were you waiting for?"

"I was afraid to approach human women. They might get scared and have me hunted. There are vampire hunters out there you know. I live in a Hasidic community in Crown Heights. Where would I meet a girl? And vampire women, well I'm really not attracted to them. I longed for a juicy Jewish girl."

"So why me?"

"You seduced me, remember?" He grinned. "I didn't have anything to do with it. I told you what I was and you wanted me anyway. I think I'm falling in love with you."

Maybe he was handing me a line, but I wanted desperately to believe him. I'd fantasized ever since my divorce about a man who would be so devoted to me he wouldn't leave. In New York City, it would take a mythical creature to fulfill that fantasy.

We talked till almost dawn. He interviewed me too, wanting to know everything about me. I told him all about my marriage, how unhappy I had been, how I got left for another woman. He listened sympathetically to my tale of living with a husband who went into rages and berated me for every little thing--a hedge fund manager I had to support because he couldn't get another job after the market crashed and his bank went under. I even told him that I wanted children but couldn't have them with my ex. We'd gone for testing and it seemed his few sperm were barely treading water, much less swimming. I found myself talking about my childhood as an overweight lonely, only child who relied on books for comfort. I told him about my mom who I rebelled against when I was a kid, but whom I was extremely close to now. He murmured sympathetically, encouraging me to go on. He barely

16

blinked as I spoke, he was so intent on every word. But then maybe vampires don't blink much.

He told me he had been a rabbi with a congregation, a wife and children when he was turned into a vampire, but had to leave his family and wander the countryside before he found a group of Hasidic vampires that took him in. His wife would have been horrified if she'd known what he'd become. I had slept with men since my divorce but Sheldon was different—he made me feel desirable, a beautiful woman who deserved to be loved. I totally forgot about being fat since he seemed so enamored of every curve I owned. I even started feeling my thighs just might be acceptable. We hung onto each other until the last moment, until he started yawning and had to go home and back his coffin to sleep.

By the time he left, he'd forgotten about the interview. I couldn't even remember where I'd left my fancy recorder. I was a goner. Not literally, thank God. When he left, he promised to call but he didn't leave me his number, which made me uneasy. As soon as he walked out the door, I started wondering if he was sincere. They all promise to call. You'd think that a vampire would follow through, but who knows? Despite all his protestations of love, maybe he was just a one-night stand like all the other bloodsuckers I'd run into since my divorce. They ravish you and then disappear into the night never to be seen again.

Chapter Three

The next morning I felt vampirized, but in a good way. My limbs were so rubbery I had to hold onto the night table when I got out of bed. I had aches and pains in places I didn't know were places. I replayed every little detail of our lovemaking as I made coffee, remembering how Sheldon looked at me, stroked me, told me how beautiful I was. I was in a reverie when I remembered that Mom had called last night. I picked up the phone reluctantly, not wanting to break the spell.

"So how're you feeling, Mom?" Still tired?"

She'd only had the surgery two months ago and I'd been down in Florida with her until recently, helping her recover. It was a slow process.

"Well, I'm not exactly a spring chicken here, ya know. I feel pretty good considering."

"Considering what?"

"That I'm still alive. Enough about me. How was the date? Give already."

"Mom, you wouldn't believe it if I told you."

"That good, eh," she chuckled.

"I wouldn't say good exactly. It was more of a cross-cultural experience." I tried to get off the hook without lying.

"Cross-cultural? He wasn't Jewish? You met him on JDate."

"Oh, he was Jewish alright. Just not the kind of Jewish I had in mind."

"Ugly? No money? Too many ex-wives? Insists on keeping a kosher home."

18

"Actually he was really good looking but I'm not sure about his financial situation. He doesn't have to keep kosher because he doesn't eat—food."

"Rhodaaaa," she whined. "Are we playing twenty questions here or what? Is this some kind of riddle?"

"Riddle is right, Ma. If I tell you what happened will you promise to believe me?"

"You're a journalist. You do your homework. Of course I'll believe you."

"He's a vampire."

"Umpire?"

My mom's hearing wasn't as good as it used to be. Especially when I said something really unexpected.

"Vampire, Mom. Think Dracula."

"You've been seeing too many old episodes of Buffy." Mom and I used to watch that show together. We both loved it. "You mean he was some kind of crazy who thought he was a vampire. I hope he didn't want to suck your blood."

"No, he doesn't feed off Jews, only goyim. He's got ethics," I joked.

"Rhoda, c'mon. This is your mother here, not David Letterman. Are you still trying to write for TV?"

One of my secret desires was to write for a show like *Sex and the City*. Or *Desperate Housewives*, or *The Witches of Eastwick*, which had been cancelled by clueless TV execs. I hoped witches were sticking pins into their TV exec dolls. Instead, I was stuck writing for *Bottom Line*, a newsletter where I had to interview "experts" and ghostwrite articles for them. At the bottom of the article it would say, "So and so was interviewed by Rhoda Ginsburg." They were the kind of dumb self-help articles that people could finish while they were on the can, as, I believe, Jeff Goldblum himself said about a fictional magazine in *The Big Chill*. I don't know what I would have done if my Word program didn't have bullets. I hated the job but it paid well, even though not well enough to cover all my expenses. And it was a steady gig, the Holy Grail for freelance writers.

"No, Mom, I'm serious, he is a real vampire."

Long silence. I could hear her breathing.

"Nah. You can't really believe there is such a thing?"

"Now I do. Sheldon convinced me. He really is undead, and Jewish. I'll send you a copy of the interview I did with him. That should convince you."

"No matter what I read, I'll think you're going nuts."

"I'll paste it into an email as soon as I transcribe it, Mom." My Mom still couldn't figure out how to download attachments—much less how to play an audio file.

"Where does this vampire live?" my Mom asked. "In a coffin?"

"I have no idea if he sleeps in a coffin but he said he lives in a Hasidic neighborhood in Brooklyn, probably Crown Heights. He took the '4' to meet me.

"Hasidic? I guess he fits in there. They all look pasty faced."

"You got it, Mom."

"Are you going to see him again? Did he ask for your number?"

"How desperate are you for me to find a guy? Would you settle for a vampire as long as he was Jewish?"

"Well maybe, as long as he has a few bucks. I guess vampires must have centuries to get compound interest. I worry about you. No husband, no savings, not even any relatives when I'm gone."

Mom was humoring me. There was no way she was going to believe my vampire story unless she saw Sheldon with her own eyes. Even then she'd be skeptical. My mom was a veteran of the New York City school system where she'd taught for twenty-five years in some pretty tough neighborhoods. Nothing much surprised her.

"I don't know how rich he is—he invested with Bernie Madoff like a lot of other Jews. I do know that he's a diamond cutter so he might have some blood diamonds stashed away someplace." I couldn't resist that one.

"Oy vey. Luckily I didn't have enough money to interest Madoff. Some of my friends lost everything to that gonif. Me, I knew he was too good to be true." She coughed loudly into the phone, neglecting to cover the mouthpiece. I had to hold the receiver away from my ear.

"Mom, you're not sounding good. You're the one who needs to be worried about."

"I'm OK, honey. Just a little out of breath when I walk too far."

"I don't believe it. I'm coming down there to take you to the doctor. I want to hear what he has to say first hand."

"Oh, sweetheart. That's wonderful. I miss you so much."

I hung up, went to Expedia and booked a flight for the next week. How did anyone do anything before the Internet, I wondered. Then I went into serious guilt mode. Why wasn't I in Florida taking care of Mom full-time? I was her only child, after all, and I could do my job anywhere? What kind of daughter was I anyway? I answered my own question. One who didn't want to live in a retirement community. One who couldn't see dating elderly widowers or guys who flipped real estate for a living. There were no dark, brooding artist types in Florida, and no vampires for sure. I wondered if they could go out in the daylight, or would they burst into flames? Or just get overheated. Did vampires tan? Sheldon sure could use some color. I hoped he could go out in the daylight, like the vampires in *Twilight*. Of course they could only go out in cloudy weather, which was why the heroine lived in the

Pacific Northwest. I don't know why she didn't move to New York City. It was January and I hadn't seen the sun in weeks.

I was on the phone interviewing the latest narcissistic New Age guru when the bell rang. I ignored it. I didn't dare put Mr. Empowerment on hold; he'd hang up and never talk to me again. This guy was a media monk, a Tibetan Buddhist who taught his acolytes how to reach enlightenment through yogic inversions. You were supposed to meditate while standing on your head. Go know! He radiated love and compassion only on Oprah, and "call my publicist, don't bother me" with the rest of the world.

The bell gave a loud buzz again. Why the hell did people assume that they could barge in at any hour of the day just because I was home? Working at home meant you were always available. Two hours later when it rang again, I opened the door and found my upstairs neighbor and closest friend Charlene, holding a huge bouquet of white roses, my favorite flower.

"Charlene, what came over you? I didn't know you felt that way about me," I said, grabbing the flowers.

"I don't. Sheldon does." She looked at me with raised eyebrows.

I looked at the card. "You are the most exciting woman I've met in a hundred years. How about a play or a night of love soon? Nosferatu and you? Sheldon." I giggled at the joke and swooned over the flowers. It had been a long time since a man had made me laugh or sent me flowers. The last laugh I got from a guy was when my ex got dumped by his twenty- five-year-old girlfriend and asked me to get back together. The last bouquet was the one my father gave me at my sweet sixteen party.

"Come on in, I'll tell you all about him."

I had no doubt that Charlene would believe every word I said about Sheldon. She was the least skeptical person I'd ever met. Having renounced her nice Catholic girlhood and become a Wiccan, the latest trendy faux religion for rebellious Catholic girls and other misfits, she had long ago abandoned normality for paranormality. Rebellious Jewish girls become Buddhists, Catholic girls become Witches. Why was that? Charlene believed in ghosts, aliens, reincarnation, spirit guides, angels, shape shifters, werewolves, and just about any other supernatural phenomenon that Hollywood or young adult fiction came up with. She would cast a spell for everything from weight loss to finding a new boyfriend. For Charlene, belief in vampires was not a stretch.

Every month she got together with her coven in the Bronx and did something called "raising energy," which was a mystery to me. She insisted she was a white witch and the spells were benign, but I'd wondered recently about the series of suspicious, if minor, accidents that had kept her despised boss out of work. Charlene had reported them to me with a strangely triumphant air. You wouldn't want to get her bad side—she was six feet tall, worked out and was ferociously loyal to her friends. Even though her height, rippling biceps and long black hair made her look formidable, her soft little girl voice was disarming, she looked like Wonder Woman but sounded like Tickle Me Elmo. She dressed in tight, sexy outfits that complimented her curves, attracting male attention wherever we went, but I wasn't jealous of her looks. Instead I basked in her reflected glamour. We were both divorced, the same age and inseparable. An affair with a vampire would be like "What else is nu?" to her.

Charlene sat down awkwardly on my tiny yellow sofa, which complemented my tiny antique rocker. I had to give up all my big country pine pieces when I left Scarsdale and downsize to dollhouse furniture that fit into my miniscule studio apartment. I was short so didn't mind their size, even though I never sat on the rocker for fear that I'd break it. Charlene's knees came almost up to her chin when she sat on my sofa.

"Does he have any single friends?" was her first question after I told her the whole story. "I want a paranormal lover, too."

It sounded like she wanted the latest fashion accessory.

"That will be the first question I'll ask the next time I see him."

"Really, Rhoda. My sex life is dead. Why can't it be undead? Wiccans are all women, there are no sexy male witches."

"Aren't they called warlocks?" I asked.

"Not if you're politically correct," she told me.

"Well, I know nothing about his social circle. For all I know he's the only vampire, certainly the only Jewish one."

"I'm not fussy," she said, "a vampire of any faith will do."

"Give it a break, Vick."

"Why don't you call him?"

"I don't have his number, or any idea where he lives except it's in Crown Heights somewhere. But I'm sure he'll call."

"Do you know his email address?" she asked.

"Damn, why didn't I think to ask for it? I could always email him through JDate He has a profile there."

"Ooh," Charlene cooed, "show me his picture."

I logged into JDate and searched for "Jewish Vampire," which, believe it or not, was his JDate username. No luck. His profile was gone.

"Isn't that a good thing?" Charlene said. "He took down his profile because he'd met you and doesn't want to keep looking. Don't you hate those guys who keep their profiles up after dating you and even having sex?"

"Yes, especially when they deny that they're still looking but you log on and find out that they've been online that day. But then how many women want to have sex with a vampire?"

"C'mon, Rhoda. Just about every thirteen-year-old girl in the known universe."

"Luckily he likes older women. Zaftig older women."

"So he's a vampire chubby chaser," Charlene laughed.

"Nah, he's just a shy vampire. He says he hasn't been with a woman in a hundred years if you can believe that. I interviewed him but I wish I'd asked more questions. There's so much more I want to know about him. Like his last name and phone number."

"And you call yourself a journalist," Charlene teased me. "The biggest story of your life and you sleep with it instead of interrogating it."

"You would have done the same thing. I tell you he mesmerized me. I totally forgot what I do for a living."

"I guess he put his vampire mojo on you, you lucky girl."

"I don't think it's lucky to be in love with a vampire. The potential complications boggle the mind, starting with, well, me getting old and him staying the same."

"Love? Are you in love?"

"Charlene, I told you to throw me in a cold shower the next time I told you I've never felt this way before. But I've never felt this way before. Just thinking about him makes me feel…well…all warm and fuzzy and secure. Like I can trust him. "

"Well, here you are on JDate for years and if the only guy you can trust turns out to be a vampire maybe it's time to look elsewhere."

"I don't want to look anywhere. I just want to see him again."

"You will, you will. Guys who send flowers always call. It's a dating rule."

Chapter Four

Sure enough, Sheldon did call, the next day, with theatre tickets for that night. He'd gotten us orchestra seats for the revival of *Fiddler on the Roof* with Alfred Molina. It had gotten great reviews and six Tony nominations. He offered to take me to dinner before the show.

"Won't that make you uncomfortable, Shel? What are you going to eat?"

"You, with my eyes, darling," he said, sounding like a bad imitation of a romantic hero in a 1930s movie.

"You have been watching too many old movies. I'm serious. What will you eat?"

"I can drink a little wine. I like to watch humans eat. I get a vicarious thrill, remembering what it used to feel like."

"What's your favorite vicarious food?"

"Jewish deli, of course. How about eating at the Carnegie?"

"Where they charge fifteen bucks for a pastrami sandwich? It's a rip-off?"

"I like to go by and smell the pastrami fumes. It will be fun to watch you eat."

I didn't have the best memories of the Carnegie Deli. The last time I was there I was supposed to interview Henny Youngman over lunch. Henny is the Borscht Belt comic who came up with the line "take my wife please." It wound up being the most humiliating experience I'd ever had as a journalist. Henny totally ignored me, refused to answer questions, wouldn't look my way, and spent the hour waving at celebrities who came by. At least I thought they were celebrities. I was sure he was ignoring me because I wasn't glamorous. If I'd been some cute, blonde, curvy TV anchor type in a miniskirt and heels, instead of a shlumpy, overweight working writer wearing jeans, maybe he would have treated me differently. Or maybe he'd have treated me worse. I could see him being crude and lewd with attractive women. I suffered through the lunch and wound up using a handout he gave me of his jokes for the story. I hoped someone *had* taken his wife—someone a lot nicer than him. I refused to let this memory ruin my dinner with Sheldon. Or ruin the pastrami sandwich I was looking forward to. Tonight I was the cute, curvy blonde – to Sheldon anyway.

The Carnegie Deli is on 55th and Broadway, a corner with wide sidewalks, which was lucky because there was such a crowd waiting to get in. I was shocked by the length of the line outside on a weekday night. Everyone looked like they'd just arrived from Des Moines—they had that Midwest *goyishe* look. It seemed the Carnegie Deli had become a big tourist attraction since the last time I'd been here. It was once a smaller place with about twenty long tables where strangers all sat together. Now it had eaten up half the block. I saw Sheldon in the back of the line and sidled up to him.

"Been here long, Mister?"

"A few minutes," he said. "Let's go inside."

"Sheldon, there's a line."

"Not for us there isn't."

He marched me right up to the front of the line, gave the hostile-looking waiter guarding the entrance a penetrating look, and we were ushered to a quiet table in the back. Considering how noisy and jammed the place was, I was stunned. The Carnegie was famous for its nasty waiters and here we were being treated like royalty.

"OK, Sheldon, how did you do it? I know you're not a movie star."

"I glamoured him. We're not supposed to do that unless it's an emergency, but I couldn't resist impressing you."

"And exactly what does glamouring involve?"

"It's a vampire thing. I can't really explain it. I just have to concentrate, stare into someone's eyes, and they do my bidding—within reason of course. He'll forget what happened afterwards. Right about now he's wondering who we are and how we wound up at this desirable table." Sheldon grinned mischievously. "Impressed you, didn't I?"

"Impressed doesn't quite cover it. Awed is more like it. Now, if you materialize a pastrami sandwich in the midst of this mob I'll really be impressed."

He snapped his fingers loudly but the waiters ignored him. I supposed glamouring only works up close. By the time the waiter brought our order it was getting dangerously close to show time. The pastrami sandwich was enormous. The Carnegie was famous for half-a-foot-high sandwiches.

I couldn't open my mouth wide enough to actually bite into it, so I removed about three-quarters of the meat and started eating. It tasted kind of dry. The pastrami I remembered was juicy and succulent. I looked at the slices and didn't see the big slabs of white marbling I remembered.

"They took out all the fat." I frowned. "I guess it's supposed to be low calorie. It's also low taste. Are you enjoying the smell at least?"

"I can't smell it," Sheldon admitted. "I don't breathe enough to smell."

"But that's why you wanted to come here."

"Well, I thought you might like it and I didn't want to make you feel guilty about eating. And now the pastrami isn't even good, so let's go to the show."

I didn't care. I wasn't all that hungry anyway. Sheldon left a twenty on the table and we elbowed our way out into the cold. "Let's take a cab," I suggested. "It's getting close to show time."

"Have you noticed the traffic, Rhoda? Let's walk. We'll get there faster, I promise."

He put his arm around me and I found as we walked that I was actually gliding. He was skimming over the ground, with me in tow.

"Hey, this is a great way to get to the theatre on time."

It wasn't very far, only ten blocks to the Minskoff Theatre at Forty-Fifth Street, but we got there in two minutes flat.

We settled into the best seats in the house, third row orchestra on the aisle. "How did you get these on such short notice, Shel? More glamouring?"

"No, this time it was a ticket scalper. Hasidic guy. I gave him a good deal on some diamonds recently."

I leaned towards him and gave him a smooch on the check. "This is so incredibly sweet of you. I never sit this close—who can afford it? I love musicals. I saw *Fiddler* in the movies but I've always wanted to see the show."

"I've never seen it. I actually haven't been to a Broadway theatre, and I never go to movies. No pun intended, but I've been dying to see this show. I never had anyone to go with. My Hasidic vampire buddies aren't exactly into Broadway musicals."

"You wouldn't go alone?" I asked.

"Nah. That's no fun. When I first came to New York, it was the heyday of the Yiddish theatre and Herschel and I went a lot. Herschel's my brother. But he never liked American culture, plus he doesn't want to be that close to humans anymore. He tries to only drink blood from animals too, but he's easily tempted. I'm stronger than him.

I made him after all. But that's a long story for another time."

I didn't have time to ask questions. The lights in the theatre dimmed, the orchestra started playing and I sat back in my seat, feeling that delicious anticipation I always experienced before a show. When I was a kid my parents took me to all the Broadway musicals, and tonight the first bars of the score made me feel like a kid again, entranced by the magic of live theatre.

Sheldon put his arm around me and gave me a little hug. I leaned my head on his shoulder, feeling thrilled to be at the theatre with a real, live man for a change, instead of Charlene or my mother. OK, maybe not live, but certainly manly. We raptly watched as Klesmer, Yiddish folk and Russian gypsy music was transformed into one of the most gorgeous scores ever written.

After about a half hour I noticed that Sheldon's shoulders were shaking. I looked at his face and saw that it was twisted into a grimace and he was sobbing. He was making gasping, honking noises that I could see he was trying to stifle. There were no tears, however, certainly no bloody tears despite the myth about vampires crying blood. It was frightening to see. His hand gripped my shoulder so tightly it hurt, but I tried not to complain, he looked so miserable.

"What is it, Sheldon? What's going on?" I was scared. I couldn't imagine what was wrong. He'd seemed to be enjoying himself immensely just a minute earlier. He'd clapped wildly after every number.

"Anatevka, Anatevka… that was my home…I miss it so much. I had no idea how much until tonight," he moaned.

"You came from Transylvania, not Russia, I whispered." Anatevka was the fictional Russian *shtetl* in the show.

"Same thing. I miss the shtetl. I miss my family. I miss my wife and children. I miss Tevye."

"Shhhh," came whispers from behind us. We stopped talking and he put his head on my shoulder as I stroked his face and held his hand while he cried. I couldn't help feeling a stab of jealousy although his wife and children were long dead. I had no idea what he meant by Tevye unless his town also had a Tevye. Eventually he stopped crying.

"Do you want to leave now?" I asked him at intermission.

"I wouldn't leave for anything on earth," he said dreamily. "I may come back every night. I feel like I've gone back in time, to when I was happy and part of a family—not lonely and hopeless."

"Who is Tevye?"

"My father was named Tevye, believe it or not. He was a big, burly guy, like Tevye in the play, with a long grey beard and the bluest eyes. We lived in the town of Bresov where he was our rabbi and I was his successor. We used to dance in lines, just like in the show, we Hasids were into joy, into ecstasy, especially when we danced. I wish I could get up on that stage and dance—I'm a good dancer."

"Maybe we could go dancing sometime," I suggested. "I'm a good dancer too. I was once told I had 'Jewish soul.'"

"The kind of dancing they do today is not exactly my style," Sheldon said disapprovingly, putting his hand to his chin as though he were looking for a beard to stroke. I could see the stern rabbi in that face. "But I'm willing to try it," he then said with an impish smile. I could see the joyous Hasid he once had been in that grin.

We sat through the rest of the show holding hands, and I saw Sheldon stomping his foot during some of the more

32

raucous musical numbers. He stopped crying and started laughing and clapping again.

After the show we went back to my apartment, where Sheldon just wanted me to hold him. Tonight was not the night for hot sex, but for tenderness. I felt so bad for the poor guy, he'd been ripped from his beloved shtetl, transported to an alien land where he was stuck with a bloodlust he couldn't always control. Of course all the Jews had to leave their homelands but at least they could start over, Sheldon couldn't. We lay down with our arms around each other until I fell asleep. When I woke up it was 4am and Sheldon was gone. I supposed he wanted to get home before sunrise.

Chapter Five

"Hi Charlene," I said chirpily into the phone the next afternoon after checking the Caller ID. "Yes, he called. We went to see *Fiddler on the Roof* last night. He broke down and cried during the show because it reminded him of home. I got to comfort him. We really had an emotional moment, but he took off in the middle of the night without leaving a note and now I'm worried again that he won't call. I was hoping you were him, but you're not. But then it's daytime so how could it be him? I don't know why I'm so anxious—but I am. I'm falling in love with the guy and it's giving me a panic attack. Why don't we go for a little shop and schmooze? I need distraction."

"I just woke up. I can't move," she gasped. "I feel like I was vampirized during the night and all the blood was drained from my body."

"I'm the one who's dating a vampire, not you. So why don't you tell me all about him while we shop. I desperately need some new clothes for my trip to Florida and my next date with Sheldon. How about it?"

"Retail therapy eh? I'm for that."

We met in the lobby and were greeted outside by a blast of freezing air. All male eyes swiveled to get a look at Charlene as we walked down 86th Street towards the subway. She ignored the attention, she was so used to it. Walking down the street with her was an exercise in invisibility. No one even saw me—no man that is. I loved her for her cleverness, warmth and original outlook on life and had managed over the years to accept her appearance as an act of God.

Despite her looks, however, Charlene's track record with men wasn't much better than mine. Yes, she attracted them by the carload, but they never stuck around. Before my marriage I, on the other hand, had a hell of a time finding a boyfriend, but when I did, they tended to linger, often past their expiration dates. My ex-husband definitely took his time leaving me—waiting until my eggs were stale. My recent spate of one-night stands was an unfortunate new post-divorce pattern than I hoped Sheldon would break.

"So tell," I asked, as we glanced at the new brownstone across the street, which was twelve stories higher than any other building in the neighborhood. I wondered how they'd got a permit for that one. "Who drained your blood last night?"

"Ooooh, I ran into this guy from the neighborhood." She batted her eyelashes flirtatiously. "We've been giving each other the eye for years, every time we pass on the street. He's tall, luscious and sinewy....you know, the catlike type who slinks along stalking his prey. I just couldn't resist getting dragged into his lair," she sighed, languorously. Charlene really had languorousness down to a science. While my movements tended to be rapid, jerky and frantic, her every gesture radiated slow-motion grace.

"Charlene, tell me something," I asked as we opened the door to Lane Bryant on Thirty Fourth Street and were happily enveloped by the warm air inside. "How is it you are always meeting men on the street who've been giving you the eye for years?"

"I think it's my dog. People always notice you if you have a dog. Why don't you get a dog, Rhoda?"

"Charlene," I replied, exasperated. "I could walk down the street with a panther on a leash and after a while people might start saying hello to the panther but ten to one they'd all be little old ladies who wanted to tell me their problems.

Sometimes I think I have 'tell me your troubles' stamped on my forehead. Men who need either a therapist or a mother or both are irresistibly attracted to me, except for Sheldon and he's from a century when weighing 200 pounds was fashionable. Outside of vampires I seem to have allure only for little old ladies and the terminally psychotic." I headed for the nearest "clearance" rack.

"It would help, Rhoda, if you'd take off a few pounds and put on some makeup. Can't you at least buy another pair of pants? The jeans you always wear look like they've been through the Boer War." Charlene helped me look through the size-22 petites, although she shopped on the second floor, in the tall section of Lane Bryant. Petite was one of the euphemisms clothes designers used to make us short, fat babes feel better. No way I was ever petite.

"A few pounds would do me absolutely no good. I'd have to lose at least fifty to even tentatively qualify as pleasantly plump. And I refuse to buy a new pair of jeans when I have at least five pairs that would fit me perfectly if I could only lose fifteen pounds but I can't lose even ten pounds so there you are." I was out of breath.

Three days later I was on a plane to Florida. I hate airplanes. The seats are too small and I get dirty looks from fellow passengers who have to sit next to me. Then I have to deal with the pain of descent when my ears explode. Gum does no good. By the time I hit the ground I'm deaf for a week. Finally, my bag is always the last one to come through the baggage carousel.

On this flight all I could think about was Sheldon. There was the usual *alta cocker* trying to make a pass at me to see if I'd be open to a little post-flight dalliance but I didn't bother to respond to his compliments. The flight attendant came around with a snack pack that actually looked appetizing but I turned it down. I asked for a vodka martini instead although I never drank on flights. What I really needed was a tranquilizer.

After our theatre date, Sheldon still hadn't and I was so desperate to hear from him, I'd started checking my cell every five minutes, but that little message icon was just sitting there not jumping up and down. I couldn't call him because he hadn't left his number and when I looked at my Caller ID list all I saw was "unknown caller" at the times he'd called me. It was incredibly frustrating. I couldn't exactly Google him—I only knew his first name. I couldn't stop thinking about his eyes, his smile, that hard body. Maybe a little too hard, but at least he didn't have to work out every day to get that way. I replayed our night at *Fiddler* in my head over and over. Why would he have cried on my shoulder and opened up with me like that if he was planning on taking off? Actually maybe that was the reason—he figured he wasn't going to see me again so he could tell me the truth. I could go around in circles endlessly with this kind of reasoning.

If I hadn't recorded our interview, I would have started doubting my own senses. What did I really know about him? Could he really be a vampire? Was I imagining the white skin, the lack of reflection in the mirror, the pointy incisors? Could he have just been trying to impress me? Vampires are so trendy these days. Maybe he was angling for a reality series, filmed at night of course. Actually, that wasn't a bad idea. I resolved when I got back to find out if there were other vampires, maybe a vampire family who would agree to having cameras set up in their lair, wherever that was. I started imagining crumbling Victorian mansions in New Orleans, and then I remembered that Sheldon was a Jewish vampire who lived among the Hasidim in Crown Heights. OK, a brownstone would do. We could film local color during the day and Jewish vampires at night.

My fantasy was to break into TV one way or another, maybe produce a reality series. It was a long shot, but I had very little going for me work-wise these days. I was tired of working for *Bottom Line* and had burned out on magazine work. Too many prima donna editors who assigned a piece, then kept changing their minds, then killed whatever I had spent months writing, paying me a mere twenty-five-percent kill fee if they paid me at all. The print industry was dying anyway. The Internet was taking over, but there were so many wannabe writers out there that websites could easily get free articles. Besides *Bottom Line*, I more or less depended on infusions of cash from Mom who was doling out my inheritance before she died so she could control how I spent it. If she kept a tight enough rein on my shopaholic habits, I might actually be able to afford an apartment where I could eat in a different room than I slept in. Or I might buy a car and put it in a garage so I could escape the City on weekends. Or I might go someplace other than Florida on vacation. Maybe Sheldon would rescue me from poverty and spirit me away to Transylvania or wherever he came from. Did Sheldon fly? If so, could he fly across the Atlantic? What did he do with his luggage on long flights?

I was lost in dreams of travel to exotic places with Sheldon when the plane bounced on the ground. My ears felt OK this time. I couldn't wait to get off the plane and check my cell. My heart sank when I saw there were no messages.

I saw Mom waving frantically from the behind the barrier they set up to keep potential terrorists away from the planes. Most of the greeters were over eighty and unlikely to be stashing bombs under their brightly colored attire, but security these days seemed to involve torturing little old ladies. Mom looked smaller than she had the last time I saw her six months ago. She'd been plump her whole life, which suited her, but now she looked thin and frail. I hugged her and felt her bones under the pretty Indian flowered dress she put on for the occasion.

"Aw Mom, are you OK? You don't look so good. You lost a lot of weight."

"I think I look great. It's the first time I've been a size ten since I was in high school."

She tactfully avoided mentioning my weight, which involved one more X in the plus size department. I'd trained her years ago to shut up about it by threatening never to speak to her again if she told me one more time that I needed to go on a diet. She now knew her place. I was feeling good about my weight this visit because Sheldon was so enamored of my size. But what if he didn't call? Would I have to find another refugee from the nineteenth century to be accepted the way I was?

My favorite part of the trip was leaving the airport and taking my first breath of tropical air. The airport looked like it could have been in any city anywhere, but even though Fort Lauderdale looked like a wasteland of gas stations, big box stores and condo complexes, the air smelled better and the sky looked bluer than it ever did in New York City. No one wore black or rushed anywhere. At least not among the retirees. When you got closer to the ocean the landscape actually started looking tropical. I guess they had to preserve some part of nature to bring in business. I felt sad because if Sheldon and I got serious I'd never be able to go snorkeling with him—my favorite sport. Maybe we could go night diving—or to those lagoons where you could see the phosphorescent fish at night. Actually, I hadn't asked Sheldon what he did during the day. For all I knew he wouldn't burst into flames during daylight, like they do in tacky vampire movies.

Maybe he'd just sparkle like the vamps in *Twilight*. In Florida no one would notice sparkling. All the girls, and boys dressed as girls, wore glitter. I wished I could call him and find out.

Mom lived in Century Village in Deerfield Beach, north of Fort Lauderdale. She and my dad had moved there from Jersey when he got Alzheimer's so if he wandered someone would find him and send him home. There were some advantages to gated communities—outsiders couldn't get in, but also the demented couldn't get out. Century was one of the oldest condos in Florida, which didn't give it any old world charm. It just looked more like an Army base than a setting for gracious living. The houses were condo complexes, low, gray concrete buildings with balconies. Trees and bushes had grown since Mom and my dad had moved in, so at least it didn't look like a settlement on the moon anymore. After being there for a while I forgot how ugly it was, and appreciated being able to swim in a pool outside my door and sit on a patio overlooking a faux lagoon—which was actually a repository for water runoff. Alligators were rumored to live in the lagoons, so you weren't supposed to get too close to them, but I suspected the alligator rumors were exaggerated. No one had actually seen one but everyone had heard of a little boy who got his arm chomped off. I wasn't taking chances. I kept away from the lagoons.

Even though Mom's apartment in Century was spacious, it felt cramped because she followed me around hectoring me about my sloppy ways. I had never been in an apartment in Century that wasn't immaculate. Most of them were furnished with white, squishy upholstered furniture and thick beige rugs. Mom's apartment, however, was a spectacular exception to the standard décor. My father had been an architect and they were both obsessed with modern furniture and design. They collected classic pieces and took them to Florida, including a huge white pedestal table, bentwood chairs and a graceful glass kidney-shaped coffee table that my father had designed. The couches were long, low-slung slabs of covered foam on spare wood frames. They were elegant but incredibly hard and uncomfortable. The entire room was stunning but it was mostly for show; there was no place to curl up and read a book. I couldn't imagine bringing Sheldon here to meet my mother; I saw him more in a *shtetl* with mud huts just like in *Fiddler*. He'd had 150 years to adjust to modern décor, but vampires and Bauhaus just didn't compute. I wasn't fond of 1950s modern myself. I much preferred country casual, with comfy couches you could sink into.

Mom was a neat freak, while I was constitutionally incapable of neatness. If I left a dish in the sink overnight I heard about it.

"Rhoda, if you leave anything out we'll have ants," she chided me the morning after I arrived. "No orange peels on the counter please."

"Jeez, Mom, I left the orange peels in the sink."

"Why didn't you turn on the garbage disposal?"

"That thing is too goddamned noisy."

We could have kept on bickering but the phone rang. The phone rang constantly at Mom's. She was a regular social butterfly, one of the most popular girls, or "goils" as they called themselves in Century. She had three close friends and many aspirants for the position of one of the goils. The gang consisted of Mom, Judy, an acerbic heavyset pushy type who did not censor her sarcastic opinions, Ellen, a sweet former social worker who listened to everyone's problems, and Miriam, my favorite, an oddball closet intellectual who often expressed her irreverent opinions in a deceptively soft, genteel tone of voice. Judy was on the other end of the phone this time. I could only hear Mom's side of the conversation.

"She's fine. She's very happy. She's madly in love." Long pause. "With a vampire," Mom said with an embarrassed laugh. Another long pause.

"No, I don't think she's lost her mind," she said into the phone, sounding defensive. "Maybe she's just desperate. There aren't a lot of available single men in New York for fortyish women."

"Well, she's my daughter and I'll stick by her even if she's a little delusional. We can't all be as sensible as you," she said sarcastically.

My poor mom was stuck defending my love affair with a vampire. That was harder than defending my marriage to a philanderer.

"Yes, I'll pick you up at five. How about the China Palace?"

The girls ate out together every night and Mom always drove. She was the only one who could still drive at night. They liked to dress for dinner as well. My mother was the most fashionable of the girls. Her walk-in closet was the envy of Century Village; unlike her friends who wore mostly pastel or beige polyester, Mom loved natural fabrics and interesting patterns. Her Indian cotton dresses and silk blouses were organized by color and type. If she was wearing purple pants, guaranteed she would have a blouse with purple in it, and a scarf and sweater to match. Her feet were still a size six and she could still wear high heels, which I never could tolerate because of my big flat feet. It was sad that her beautiful clothes were now too big for her. Most of them were size fourteen's. It was even sadder that they didn't fit me because I was in the XX's.

My visits were a big deal to the 'goils', who looked forward to hanging out with me. They were in their eighties and at forty-one, I was the voice of "young people" to them, even though in New York, where the happening crowd was in their twenties, I was already a dinosaur. Women my age lived in the 'burbs or Park Slope with their first husbands and kids. My first husband didn't stick around for the kids. But I liked being treated like a kid again by Mom's friends--being fussed over and catered to.

I suppose most New York women my age would have dreaded keeping company with a bunch of eighty-year-olds in a Florida condo, but I loved spending time with the girls. They were funny, irreverent, and had a great time doing just about anything. Mostly we went out to lunch somewhere nice, since lunches were cheap, then to a museum, or shopping, then home for a nap, then to dinner before six, never missing the early bird. After dinner we'd take a stroll on the beach. Deerfield was famous for its scenic non-commercialized beach, and long pier that stretched out into the Atlantic. Mom and I had scattered my dad's ashes off that pier. I said Kaddish and we cried and cried. Then we went for ice cream, Mom's favorite indulgence. Hanging out with the girls was easier than being with my own fellow journalists, who made me feel inadequate because I didn't work on a TV show or at the *New York Times*. They also made me feel fat and frumpy, since they worked out obsessively and dressed in the latest boho fashions. There were no expectations with Mom's friends except that I be sociable and amusing, which was easy.

At the China Palace they started grilling me about Sheldon. Judy had wasted no time in spreading the word about my latest exploits.

"Rhoda, I hear you're keeping company with a new guy these days?" Ellen asked politely. Unlike Judy she was always polite.

"He's new to me all right," I replied. "But he's been around for a while, 150 years or so but that's young for a vampire."

"C'mon, Rhoda," Judy chided. "You can't kid a kidder. What's the deal with him? Vampires, shmampires, what does he do for a living?"

"He's not exactly living, but he was a rabbi once upon a time. He lives as a Hasid and works as a diamond cutter, a night job." I hadn't told my mom yet about Sheldon's job since it was a trade, not a profession. Even though she was a Socialist, she was still a snob. Only the Orthodox worked in the diamond district and they were as foreign to Mom and her friends as vampires. She was an atheist who disapproved of rabbis, priests, and other true believers.

"Noooo," Miriam said in disbelief. "You're not the kind of girl to get involved with a rabbi. Much less a Hasidic Jew. I thought you were an atheist."

Miriam was humoring me, and so were the rest of the girls. She just ignored the whole vampire thing, which was her way. She was very polite and wouldn't have wanted to make fun of or contradict me. The girls were obviously not going to believe my story about Sheldon. I don't know why I'd told them the truth—I guess because I wanted to make it easier on Mom, so she wouldn't have to lie to them as well. I couldn't lie to her—I'd never been able to lie to her.

"That's my mom you're thinking of, Miriam. She hasn't been in a synagogue since she was a kid, even though you'd never know it considering how she carries on about me marrying a Jew. Rabbis are supposed to be married and have kids. Vampires are supposed to be solitary creatures of the night. Poor guy has got to be dealing with a severe identity crisis. I'm pretty confused myself."

The Chinese food arrived, smelling garlicky and delicious. I put my napkin around my neck and dug into the lobster with black bean sauce, a specialty of the China Palace. What would it be like to never eat lobster with black bean sauce again, or anything edible again? It didn't seem to bother Sheldon when we were at the Carnegie Deli, but he was slim and probably never had an eating problem even when he ate real food. I supposed it would be reassuring to know you couldn't ever gain weight. I decided that if I was ever going to become a vampire I'd have to lose at least fifty pounds first. I could not imagine spending eternity in plus-size clothing.

After dinner, we drove to the beach to take our usual two-mile walk. Mom made it a few blocks before she suggested we sit and look at the ocean. She pretended she wasn't tired but I could see that she literally couldn't take another step. She was gasping for breath. I sat with my arm around her protectively. The girls walked on without us. After they got back, Judy suggested she and I walk to the ice cream stand at the end of the pier and get ice cream for everyone. Mom said she'd wait till we got back, looking grateful that she didn't have to get up.

"Rhoda, your mom isn't doing so good, I guess you can see that," Judy said. "She may need another surgery. You're going to have to take her up North with you, or get her help down here. She can't manage alone much longer."

"She's already had a quadruple bypass," I said. "She doesn't have any blood vessels left to bypass. She's very independent. I don't think she'd accept help—except mine, and I don't want to move to Florida. I have no space for her—I live in a tiny studio."

I didn't think I could bear to lose Mom. She was all I had in the relatives department, I'd tried to have kids with my ex—but not very hard. We were both too busy with our careers and his career included the *shiksa* in the next cubicle. My mom waited till she was in her forties to have me, and was grateful not to have any more kids because she said that taking care of my dad and me was enough, but I think she just wasn't the nurturing type. In another era she

45

would have been a CEO. She liked running things, which didn't make her the easiest mom to get along with when I was a kid. But she was fiercely loyal and was always there when I needed her. Now it was my turn to be there for her. She was dependent on me and I had to save her life. I didn't care that she was in her eighties, I couldn't let her die.

Chapter Six

I got home after a week in Florida, even more frantic that I hadn't heard from Sheldon. While I was in Florida I'd obsessively checked my cell phone and called my home phone for messages from Sheldon. Nothing. I couldn't understand it. We'd gotten so close that night when we saw *Fiddler on the Roof.* He'd opened up to me, showed me his tortured Jewish inner child. Then again, what could I have been thinking? The guy was a vampire, or he said he was a vampire. The real question was what was wrong with me? Was I so desperate for a man who treated me decently that I'd buy any story I was told? Betrayal by my ex had undermined any trust I'd ever had in men—which wasn't a lot to begin with. Right now I wasn't sure of anything. Maybe Sheldon really had been putting me on. What proof did I have of his real identity—phony fangs, a trick mirror that didn't fog up, a low body temperature? What was wrong with me? Why did I believe him in the first place? Maybe he was just another player trying to get laid. But last time he didn't want sex. What was that about? Men—alive or dead—had always been a mystery to me—they still were.

I traipsed upstairs to Charlene's apartment, forcing myself to walk rather than take the elevator. I desperately needed the exercise.

"No call, no email, no nothing, Vick. I'm desperate. What should I do? I'm sure he's seeing someone else. He probably lied to me about me being his first in a hundred years. It was just a really good line."

Charlene was nonchalant. She never got worked up about men, except her ex-husband who had left her for his

47

secretary. Once you got her on the subject of what a rat he was she never shut up. She didn't worry about attracting men because, unlike me, she had the "it" factor, that mysterious allure that drew men to her no matter what she did. Charlene could stand in the corner at a party and, while I was frantically circulating, trying to flirt, men would congregate around her vying for her attention. What the hell was her secret? OK, so she was tall, voluptuous, with long black curly hair and could have been a swimsuit model. OK, so I was short, plump and could have been a Jennie Craig "before" model. But looks weren't everything. Who the hell said that? Not my mother, who was always trying to get me to lose weight.

"Jeez, I don't know why guys think they have to feed you a line even after they get you into bed. Or tell you they'll call if they have no intention of calling. "

"Charlene, Sheldon was different. Not just that he was a vampire, or said he was. He really seemed enthralled with me."

"Has it occurred to you that maybe that's why he's had second thoughts about pursuing a romance with you? He's a vampire. Think blood-sucking, painful death, maybe arising from the dead, maybe not. He may not really be a vegetarian vampire like Edward Cullen. Maybe he's a Dracula vampire like, well, Dracula. Maybe he's tempted to kill you, or doesn't want to kill you, or is afraid of falling in love with a mortal, or maybe his Blackberry died and there aren't any pay phones that work in Brooklyn anymore. Who the hell knows?"

She took a long drag from her Marlboro and I coughed. I'd begged her to stop, I finally had given up smoking when I couldn't breathe anymore but Charlene thought she was immortal. She jogged every day and thought that magically made up for smoking. I kept trying to explain that her lungs didn't care if she jogged—they longed for clean air. I wanted her to stop for selfish reasons—I couldn't stand to be in her smelly apartment. When she visited me I enforced my no smoking rule.

"Could you please blow the smoke out the window while I'm here?" I begged her.

Charlene opened the window and blew out amazingly round smoke rings.

"Maybe he's just not into me—literally. He doesn't go for my blood type. It's hard enough to figure out why a regular guy doesn't call, much less a vampire."

Charlene laughed. "I wish that during a first date you could implant a remote recording device on a guy and find out what he's saying about you."

"Guys don't talk about women to their friends, at least that's what they claim."

"I wonder if he hangs out with other vampires?" Charlene speculated. "Maybe someone knows him."

"I doubt it," I said. "If he does hang out with other vampires they've got to be Jewish. I can't see Sheldon with a bunch of *goyishe* vamps. He's just too ethnic. He dresses like a Hasid and lives in Crown Heights. Or that's what he said."

"I'll ask my coven," Charlene offered. "I bet someone knows a vampire who knows other vampires who know Jewish vampires. There's got to be a vampire underground. Haven't you read Anne Rice? They even have secret vampire balls. Now that would be a trip."

"OK, go ahead and ask. What have I got to lose? But I can't exactly hunt him down. If he doesn't want me too bad; it's his loss. I'll move on. I always do." I sniffled a little. I was tired of moving on. I would have liked to move in for a change.

More bad news arrived when I got downstairs—a voice mail from Dr. Cohen, Mom's doctor, asking me to call him. Ominous. Cohen never called unless he wanted me to pressure my mom into doing something she was refusing to do. He was a cute young Jewish doctor who was very fond of my mother, flirting with her whenever she went to see him, which was often. Even though I'd been to his office with her numerous times, he never flirted with me, more's the pity.

"So? What's going on?" I asked anxiously when I heard his voice.

"Has your mother told you the results of her echocardiogram?" he asked.

"No, I didn't even know she had one."

"You've noticed her being out of breath a lot, haven't you?"

"I've been worried about that. I thought it was due to the bypass surgery."

"No, the bypass went well, but the latest echo shows she has a faulty heart valve which needs to be replaced."

"Why hasn't she told me?" I asked him.

"She was afraid to tell you because she doesn't want another surgery. She's refusing to do it. I can hardly blame her. She's already been through two heart surgeries. I'm hoping you can talk her into it."

"What will happen if she doesn't have it?"

"She'll have a heart attack and die. I'm not sure when, but it could be soon."

"Oh no, no. She's going to have that surgery."

"You're a good kid," he laughed. "She's lucky to have you."

"She's all I've got. I'm lucky to have her, too."

I collapsed on the couch and sobbed when I hung up. How could I ask Mom to go through another major surgery, the last one was horrible. I had to try, though, so I picked up the phone.

"Mom, it's me. Dr. Cohen told me the news."

"Dammit. I told him to keep it to himself. I didn't want to upset you."

"What kind of *meshugenah* are you? You're dying and you don't want to upset me. What would be sufficient reason to upset me?"

"I'm not dying. I'm fine."

"You can hardly walk a block without gasping for breath. You will have a heart attack and die if you don't have this surgery."

"I'm eighty-one years old. I have to die sometime."

"Eighty-one isn't that old anymore. Angela Lansbury is eighty-four and she's doing eight shows a week on Broadway."

"If I had her stamina I'd join the senior Rockettes. I bet you didn't know we have a bunch of ex-Rockettes down here who put on a show every Christmas."

"Stop changing the subject. Ma, you can't do this to me. I need you. You're the only family I have."

"Oh, Rhoda, why didn't you stay married? I'd feel so much better if you were married."

"He left me, ma, for a bimbette, don't you remember?" I wondered if she was losing her mind as well as her body.

"Didn't he break up with that girl? Can't you get him back?" She remembered.

"I'd rather put on a burka and live with the Taliban."

"Well, he probably wouldn't have left you if you'd worn a burka," she laughed. "He always wanted you barefoot and pregnant."

"That's another thing. I never got pregnant due to his sluggish sperm, but he blamed it on me. The bimbette never got pregnant either. Ma, will you think about the surgery, just think about it. I'll call you tomorrow."

Chapter Seven

It was a dark and stormy night. Or it should have been. I felt really foolish standing in a circle, holding hands with a bunch of witches. Charlene's coven meeting was in the large living room of a condo on the Grand Concourse in the Bronx. The apartment was furnished with expensive couches and antique throw rugs. Having been brought up by parents who were obsessed with design I noticed these things. We had to schlep to the Bronx because the Manhattan coven members had apartments that were too small to accommodate the entire thirteen members. Usually they didn't let a stranger go to their private ceremonies but since I was Charlene's best friend and Charlene was the High Priestess they didn't have much choice. Actually she'd been trying to talk me into joining for years but I'd refused, partly because I felt that if I was going to get religious I'd go to a synagogue and partly because it was in the Bronx.

I'd allowed Charlene to drag me up there on this freezing night in December—which actually was the darkest night of the year—to a winter solstice ceremony because one of the coven members claimed acquaintance with a vampire, who maybe knew Sheldon. Maybe they all knew each other, there might be some vast vampire network, or at least a telephone tree. Even though I still couldn't stop thinking about him, I wasn't planning to throw myself at him in desperation; I was no stalker. I'd been ready to accept that he was just not into me after a week with no call, when Charlene had another idea. After Dr. Cohen called I'd raced up to her apartment, gasping for breath through my tears.

"I know I'm supposed to be resigned to my mom dying, Charlene, she's eighty-one and she's not going to live forever. But I just can't deal with it. I can't. I've lost too much—a husband, the family we were supposed to have. I'm forty-one, I'll probably never have kids. She's all I've got—and you of course."

"Wow. Living forever. Now there's a concept."

"What on earth do you mean?"

"Don't you know someone who lives forever?" she suggested coyly. "And couldn't he... arrange for other people to do the same."

"What? Turn my mother into a vampire? That's the most grotesque idea I ever heard."

"And why is it grotesque? Is Sheldon grotesque? From what you told me he's a real gentleman. Just because you're a vampire doesn't mean you have to be a killer. Haven't you read *Twilight*? Maybe he could teach your mom his secrets—make her a de-fanged immortal."

"Can you just see my mom as a vampire?" I had to laugh. "She'd be mortified. She's so conventional. How could she keep hanging out with her friends? That's the only thing she likes to do. They're all in bed by sunset."

"I'm sure they'll adjust. They love her and want to keep her around too. If they have to give up early bird specials they'll survive. I'm sure the food later at night is a whole lot better."

"But my poor mom won't be able to eat it. She'll be cruising the streets looking for poor, unsuspecting victims." I couldn't imagine my kindly mom, who volunteered at the hard of hearing association and mentored ghetto kids, tracking down human prey. What if she attacked those kids?

"Sheldon sounded eminently civilized," Charlene reassured me. "He hardly attacked you, and showed no interest in sucking your blood."

"I have no idea how he gets blood," I said. "He says he gets it from animals. I hope that doesn't mean he kidnaps people's pets. Maybe he goes hunting for big game in the Catskills, like the Cullens. Can you see my mom doing that? She's strictly a City girl."

"C'mon, Rhoda, you have no idea how he survives or how she would. The first step is to find him and ask him."

"That seems to be the problem. He's disappeared."

"I bet Karen knows him. She's networked up the wazoo. She's even been invited to dinner at the White House. OK, she crashed, but she didn't get caught like that blond broad who crashed the White House state dinner. She knows everyone and as soon as vampires got hot she starting bragging that she knows some personally."

"You believe her?'

"You would too if you knew her. That girl is the Arianna Huffington of the paranormal. She actually was a consultant on the set of *Buffy the Vampire Slayer*. How do you think they came up with all that ancient vampire and monster lore?"

Finally I agreed. Maybe Sheldon could save Mom by bringing her into his undead fraternity. If turning her into a vampire was her last chance at life—maybe eternal life was pushing it, I just wanted her to live a few more years—what other choice did I have? Plus, let's face it, I was desperate to see him. One night with a vampire was worth years with most Manhattan men, who talked incessantly about their boring jobs and couldn't get it up half the time, or couldn't keep it up if they did. Sheldon didn't talk about his job, and in bed, well there was no contest.

So that's how I wound up on the Grand Concourse in a white robe reciting ancient Celtic verses. At least they sounded like ancient Celtic verses. Charlene gave me a cheat sheet and I recited:

> *Lady spin your circle bright, weave*
> *your web of dark and light; Earth, Air,*
> *Fire and Water, bound here as one;*
> *Rune and rock and blood and bone,*
> *power of sea and power of stone, bound*
> *here as one*

I was hoping there would be some spell casting, and there was. After creating a circle by marking off the four directions, and creating an altar in the middle of the circle, the coven cast a healing spell for my mom, which I thought was very nice of them. I also asked for a spell to find Sheldon and they graciously burned some herbs, which smelled delicious, and recited:

> *I conjure thee oh creature of darkness, that thou beest*
> *at a meeting place of love and joy and truth; a shield against*
> *death; a boundary between men and the realm of the*
> *Mighty Ones; May our Rhoda, queen of the night, in all*
> *your beauty bright, find your lover wherever he be.*

Afterwards we had a potluck dinner with scrumptious food—witches love to cook and eat, Charlene told me later. I felt right at home in the group when I noticed that the majority were on the hefty side after the robes came off. Karen, however, was not only not fat, but looked like she worked out regularly, and wore a very fashionable jeans outfit, with a fitted sweater, bolero jacket and high heels that I would have keeled over in.

"So you're the infamous friend who had a fling with a vampire?" Karen asked.

"I guess word gets around?"

"Charlene isn't known for her discretion, and this bit of gossip is more than juicy, it's well, Page Six worthy. I am so in awe of you. I have never met anyone who has actually had sex with a vampire. How was it?"

I'd always admired Charlene for being so open, but not with my love life.

"I really don't want to share the gory details, except that there wasn't any…gore I mean. I just want to find him. He left me flowers and a promise to see me again but not a word since. It's been two weeks. I would never track down a guy who didn't want to see me because despite frequent lapses, I do have some pride. But now there's another reason I don't want to go into."

"What do you know about him?"

"He's Jewish, works in the diamond district, lives as a Hasid in Crown Heights."

"That's a great cover," Karen observed, obviously impressed. "I've heard rumors about Hasidic vampires, that there may be a whole nest of them in Crown Heights."

"Where did you hear that rumor?"

"I took the tour."

"The tour? Is there a Hasidic vampire tour?"

"No, but there's a tour of Lubavitcher Hasidic sites in Crown Heights. The guide told us about some very mysterious Hasids who only come out at night," Karen said. "He showed us their lair—I vaguely remember where it is. I asked him a lot of questions but all he would say was they were just dedicated Talmudic scholars, he knew very little about them and neither did anyone else. He said that as long as they observed Jewish law and didn't bother anyone the rabbis wouldn't bother them. Then I asked if they were married or had kids. He looked at me very suspiciously and clammed up. It was weird."

"We're going to have to take the tour, obviously," I said. "Karen, would you come? Maybe you'll remember the building he pointed out. And Charlene, I'm sure you wouldn't miss it for the world."

Charlene nodded enthusiastically. She was always up for an adventure, no matter how bizarre the destination.

Chapter Eight

We arrived for the Hasidic tour promptly at the ungodly hour of 10:30 a.m. At least it was ungodly for me. I was usually barely up by that hour, and certainly was never on the subway to Brooklyn by 9:30. Maybe I could keep waking up later and later until I adjusted to Sheldon's schedule—once I found out what his schedule actually was. Charlene and Karen came with me for the tour. I'd never been to Crown Heights. It felt like we'd gotten out of the subway from twenty-first-century New York and exited into a time warp—eighteenth-century Europe, but with some visitors from Harlem. Hasidic men, wearing black suits and hats with long beards and side curls, shared the streets with black youth in baggy pants and over-the-ear wool caps. The Hasidic women—in kerchiefs, black stockings and long coats-- were all pushing baby carriages and had three or more kids hanging off them. The stores had Yiddish as well as English signs.

The tour participants consisted of us and a group of very Republican-looking white couples dressed up in their Sunday best, and their excessively neat children, all of whom could have been transported straight from 1958. The three of us stood out like exotic birds in a henhouse. I asked the big blonde woman next to me where they came from. "We're from Pastor Hagee's Church in San Antonio, Texas, dear," she said with a southern drawl, assuming I knew what she was talking about. She stuck her face too close to mine and said loudly, "This tour is just fascinating. We went to Israel last year. We just love Jews."

"What?" I was stunned. "Why would you love Jews?"

"Well, you know the Bible says that the End of Days will come after the Jews return to the Land of Israel. Then there will be a second coming of Christ and we Christian faithful will go up to Heaven during Rapture. The rest of humanity will just go to Hell. We came on this tour to be more Rapture ready."

I'd heard something about the Rapture but never met anyone who believed in it. "How about the Jews?" I asked, not really wanting to know the answer.

"Oh, we wouldn't harm a hair on your dear little heads. All you have to do is convert and you can come up to Heaven with us."

"How did you know I was Jewish?"

"The nose, darlin'."

For a moment I wondered why I'd never gotten one of those ski jump noses like all the girls I grew up with. Because I liked my nose, that's why. I thought it was aristocratic.

"We're stuck on the tour with a bunch of born-again nutcases," I whispered to Charlene.

"I heard that broad. You know George Bush and Sarah Palin believe in the Rapture."

"Let's hope it works. When the Rapture comes they get transported to heaven and we get to stay here with all the liberals, atheists and other apostates."

I turned towards our tour guide who was lecturing about the history of the Chabad movement. "Most people assume Hasidim are sort of like the Amish—but Jewish," he said. "Nothing could be further from the truth. We may have black hats, speak Yiddish and have as many children as God grants, some of us have ten or more, but we also have one of the most popular sites on the Internet."

"Why am I not surprised?" I nudged Charlene again. "There's no way Jews could resist modern technology no matter what kind of clothes they wear."

Our guide was a little, skinny, very young guy with the requisite beard, except his was short and scraggly. His Yiddish accent was incongruous on such a youngster. In my world only people over eighty had a Yiddish accent. He introduced himself as Rabbi Yisroel, the former rabbi of Woodstock, New York. Like Mormons, the Lubavitchers are missionaries. They set up shop in cities and towns all over the country and try to convert Jews who have strayed from the fold back to their religion.

"Why did you leave Woodstock?" I asked, wondering why anyone would come back to this dreary neighborhood when he could live in the beautiful Catskills.

"Family problems, don't ask! Plus there was a war for the local Jews. A rival Chabad rabbi in Kingston a few miles away had more money and support. Between him and the Woodstock Jewish Congregation folk singing rabbi, no one came to my services. I'm a musician too, but I play rap music."

"What???" The day was getting stranger.

"You didn't know there were Hasidic rappers, did you?" he laughed. "I play back-up for Matishayu, the famous Jewish reggae rapper. He was on Letterman a while ago."

"No, I didn't know." Hey, if there were Hasidic vampires, why not Hasidic rappers.

The first stop was the balcony of the Lubavitch synagogue where we were segregated by Plexiglas from the two hundred or so long-bearded Jewish men swaying wildly and *davvening* off-key. It turns out the Plexiglas was the *mehitza*, the barrier that separated the women from the men below. When it came to sexism even Muslim fundamentalists don't have much on Hasidic Jews. At least Orthodox Jewish women don't have to wear veils, but they do have to cover their heads. In olden times they wore kerchiefs but today most of them wear wigs, which makes no sense at all in an era where wigs are sexier than real hair.

The next stop was fun--a matzoh bakery where they were making *shmura* matzoh that was kosher for Passover. In the obsessive-compulsive tradition of Kosher food the matzoh has to be made in less than eighteen minutes so the dough won't rise, not even one millimeter.

"Try not to get in the way," Yisroel instructed us as the group stepped from the freezing sidewalk into a loud, hot, dizzying flurry of activity. Twenty-five women in kerchiefs stood side by side at a paper-covered table furiously rolling dough into flat round blobs that were then tossed to another table where a four-man team punctured them with tiny holes, lined them up on wooden poles and handed them to a baker who slid them into a coal- burning oven for precisely twenty seconds. The workers greeted each batch with shouts in Yiddish and bursts of applause. We got to taste the matzoh which, though slightly burnt, was a lot better than Manischevitz.

The next stop was a tiny living room where a wizened old man was painstakingly penning a Torah scroll with a quill on parchment. I was fascinated by his artistry. Our guide explained it took a year to make these scrolls and synagogues all over the world ordered them.

We wound up at the visitors center at the Rebbe's headquarters. Rebbe Menachem Schneerson had been the spiritual leader of the Chabad movement until he had the temerity to die in 1994 without naming a successor, which occasioned a huge battle between two factions of Lubuvitchers. I had no idea who won. A lot of Lubuvitchers thought he was the messiah, even after he died. I wondered how that would jibe with the second coming of Christ according to the fundamentalist Christians. I could imagine the spirits of Schneerson and Jerry Falwell battling it out during the Rapture. Who would get into heaven and who would have to convert? I'd put my money on the Rebbe.

On the way to the deli for lunch, which was included with the tour, Karen shouted out, "That's it. That's the place where the scholars only studied after dark. I'm sure of it."

We were on St. Marks Avenue. She pointed out a nondescript brownstone with blackout curtains on the upstairs windows.

"Who lives there?" she asked our guide.

"That building is cursed," our guide said in a low voice.

"Who cursed it?" I asked him, hoping to get some useful information.

"There are rumors of some strange goings-on there," he stroked his beard thoughtfully, raised his eyebrows and nodded in a scholarly way. "Local Kabbalists tell stories about *estries* who fly and subsist on blood, especially the blood of children. Maybe vampires. It's probably just superstition, but you never know." He gave a ghoulish laugh to see how the kids on the tour were reacting. They had been pretty bored so far but they perked up at the word vampire. Even fundamentalist Christian kids weren't immune to the gospel according to Stephenie Meyer.

"Unholy creatures," one of the suits said vehemently. "They should be burned at the stake."

"You just need the stake, not the bonfire, I believe," I said to him sarcastically. "Don't be ridiculous. There's no such thing as vampires."

"That's the place he pointed out during the last tour. He seems to have conveniently forgotten," Karen whispered to us. "We'll go back there tonight. But let's finish the tour. I'd hate to miss the deli lunch."

By the time we got to the deli I fell into the chair, exhausted. That was a hell of a long tour. Unfortunately today's Hasidim may speak Yiddish but they know nothing about real Jewish food. I was hoping to get some good kosher food, but the pastrami was dried out and the corned beef was worse. The bagels were the big puffy kind, not the little chewy old-fashioned ones. You have to go to Katz's on the Lower East Side for real pastrami.

That night we took the subway back to Brooklyn and braved the streets in Crown Heights, which looked much less Jewish as the sun was setting. Crown Heights was still the ghetto. When we got to St. Marks Avenue I relaxed since it was across from the 77th Precinct. We could always yell and maybe a cop would come running. Or maybe not. Why, I wondered, were streets named after saints, especially in this neighborhood. Why not Rabbi Akiva Avenue or Golda Meir Boulevard? Harlem had Martin Luther King Boulevard or W. E. B. DuBois Avenue. The building in question looked even more ominous at dusk, with those black curtains and a stoop that looked like no one ever sat on it.

"Can we go home now?" Charlene's voice quavered.

"C'mon, you big sissy." I wasn't easily scared especially when this close to possibly finding Sheldon. "You're six feet tall and know karate and kickboxing." Charlene was always taking the latest aerobic fad. "What're you so afraid of?"

"Things that go bump in the night, more than getting mugged. Though that's crossed my mind as well. That building might have some nasty vampires along with your de-fanged boyfriend."

"Get a grip," Karen chided Charlene. "We're big bad witches remember. We can always cast a spell."

"Spell?" Charlene squeaked. "I don't know any spells against vampires. Do you?"

63

"How about the divine light invocation?"

"What's that?" I asked. Charlene also looked bewildered.

"OK here's what we do just in case," Karen instructed.

"Raise your arms, hold your breath and affirm to yourself with all the concentration possible:

I am sustained by Divine Light
I am protected by Divine Light
I am surrounded by Divine Light

"Now use your imagination to see yourself standing in a shower of brilliant white Light. If that doesn't work run across the street and into the precinct, shouting, vampires are after me. At the worst you'll get locked up in Bellevue."

"It's freezing," I said, all of a sudden noticing that we were standing on the street shivering. "We can't just loiter in the street. Women do not loiter in this neighborhood. We'll probably get arrested for prostitution."

"Three nice Jewish girls like us?" Charlene said.

"You're not Jewish," I reminded her.

"Two and a half nice Jewish girls. I'm Jewish by association. It's catching."

Karen laughed. "I'm not Jewish either. I'm a nice Italian girl, Catholic of course, but since I'm a New Yorker I'm Jewish. You remember what Lennie Bruce said, 'If you live in New York, you're Jewish, and if you live in the Midwest you're a wasp—well I'm a native New Yorker."

"Let's hail a cab to sit in," Charlene suggested, like the half-Jewish princess that she was. "We'll wait for Sheldon to come out of that building. It's almost sundown. He probably goes out at night, wouldn't ya think?" Charlene asked me. "You told me he works at night."

"It's forty cents a minute. We could be here for hours," I complained.

"I'll spring for the fare," Karen offered. "I just got a job on Wall Street. Hedge fund manager."

"What kind of job is that for a witch?" I asked.

"The best kind. I'll be a rich witch."

"OK, if he doesn't come out in an hour we'll go in and look for him."

"You'll go in," Charlene said.

The cabdriver's ID said Khalid Mohammed. He had a menacing look and a prayer rug next to him in the passenger seat. If I'd been sitting next to him on a plane I would have checked out his midsection for explosives. I was nervous. What would he think of three women sitting in the back of a cab in Crown Heights casing a building with blackout curtains?

When I told him we just wanted to sit here he took it as an invitation to interrogate us. Unfortunately he spoke English—with a thick Brooklyn accent.

"So, whadda three nice girls like you doin' in a dump like this?" he asked. "You should be clubbin' in Brooklyn Heights. How's about I take you to this high rollin' club I know about. Lotsa older guys there. Gamblin' in the back room. You might meet a guy with moolah."

Was this guy with the Muslim mob or with a road company of *Guys and Dolls*?

"Where do you come from?" I asked him. "You're sure not from the Middle East."

"I'm from Joisey."

"A Muslim from Joisey?"

"I'm Italian."

"A Muslim Italian from Joisey?" I was beginning to feel like we were doing a Marx Brothers routine.

"Doncha believe in diversity? Whas wrong with a Muslim Italian from Joisey?"

Charlene elbowed me in the side and whispered, "He's probably nuts. Just humor him."

"Whaddya doin' here anyways?" He kept talking. "Just black hats around here, no good lookin' dames."

"My boyfriend is a black hat." I leaned forward conspiratorially. "He's hiding me from his family."

"Whaddya doin' with a married man, a black hat to boot? Them guys is good for nothing,' I never got a decent tip from one yet."

"My boyfriend's rich. And he's single." I leaned back confidently as if I knew what I was talking about. "And my girlfriends wanted to meet him." It was a lame story but he didn't look bright enough to figure that out.

After sitting in the cab for an hour with Khalid asking us a long string of questions, including how old we were, where we worked, how much we made, who had a boyfriend, why we weren't married, why we got divorced (me and Charlene, Karen had never been married), why we didn't have kids…why, why, why, I finally told him that he should check out our Facebook pages if he wanted more information. We promised to confirm him if he friended us. I, for one, was lying. No way was that guy ever going to be my friend on Facebook or anywhere else, but the suggestion seemed to mollify him. Then he went into a long rant about how he hated being a taxi driver, how his back hurt constantly, how the Bloomberg administration was trying to drive honest cabbies out of business, how it was impossible to make any money after he leased the cab, yadda, yadda, yadda. By that time he'd gotten on my last nerve and I couldn't have cared less if he wound up homeless.

"Someone is coming out of the building," Charlene whispered. "A tall guy. Black hat."

"Omigod it's him!" I shrieked. I couldn't believe it. I ran out of the cab and down the street. He moved really fast and I was out of breath by the time I caught up with him on the next block. I was yelling his name but he kept on walking.

"Sheldon, why are you running away from me?" I gasped.

"Rhoda, you're blowing my cover," he said turning around while he kept walking. I noticed he had a long beard. He must have let it grow back since the last time I saw him. "I'm a Hasid," he growled. "I'm not supposed to be seen talking to a woman I'm not married to on the street."

"Then get into the goddamned cab." I growled back.

Charlene and Karen had told the cabbie to follow me. That was a smart move. I opened the passenger door for him and pushed him into the front seat. I got into the back with the girls and gave Khalid my address in Manhattan.

"Who is this pasty-faced weirdo?" Khalid turned around and asked me. "He doesn't look like a Hasid to me. He looks like he's got AIDS. I'm not gonna sit next to him. Maybe he's catching."

"Ok, stop the goddamned cab. Charlene, go sit in the front, Sheldon come back and sit next to me."

"Can we please get out of Crown Heights first," Sheldon begged. "I'm in enough trouble already."

"If you get out of here quick you can have the tall girl with the curly hair in the front," I told Khalid. "How's that?"

"You're gonna owe me for this," Charlene whispered to me. "That cabbie creeps me out."

"Name your price."

"Permission to smoke in your apartment, in perpetuity."

"Aaaargh. OK." I would have promised anything. I'd take it back later.

Karen poked me and whispered, "Sheldon's really cute. Pasty face and all. He looks just like Sasha Baron Cohen. Not as Borat--as himself. Sasha is to die for."

"They say Sasha's an Orthodox Jew like Sheldon," I said, "though I find that really hard to believe. I can't imagine Orthodox Jews would approve of sticking your face in a fat guy's butt."

"I didn't see that movie," Charlene said, "now I'm not going to."

"I wonder if Sheldon would like it?" I mused aloud.

"I've seen it." Sheldon turned around. "Disgusting!"

When we got to Bed Stuy Sheldon got into the back, grabbed me and kissed me. I kissed him back because I couldn't help it but I wasn't forgiving him that fast. "How did you find me? Did you hire a vampire detective or what?"

"Why didn't you call? How could you cry on my shoulder and open your heart to me and then disappear? What kind of game were you playing?" I shot back at him. I had no intention of answering his questions until I was good and ready.

"I don't play games, Rhoda. I was just protecting you. Wait until we get to your apartment—I'll explain everything. I swear I'll make it up to you."

"You shouldn't swear—I think it's a Christian thing. But there's something very important you need to do for me and you sure as hell are going to do it."

"What is it?"

"I'll tell you later. I want you to promise you'll do whatever I ask no matter what it is." I felt I had the upper hand at the moment but might not get it again.

"OK, as long as you tell me how you found me," he said. "I have a feeling I may be sorry, but I promise."

Chapter Nine

I was half-afraid Sheldon might fly away before he got back to my apartment, assuming he could fly, which I'd never seen him do.

"Sheldon, can you fly?" I asked him as we trudged upward. "If you can I wish you would fly me up these stairs. I'm exhausted."

Charlene and Karen had discreetly disappeared into a neighborhood bar when we got out of the cab.

"If I could fly why would I have to take a cab to Manhattan from Brooklyn? Or worse, the subway, which is how I get to work every night." Sheldon said.

"You take the subway?"

"Unfortunately yes, I have my limits transportation-wise. I'm not Superman, just a lowly Jewish vampire who works in the diamond district."

I unlocked my door, and led him to the couch where we sat side by side. He took my hand, gazed into my eyes and smiled. "OK, that wasn't what you wanted to ask me, was it?"

"No." I felt very sullen. I didn't want to give him the satisfaction of letting him know how much I cared.

"You don't have to ask me. I know." He looked into my eyes soulfully. "You're my little knish."

"Knish!! You're calling me a knish."

"If I could have anything in the human world I'd have a knish, so you're it." He gave me such a big boyish grin that I almost forgot what a faithless bloodsucker he really was.

"Answer the question. You know what the question is." I put my legs up on my coffee table and pretended to relax. I didn't want him to know how anxious I was about his answer.

"No, you were not just a two-night stand for me. But in all these hundred years I have never let myself fall in love with a human woman. I didn't want to ruin your life. Seeing *Fiddler* reminded me of what it's like to lose everything you love. I didn't want to put you through that. You deserve to find a nice Jewish guy, settle down and have babies."

"I'm too old for babies." Actually my mom had me when she was forty so maybe late-life childbearing was in my genetic inheritance.

"Forty-one is not that old. If you can't have one you could always adopt," he said.

"We could adopt together."

"I doubt there's an agency that would approve a vampire."

"C'mon, Sheldon, that's not the real reason."

"Rhoda, you deserve better than me. What kind of life would you have with me? I don't have a life. No way you would move to Brooklyn, much less Crown Heights. I can't see you in a wig pretending to be Orthodox. You'd hate going to synagogue, much less standing behind a *mehitza*. You like to dress in jeans not long skirts. I'm sure you wear a bathing suit and go swimming now and then. Well, not if you live with me—unless you just swim with women. And I haven't even mentioned the hours I keep."

I ignored that. "Why would I have to wear a wig? Why do I have to stand behind a *mehitza* or go to synagogue at all? How does anyone know those women are wearing wigs anyway? All I'd have to do is put on a dress with long sleeves and push a baby carriage."

"And rent about ten kids," he laughed.

"OK, you'll have to leave Crown Heights. Why can't you be a Manhattan metrosexual vampire?"

"I can't leave Crown Heights. Can't we just date for a while?"

"You're the one who didn't call." I started sulking again, turning away from him. I hated myself when I did that. It was so unattractive.

"Rhoda, being a Hasid is my cover, it's worked for a hundred years and I'm used to it. I'm set in my ways. I have responsibilities to be there for the vampire *minyan* who live in my building and to Goldie. There are folks out there who would like to kill me. Fundamentalist Christians for starters. And vampire hunters—you don't even want to know about them."

"I ran into a bunch of those Christians on the tour."

"So that's how you found me. That *fershtunken* tour. They're always pointing out our building to scare the tourists. Those Lubuvitchers will do anything to seem cool and hip."

"Our tour guide was a rapper."

"He was a ghost?"

"Not a tapper, a rapper. You are really from another century. Rap is music. The kids love it."

"I never listen to music. I prefer audio books, except when Goldie is reading to me."

"That's another thing, Goldie. Does she go wherever you go?"

"She has for a hundred years. Without me she'd disintegrate. I wouldn't want to destroy Goldie. She's been a faithful servant and a good friend. "

"You are truly weird, and not just because you're a vampire. Who has a golem? I thought they were mythical creatures?"

"And I'm not?"

"You're not mythical to me." I went over to give him a hug, but he moved to the window, pulled out a cigar and lit it.

"Put that goddamned thing out. I didn't know vampires smoked."

"What other pleasures have I got left? I can't eat or drink. I don't have sex—much. Although now that you've tracked me down I'm not responsible for what happens between us anymore—you are. I love smoking. I especially love cigars. Why shouldn't I smoke? I can't get cancer."

"I can. Ever heard of the dangers of second-hand smoke?"

"OK, I'll put it out." He sighed and threw the cigar out the window. "Sheldon, you don't throw lit cigars out the window. What if you hit someone?" I could imagine my neighbors being scandalized if any of them happened to be leaving or coming home at the moment.

"Rhoda, you seem to expect me to behave properly. I have no idea how humans are supposed to behave these days. I don't hang out with humans. In my day people threw garbage out windows."

Suddenly I realized I not only had a vampire on my hands but an unsocialized vampire. I was going to have to teach him how to act human. I supposed it was no worse than getting any guy to pick his clothes up off the floor but I had no idea what other bad habits I might have to deal with. Did he piss out the window too? Oh, he probably couldn't piss.

"How do you know the expression 'hang out' if you're from the eighteenth century?" I asked him.

"I watch TV, what do you think? And I know how to read. I've read all the vampire novels so I know how I'm supposed to act. They're a little dumb, don't you think? Do they write them for kids? Except for Anne Rice of course. I wish I could be like Lestat. He's my hero—so courageous. Can you believe he became a rock star?"

"No, I can't. That was fiction. In real life vampires don't play the Palace. Or maybe they do. What do I know? What else do you do with your spare time?"

"I surf the Web. I davven, study Torah, kibbitz and play chess with the guys I live with."

"Torah? Guys. What kind of guys?"

"Vampire guys. Jewish Hasidic vampire guys. Who do you think I live with?"

"Sheldon, I have no idea. I really know nothing about you. Or almost nothing."

It immediately occurred to me how thrilled Charlene would be to find out there were other vampires, hopefully single ones. We could double date.

"Are they single vampires?"

"Why do you want to know?"

"You met Charlene in the cab. The tall brunette with the curly hair. She's my best friend and she wants to date a vampire too."

"The vampires I know are all Hasids. They'd never date a shiksa, human or vampire ...well maybe Mendel would."

"Who's Mendel?

"My brother Herschel's roommate. He's sex-crazed. Herschel is engaged."

"You have a brother?" That sure complicated things. Would Sheldon be willing to leave his brother in Crown Heights and move in with me?

"How did you wind up with a vampire brother?"

"I turned him into one. He was dying of consumption. He begged me, he didn't want to die. I didn't want to go through eternity without a family."

I started sobbing. I didn't plan to, it just happened.

Sheldon looked alarmed. "Rhoda, what did I do? Did I say something to upset you?"

"Just thinking about my mom. She's been sick lately and I worry about losing her. She's my only family."

"Poor baby," Sheldon said sweetly, hugging me.

"Maybe you can save her."

"Me! I'm not a doctor. I thought about going to medical school but there's too much blood, I might faint. Or kill my patients."

I didn't explain. I decided to wait awhile, until we'd spent some quality time together. I'd made the mistake of introducing my ex to my mom too fast—she really liked him and pressured me into marrying him. Charlene was always reminding me to take it slower with guys so I wouldn't scare them away. Introducing a guy to Mom too fast was one thing, asking him to turn her into a vampire was quite another. Who knew how he'd react? I had to make sure he was really mine—that he was totally committed to me—before I brought it up.

Sheldon kept stroking my back. Then he sneakily moved from my back to the rest of my body. That boy sure knew how to change the subject. Mom ceased being a topic of conversation as we fell onto the floor and ripped each other's clothes off. I wished I'd cleaned the floor. I felt dust balls on my tush. I didn't think Sheldon would notice as he started moving inside me. At that point I forgot about everything except how wonderful he felt.

Chapter Ten

"I want to make it up to you," Sheldon said after we made love. "I want you to forget that I made you suffer, that I didn't call."

"I'm still not totally buying your explanation about why you didn't call." Now that we had made love I felt bolder about confronting him.

"Rhoda, it was for your own good. Don't you understand that?"

"No, I don't. Disappearing with no explanation is never good for any woman." I propped myself up on an elbow and stared at him, as if I could tell by looking at him whether or not he was telling the truth.

"Would you have accepted it if I told you I didn't want to hurt you?"

"No, when guys say that it means they do want to hurt you, and they always do."

"In my case it was the truth," he looked back at me with such a sorrowful expression that I not only believed him, I felt bad for him. "I just couldn't see any way I could make you happy. I'd have to leave you one way or another so you could lead a normal, human life."

"Why didn't you tell me what was going on. How could you just disappear with no explanation?"

"I may be a vampire but I'm no match for a determined Jewish woman. I knew you wouldn't accept my explanation--you'd suck me back into your web," he licked his lips and raised his eyebrows in a silly approximation of a lustful look. "And I was right, you have."

"Are you sorry?"

"No. I can reassure myself that at least I tried to get away—now whatever happens I won't blame myself. You went after me so I'm off the hook," Sheldon gave a sigh, which sounded like a sigh of relief. "Does that make sense?"

"Not really, you should have called. But I can't resist you so yes, you're off the hook."

We'd gotten off the floor finally and were sitting naked on the couch. I usually lunged for my bathrobe after lovemaking, but he reassured me constantly that he loved my body the way it was—poochy stomach, flabby thighs and all—because I had a natural advantage in this relationship—I was alive and he was dead. He would always love my body no matter how it looked because I had blood running through my veins and he didn't. He would always want that blood although he could resist sucking it. That made me feel secure in a perverse kind of way. It was like being with a much older guy. Just being young was enough, it didn't matter that my cups runneth over with cellulite.

"What's the most romantic thing you've ever done, Rhoda?"

"My ex once took me to Nathan's on Coney Island for a hot dog at midnight and then we made love under the boardwalk. I wound up scraping sand out of my private parts for days. How about you? How many women did you have—when you were human?"

"Let's just make believe we are each other's first love." Sheldon leaned on his elbow and hovered over me. I would have felt his hot breath on my face if he'd had any hot breath, but breathing wasn't one of his habits. "Let's pretend tonight is the first time for both of us and we're going to be together forever."

"Forever is a hell of a long time for a vampire."

"Never long enough to spend with you."

If anyone but him had fed me that line I would have dismissed it as flattery--but Sheldon was obviously so sincere that I couldn't conjure up even a hint of sarcastic comeback.

"Rhoda, why don't we do something really romantic? Let's go out on the town to celebrate our reunion."

"Don't you have to work tonight?"

"I can take off. But I don't know what to do about clothes. I'm not dressed for going out. You wouldn't want to be seen with me looking like I'm ready to *davven* rather than dance."

"I'll fix you up. Shave the beard, ditch the hat, and you'll look almost normal. I'll give you a snazzy tie. I bought it for my ex but he never wore it—he was a crappy dresser. The coat's a little long but if you wear it open maybe you'll look cool—like a refugee from a spaghetti western."

"I'll try." He went into my bathroom and came out shaven and not pasty.

"How'd you get that color on your face?"

"Spray-on-tan. You had some in the bathroom. Doesn't it look great?"

"Better on you than me. It makes me look orange."

"What else do you have that I could put on?" Sheldon asked. He'd put on the clothes I'd given him and was staring at himself in the mirror. He looked almost normal.

"I didn't realize you could see yourself in the mirror?"

"I can now that I'm tan. I can see my face with this stuff on it. I haven't seen my face in a hundred years. I'm a handsome Jewish boy, aren't I?" He winked at himself.

"You look just like Jeff Goldblum."

"Karen said I looked like Sasha Baron Cohen. Isn't he better looking? And younger?"

"You watch too much TV. Let's get out of here. I want to show you the town."

Sheldon laughed. "The night is ours. What's our first stop?"

"Central Park," I said. "I've always wanted to go there at night but I never had a vampire to protect me."

"What makes you think I can protect you?" Sheldon asked coyly.

"Fangs. Superhuman strength. Chutzpah."

"OK, let's go." I led him out the door.

"Not yet," he said. "I want to see you in something besides those shlumpy jeans. Now get dressed."

"But I hate getting dressed up. I'm a jeans kind of girl."

"Nope. I want to see you in a sexy dress. Wear this?" He held out a black, low cut cocktail dress that I'd worn once to a New Year's Eve party. He'd snuck into my closet when I went to pee.

"I don't even know if it fits."

"Wear it." He wasn't letting me off the hook so I put it on. It was a little tight, but it did fit, and it showed off my impressive cleavage, which had gotten more impressive lately with my extra poundage. Thank goodness some of it had landed in the right place. I put on a pair of stockings and high-heeled boots, went into the bathroom, applied lipstick and mascara, and fluffed my hair.

"Rhoda, you are a vision." Sheldon grinned when I came out.

"But I can't walk in these boots."

"Don't worry, we'll fly."

"You said you couldn't fly."

"I've been practicing. I can glide around a bit on the ground. Just hang onto my arm."

I put on the gorgeous cashmere coat that I'd snagged for twenty bucks from my favorite Upper East Side thrift shop but never wore because it didn't really go with jeans. I

78

looked in the mirror and had to admit I looked pretty terrific, even with my extra X's. Sheldon took my arm in a very courtly gesture and we floated down the stairs. I was prepared to walk, but he hailed a cab, which stopped for us immediately, probably because he didn't radiate weirdness when he was with me—or maybe it was the tan.

"Central Park, please."

"It's a big park. Where exactly? The cabbie asked politely. A polite cabbie in New York, what a concept.

"Where do the hansom cabs park?"

"You could try the Plaza. There's usually a couple there."

"To the Plaza then." Sheldon turned towards me. "Champagne at the Palm Court. I saw this place when it was built a hundred years ago."

"Do you drink champagne? Can you drink at all?"

"I can have a little, as long as I don't overdo it. It evaporates in my system but the bubbles tend to fizz out of my nose. I wish they'd made champagne when I was human. I mostly drank sweet wine on holidays like the rest of the Jews. Until I died that is. Then I could only take a few sips."

"You have to tell me the whole story," I was eager for the details.

"Over champagne, darling."

The taxi pulled up in front of the Plaza and Sheldon ushered me up the broad stairs into the elegant lobby. I showed him the portrait of Eloise, whom I adored when I was a child. He was mystified,

"I've always wondered why this silly picture is in this elegant hotel."

I could see that life with Sheldon was going to involve some cultural dissonance. How could he understand what it was like to grow up as me, or vice versa? Oh well, I guess

I'd just have to pretend he was from the older generation. Actually older by about four generations.

"She's a character from a beloved children's book. She lived at the Plaza and did naughty things like ordering two peanuts on a spoon from room service, swinging on the chandeliers in the ballroom and pouring water down the mail chute."

"You thought this was cute maybe? She sounds like an annoying little *pisher* to me."

"You had to be there."

We sat in the Palm Court right in the middle of the Plaza lobby drinking champagne, or at least I drank champagne; Sheldon sipped a few bubbles. He bought me caviar, real black beluga, which I'd never tasted before, and I wolfed it down. I know you're not supposed to wolf caviar but I couldn't resist, despite feeling self-conscious about stuffing myself in front of Sheldon. For all I knew he could have lasted weeks without a blood donor, but I needed food three times a day and at least two snacks. This counted as a snack. "So, you promised to tell me more about becoming a vampire, Sheldon."

He shrugged and said, "I lived in a *shtetl* in Transylvania, near Count Dracula's castle. Actually Transylvania was part of Hungary at that time. He liked feeding off Jews because no one cared what happened to us. He knew I couldn't fend him off. Stars of David have no effect on Christian vampires; you have to have a cross, a large, silver cross. We Jews were pretty short on crosses and even though I was a rabbi, the local priest wasn't going to lend me something that valuable. So that monster fed off me and my people regularly until I died and came back as a vampire, like him. He made vampires out of the most pious men in the shtetl, he thought that would be a good joke. The joke was on him. The villagers eventually went after him and staked him in his coffin. They had no idea I was a vampire too, so they left me alone. But enough about me. How did you become Rhoda?"

"I was born that way, in New Jersey, the child of Jewish left-wing parents. They didn't believe in religion. Any kind of religion. We used to go on picnics and eat ham sandwiches on Yom Kippur. They did believe in books, though, and I was a bookish kid. I spent all my time reading and avoiding sports because I was afraid no one would choose me for their team."

"My poor baby. You've been chosen now, by me."

We looked outside for a hansom cab, but there weren't any. Maybe it was too cold for romantics to sit still while being hauled by a horse.

"Why don't we just take a walk in the Park," Sheldon suggested. "We could use the exercise."

He was just being polite. I was the one who needed the exercise.

Walking in the Park with Sheldon was sublimely romantic, especially since I'd never seen it at night before. I loved Central Park, had spent many hours wandering around there, usually wishing I was a couple like all the other arm-in-arm couples. Well now I was but we were the only couple, which was a bit disappointing. I would have liked to show off Sheldon to all those snooty New York girls who hung onto their handsome dates, showing them off as if they'd bought them at Saks. The Park was scary at night. The streetlights cast long yellow shadows and the dark leafless trees looked a bit menacing. When we got to the Wollman Ice Rink, which of course was closed, I told Sheldon I wished we could skate. I loved to skate and wasn't half-bad at it.

"Why not?" he said. "Let's skate."

"Has it occurred to you that the rink is closed, plus we have no skates?"

"No opening, no skates, no problem," he said, lifting me up and flying me right over the stone wall that separated the rink from the park walkway around it.

"Wow, you really have been practicing. Now, what do we do for skates?"

"We depend on my magical powers," he said, heading for the skate rental department at the back of the rink. "Just watch me."

He broke in. No magical powers were involved, just a bit of skill in breaking and entering that he'd probably gathered over the centuries. Not really kosher but who cared? We grabbed two pairs of skates in our sizes, put them on and ice-danced together. Sheldon zipped around the ice, spun me in circles, and even lifted me over his head and twirled me. It was thrilling. I felt like Torvill or Dean. I wish I remembered which one was which.

"How did you learn to skate like this?" I gasped. I was out of breath from trying to keep up.

"It's cold in Transylvania in the winter, and we skated on the rivers to get around. I always loved it. Now it's much easier since I'm so fast."

"I wonder if we could try out for the Olympics," I joked. "For the night events only, of course."

After our skate we went back to walking through the park, but while we were in one of the tunnels, two real live muggers actually did jump out at us. They were both just kids, dressed in baggy jeans, bomber jackets and caps, but scary kids because one had a knife and the other had a baseball bat.

"Where's your wallet, whitey?" the bigger one demanded. Obviously Sheldon's tan hadn't impressed him. "You give me that bag, bitch." He grabbed for my bag.

Sheldon reached for his wallet. Then he moved so fast I couldn't even see him. He became a blur and all of a sudden we were on the other side of the tunnel and the kids were both gone. When I looked at him he was shaking and I could see the white under the fake tan.

"You were amazing." I was numb with fear. "What did you do to those kids?"

"I threw them. If you look, you'll probably find them on the other side of those bushes, and not in good shape."

"So why do you look scared?"

"They tried to mug us. What if they'd hurt you. Or me? I'm a rabbi, not a policeman."

I forgot I was afraid too and started to laugh. "Scaredy-cat vampire, eh. Let's go back to my place," I said. "Between the champagne, the ice skating and the fear, I am really lusting after your undead bod."

"I'm sorry, Rhoda, I have to go to a meeting. I don't want to miss B.A. tonight. I've committed to ninety meetings in ninety days. I had a relapse a month ago. I raided a blood bank."

"What? What do you mean?" I was stunned at this new information.

"My B.A. meetings, Bloodaholics Anonymous. It's how I keep my impulses under control. You can come with me if you want to."

It was 2 am and I wanted nothing more than to get into bed with Sheldon and do the nasty, but I certainly didn't want to get in the way of his sobriety. Plus I couldn't imagine what a B.A. meeting could be like and my curiosity got the better of my lust.

"I'd love to go. Where is it?"

"Not in a church basement," Sheldon laughed. "Follow me."

Chapter Eleven

I wasn't surprised when Sheldon led me to the basement of a ratty little synagogue on the Lower East Side: Temple Beth El. You never would have known it was a synagogue unless you looked closely for the Hebrew lettering on the door

We went down some stairs to a basement entrance, to a room with about forty people in it—all vampires, I supposed. The smoke was so thick I could barely see their faces. Just like alcoholics, I thought. They had to have something in their mouths and if it wasn't people's necks it was cigarettes. I started coughing so hard that Sheldon had to lead me to a chair.

"Smoke this." Sheldon handed me a cigarette and told me to smoke it to mask my human odor. Otherwise the scent of my blood might cause some unwanted attention.

"I hate cigarettes, they make me sick." I protested weakly, still coughing. .

"You'll be even sicker if some of these bloodaholics get a whiff of you. Just puff, you don't have to inhale."

The group leader got up and introduced himself. "Hi, my name is Jerome and I'm a bloodaholic."

The group all said in unison, "Hi, Jerome."

He continued. "Tonight we're working step nine, making amends to those we have injured through our behavior. My sponsor said that could be a letter, a phone call or 'popping around' to see them. Most of my amends were made at a personal level. Now that I sponsor vampires myself, I tell them not to confess to loved ones about those we've killed as that could really hurt them or put them in a bad position. Why confess to something that could get you put in jail! You can do more good passing on the twelve steps, than being stuck behind prison bars. In short, say you're sorry when and if you can. If you can't go to someone just become willing. A change of attitude, a change of heart, that is what it is about!" Jerome sat down.

Then a pretty blonde stood up and announced, "My name is Tiffany and I'm a bloodaholic." She then went on to describe some of her more reprehensible behavior. "Last week I lost control, left home and wandered the streets looking for a victim. I found a poor homeless man who was sleeping in front of Bloomingdales at 3 am. He fought me off but of course I was too powerful. He smelled really nasty, but tasted so delicious I almost killed him. Thank God I stopped myself."

A tall very skinny man dressed in jeans and a sweater stood up and declared, "My name is Terrence and I'm a bloodaholic. I try and try to stick to animal blood but the stuff just tastes horrible. Plus I'm in PETA and feel worse about killing animals than I do about killing people. Actually I think it's more ethical to kill people—poor little animals can't defend themselves. I try to kill rats but you know how intelligent they are and when they twitch their whiskers and give me that "please don't hurt me," look, half the time I release them. But I have to eat something so I raid blood banks, which I know is terribly wrong. Sick people need that blood, but so do I. I'm sick too if I don't eat. So what should I do, tell me that? I have to survive."

"He's got a terrible dilemma," Sheldon whispered to me. "You can't be an animal rights activist and an abstinent vampire without getting in a lot of trouble."

Just like in AA, no one responded. No cross talk was allowed, which was probably a good policy because what could anyone have said to this guy?

I watched as vampire after vampire stood up and confessed their irresistible lust for blood. Many of them fell

85

off the "wagon" and stalked muggers and other criminals for their fix. Others weren't so ethical.

"My name is Veronica and I'm a bloodaholic." Veronica was a stunner. Tall, with long brown hair and a curvaceous figure, she resembled Ava Gardner in *Night of the Iguana*. "It's just too easy for me. Men pursue me, will do anything to be with me. They literally throw themselves at my feet. I'm a weak person, I've always been weak. That's how I wound up a vampire in the first place. I loved the bad boys, I was bored with the preppy types who went for me, I lusted for danger and I got it. One day a vampire came on to me. Let me tell you he was irresistible—looked just like Robert Pattinson. I couldn't say no, so here I am. I let him suck on me for weeks and vice versa until finally I died and came back as a vampire. I don't mind being immortal, but I don't like having to fight my impulses all the time. Yesterday I had sex with a musician, you know how irresistible they are. I always wind up with musicians because they stay up all night, and I find them in clubs. Well, he was an electric guitarist in a heavy metal band. A real hot one. The sex was so incredible that I lost control and sank my fangs into his neck and just sucked him dry. It was too late to save him so I had to dispose of the body in a Dumpster. They found it the next day. You probably read about it on the news. I had to disguise it as a drug overdose so I left heroin and a needle on him before I dumped him. I am so, so sorry for what I did, but like I said, I'm weak. I might have to go into rehab."

"Is there rehab for vampires?" I whispered to Sheldon.

"Yes, I've been through it. I'll tell you about it later."

At that point it was break time, and all the vampires got up and milled around a table with foam cups and one of those big carafes with push-button pumps that usually dispense coffee. The substance coming out of this carafe was definitely not coffee.

"What is that stuff?" I asked Sheldon, who hadn't made a move to get any for himself.

"It's blood, but the lowest-quality stale stuff that's been in a freezer for probably months. They get it from a butcher so it's from long-dead animals. Totally disgusting. I'd rather sit under a sunlamp than drink it."

"Sounds like the coffee they serve at AA meetings," I laughed. I'd been to Al-Anon a few times when I was involved with a guy who drank too much and I knew about the whole twelve-step thing.

I didn't talk to anyone during the break, but they were certainly animatedly talking to each other. I noticed the vampires were a motley bunch—all ages, races and sizes. All socioeconomic groups as well. Some wore Walmart, others Sears and others Versace. Just like at a real New York AA meeting. They weren't any better looking than the general public, though, despite the myth that you got better looking after changing into a vampire.

After the break we sat down again and the leader got up and said, "This is a step meeting. Has anyone been working the ninth step this week? Has anyone made amends to people you have hurt?"

Sheldon got up and said, "My name is Sheldon and I'm a bloodaholic. I hurt the woman I love. "He gave me a sidelong glance. " By getting her hopes up about having a relationship and then letting her down by not calling her. She had to track me down. I'm not afraid of hurting her physically. I've been a vampire for a very long time and I can resist human blood. OK, occasionally I lose it and raid a blood bank, like I did recently, but I don't kill anyone. I'm used to hunting small animals like rats and mice in the winter—and the occasional suburban raccoon." He turned towards me. "No, Rhoda, I don't kill dogs or cats. In the summer I kill a few squirrels in the country. And deer, I love to hunt deer. There are too many deer anyway. I haven't hurt a human for a very long time, though I used to. I keep my impulses under control by coming to meetings. But a relationship, that's scary. I'm afraid of being hurt."

Sheldon sat down. I felt both happy and scared. I realized that this was a commitment I was making to a very dangerous way of life. I might be stalked by animal rights activists. PETA could send bomb threats. Or worse. Could I keep it up, I wondered. Could I love a vampire and not turn into one? Did I want to turn into one? It was very confusing to a nice Jewish girl who once upon a time just wanted to marry a doctor and live in Scarsdale. I might be marrying a Jewish vampire who sleeps in a coffin in Crown Heights instead.

I was distracted by another vampire, this time an elderly lady who looked like my mother. "My name is Zelda and I'm a bloodaholic. Although I never meant to be a bloodaholic. I always wanted to do good in the world, to help people, and now here I am hurting them." Zelda started crying. I wanted to go over and hug her, but that wasn't allowed in these meetings.

"I may look old," she said, "but in vampire years I'm young. I was turned into a vampire against my will by the Golden Grandmas. I started going to Golden Grandma meetings because my friend Edith went. I was lonely, my husband Herman had died the year before, my kids were all living far away and didn't want to be bothered with me. After Herman died I just fell apart. Edith rescued me, she took care of me. My arthritis was killing me, not literally but you know... Or maybe you don't--you're all so young. Anyway they say getting old isn't for sissies and I'm a terrible sissy.

"I thought it was strange that the Golden Grandmas met at night--I mean most of us can't even drive at night-- but I didn't ask questions. I had no idea that these ladies--

who were very refined by the way--were really a nest of bloodsucking vampire AARP members. I felt so foolish when I found out. We'd sit around and talk about our grandkids, play mah-jongg, show movies. They talked me into joining them—into becoming a vampire. Edith was my only friend and she insisted. I never could say no to anyone, especially a good friend. But I don't like the lifestyle. Not the bloodlust—that's not a problem for me. I'm post-menopausal, I don't have a lot of lust. I'm fine with animal blood, I trained my cat Tiny to give me the mice she kills. I suck the blood and he eats the body. It's disgusting but I survive that way. But I'll never get used to not eating food. I used to live for bagels and lox and chopped liver and cheese cake and steak and..."

Everyone in the room started shushing her. "Mentioning food is considered terrible manners in vampire society," Sheldon whispered to me. "It's the hardest thing for us to give up. But it's been so long for me I hardly miss it anymore. As long as I can still have sex I'm happy." He leered at me.

"I need to make amends to my kids," Zelda said sorrowfully. "I just disappeared, moved in with Edith and never told them where I went. They called and wrote and I didn't answer. They even sent private detectives and put up posters all over town. I was ashamed, how could I tell them the truth? I was so weak. I didn't want to die, I didn't want to be dependent on them, or on anybody. Is that a crime? I still don't know what to do but I have to make amends." She sat down, put her head in her hands and sobbed.

I felt terrible for her. She was in a real pickle. What could she tell her kids? "Hey there Sonny, I've become a vampire. I'm going to live forever and you're not—get used to it." Poor Zelda. But her plight gave me an idea. I determined to talk to Sheldon about it after the meeting, as soon as we got home. But where was home? The Upper

East Side or Crown Heights? Where did Sheldon sleep during the day? Could he sleep at my apartment or did he have to go back to his? Did he actually have to sleep in a coffin? Maybe I'd order a doublewide coffin that we could share. The only problem was I had severe claustrophobia. I found my mind wandering as more vampires talked, most with the same story. Uncontrollable blood lust, killings of innocents mostly accidental, and a lot of guilt and breast-beating. I supposed there were vampires who were remorseless killers but they weren't in this room. It got boring after a while. I felt guilty about being too tired to be horrified continuously.

I woke up abruptly when a disheveled young vamp with long uncombed black hair, who was smoking a hand-rolled cigarette that looked suspiciously like a joint, got up and said with a scowl, "My name is Luther, I'm a bloodaholic and I don't want to be here. I don't think there's anything wrong with sucking human blood. That's why we were made and that's what we're supposed to do. I was forced to come by Vampire Court—they said they'd lock me up in the dungeon and throw away the key if I didn't change my ways. I've been sober for a week now, sucking rat blood, yuck!"

"You have to fill me in on Vampire Court," I whispered to Sheldon.

"Later. I'll answer all your questions."

"Can we leave, Sheldon?" I yawned. It was late and I was exhausted.

"Not yet, be patient, it will be over soon. I'm a sponsor and Gary, my sponsee, wants to talk to me. There he is over there."

I saw a tall, slender, very handsome vampire with granny glasses, long messy blond hair, and a rumpled corduroy jacket with leather elbow patches looking at Sheldon expectantly. He was a professor type—Charlene loved professors. I decided to stick it out for her sake. Maybe I could fix her up.

Eventually they got to the Serenity Prayer, and if there was ever a group who had to accept what they couldn't change it was vampires.

"So, Rabbi, how's it hanging?" the cute blond guy said when he came up to Sheldon after the meeting. How's it hanging? I hadn't heard that expression since the late eighties. Some vampires must try too hard to sound cool and get their slang stuck in the wrong decade. I wondered how old this one really was.

Sheldon introduced him to me and then took Gary aside to give him advice. I was impressed at his fatherly demeanor. He obviously cared for his sponsee, who may have been younger than him but in vampire years, who knows?

I cornered Luther. "What's this about Vampire court and Dungeons?" I asked.

He stared at me like I was a bug. "You're human, you don't want to know."

"Oh yes I do," I said. "I have a personal and professional interest in the vampire life."

"Well, I don't want to talk about it. Not to a human, and certainly not to you. It's none of your goddamned business." He stalked off angrily. I decided to ask Sheldon what he knew, or if there was someone else who could explain it.

He looked worried when he came back to me. "Gary is a troubled soul," he explained. "He's killed quite a few humans. He picks up prostitutes because he loves sex, then he wants more and can't help himself. He was ordered to go to B.A. by Vampire Court quite a while ago. He's seriously in denial."

"What is Vampire Court? Obviously it doesn't do much good if Gary is still killing people." I decided maybe this wasn't someone I wanted to introduce to Charlene. "He's a killer. Why don't you turn him in to the police?"

"That's something you need to understand right now, Rhoda, we NEVER turn each other in. The police don't know we exist and we'd like to keep it that way. Some retired FBI agents know about us, but they keep it quiet because we police ourselves. Can you imagine what kind of hysteria would go on if people knew about us?"

"Nah, not these days," I said. "Everyone's in love with vampires. No one would care about a few dead hookers. A TV producer would show up to do a reality series. You could make a fortune."

"Maybe that's true but I still wouldn't want to take that chance. In my day the people who hunted us weren't paparazzi. We almost got wiped out by a group of vigilante FBI agents back in the days of J. Edgar Hoover. They were running around with stakes opening coffins all over the place."

"How come I never heard about this?"

"It was covered up, like Roswell. No one wanted to alarm people."

"What happened?"

"FBI agents arrested some vampires back during Prohibition thinking they were bootleggers and the vampires wiped them out. J. Edgar took it personally. He went to war against us. It went on secretly for years, like his war against gays. He sent agents to stake us in our coffins, he assigned double agents to pretend they were vampires and out us, he forced us to walk into the light. Very ugly."

"Maybe J. Edgar was a vampire, a self-hating one, just like he was a self-hating homosexual," I joked.

Sheldon didn't think it was funny. "That would explain a lot. Hoover seemed to know all our secrets. His agents would show up in places we thought only vampires knew about. Eventually we figured out some Feebs were vampires. The only solution was to police ourselves. When a vampire goes rogue the V.B.I, Vampire Bureau of Investigation, goes after him and he's forced to go in front of Vampire Court. He gets sent to B.A., shapes up or is sent to the dungeon. By the way, B.A. was started by some Feebs who got turned. B.A. is pretty lenient these days though—now that J. Edgar is long gone. They give everyone a lot of chances—first to go to B.A. and then to rehab and then they get locked up if they don't escape first. One day my brother will synthesize blood and then we can come out of the closet, like on *True Blood*, but so far the stuff he's come up with tastes good but lacks enough hearty hemoglobin. You couldn't survive on it. It's more like an aperitif than a main course."

"How about that blood in the coffee machine? Why can't you survive on that?"

"That would be like you drinking piss to survive, you would probably kill a human sooner or later for the real thing."

"I guess immortality isn't easy."

"Neither is the alternative. Let's get out of here, sweetie." Sheldon gave me his adorable lustful leer. "I have plans for you before sunrise."

Chapter Twelve

Once we got out on the street we had the "your place or mine" discussion. Unlike most such discussions, which usually involve a secret agenda of who wanted to be in a position to escape in the morning, this one hinged on where the coffin was located.

"Rhoda." Sheldon looked at me apologetically. "We don't have time for me to go to your place and then go home. It's already 4 a.m. and I might not make it. I'd hate to wind up on the subway at daybreak and then find it's too light to get home when I get to my stop. I'd have to spend the entire day sleeping on the subway. I might wind up in jail."

"OK, but why can't you sleep at my place? How about if I draw the blinds and the curtains—it's dark."

"Not dark enough. You'd have to get blackout curtains. And I'm not sure that will work for the entire day. I take my old coffin wherever I go with dirt from Transylvania in it. I wouldn't be comfortable anywhere else. My coffin is like a broken-in pair of shoes."

"Yuck," I said. "Maybe dirt from any graveyard would do?"

"I'd be willing to try it—for you. But for tonight, why don't you come with me to Crown Heights? You can go home when it gets light. I'll give you cab fare."

I sighed. The last thing I wanted was to schlep to Brooklyn, but there was no way around it. Sheldon hailed a cab. At least I'd be going there in comfort. If I had to stand on a smelly subway platform at 4 a.m. I would be miserable.

We pulled up in front of Sheldon's building and he escorted me up three flights of a walkup. Three flights and no elevator. He didn't offer to fly me up either. Maybe he thought I could use the exercise. Not what a Jewish princess was used to! I wanted to complain but kept my mouth shut—I didn't want to ruin the mood. The inside of Sheldon's apartment looked pretty barren, like a typical bachelor pad except for the ornate coffin in the middle of the bedroom. There was no bed, but there was a ratty old couch that he pulled me down on as soon as we got inside. The only decoration was a large life-sized whitish statue in the corner, of a woman with a babushka. I guess she reminded Sheldon of home. Or he was an art collector. I forgot the surroundings very quickly under his expert hands. I could have been in the middle of an earthquake and wouldn't have noticed. Actually I was in the middle of an earthquake, my own, and I was screaming with pleasure. Sheldon broke the mood by putting his hand over my mouth.

"Rhoda, shhhhh. People will think I'm killing you….literally."

I gasped for breath and said, "Who would think that?"

"This whole building is filled with Hasidic vampires, including my brother Herschel. They'll get suspicious. They know I'm in B.A., but they'll think I fell off the wagon."

I sighed, got up and put my clothes on as Sheldon looked at me appreciatively. "Might as well get dressed," I said. "Just in case another vampire comes by."

"Herschel tends to drop in a lot. He looks out for me."

"You're lucky you have a brother," I said. "I'm an only child and my only family is my mother." I took a deep breath and decided to ask him if he'd change Mom. "She's dying, Sheldon, of heart disease. I don't know what to do to save her. She refuses to have another surgery—she already had two coronary bypasses."

"I wish I was a doctor, but I can't help you there."

"Yes you can, you can save her, you can turn her into a vampire."

Sheldon backed all the way across the room and stared at me. "You want me to turn your mother into a vampire? You have to be kidding." He stared at me. "You're not kidding."

"Not kidding. I've been thinking about it for a while, and when I heard Zelda at the B.A. meeting, that convinced me. She's an old lady vampire."

"She's a miserable old lady vampire," Sheldon said. She can't see her grandkids, she can't have bagels and lox, she....well she does have friends but she's not happy.

"My mother doesn't have any grandkids, she has me, and she can't eat bagels and lox anyway because of her heart."

"How about friends?" he asked. "What will she do with herself as the only vampire in Century Village?"

"Her friends love her. They'll accept her the way she is. They'll get used to going out late. They never go out during the day anyway, it's too hot. She'll miss the early birds but she can walk on the beach with them in the evening. She can still play mah-jongg and visit after dark. She won't be able to go to museums but she can still see movies and plays. The most important thing is she'll be alive—I'll still have a mom." I started crying, not on purpose but it did a job on Sheldon. He got very upset. Maybe he wasn't used to women weeping.

"Please don't cry, honey, please, please." He threw his arms around me, pulled my head on his shoulder and started patting my back.

"I don't know what to dooooooo ..." I moaned. "I don't want to lose Mom. She's all I've got."

"You've got me, baby," he said comfortingly.

"You're not my Mom. No one will ever love me like my Mom."

Then Sheldon started crying. He was heaving and sobbing loudly, this time not holding back like he had at *Fiddler*, but there were still no tears. We had our arms around each other and were both crying.

"I miss my mother too, Rhoda. When I became a vampire I had to disappear. It would have scared her to death, knowing I was a dybbuk, or some other evil creature. She was very religious. It was easier for her to think I'd died. Or that's what I thought. She went into mourning for me and never stopped. Eventually she died too, of consumption. Everyone died in those days of consumption. When Hershel got it and it looked like he was going to die I turned him into a vampire so I could have a family. He begged me to do it. I understand what you're going through. I will always regret not changing my mother. I love that you're so devoted to yours."

"Will you do it?" I begged.

"I want to do it for you. If I couldn't save my mother at least I could save yours. But let me think it through. An old person shouldn't become a vampire. They'll be old forever."

"She won't feel old, will she?"

"Yes and no" he said. "She'll have some vampire powers, and her heart will be OK because it won't beat anymore. She'll still have arthritic knees and wrinkles, but no aches and pains. I once talked to Zelda about her change and that's what she told me. She said she didn't like having to hobble around forever but her joints didn't change when she died. But she was really strong and could knock out a boxer if she had to. She could fly a little too. Actually vampires can develop different skills. She needed some way to move fast so she developed flying."

"I won't tell mom that she's not going to become young again, or she won't do it."

"What are you going to tell her?" Sheldon asked.

"Ummm. Not sure. I guess I'll play it by ear. Actually you'll be the one telling her. We're going to Florida together."

"Florida!!" Sheldon almost shrieked. "That's rogue vampire territory."

"What do you mean?"

"Vampires who don't want to play by the rules move to Florida—or Mexico. Also vampires who like warm weather. Florida is more—well—easygoing than New York. All those drug dealers and drug wars—you can get away with murder there, and a lot of vampires do. I'm a New York vampire through and through."

"What's a New York vampire?"

"I have a terror of beaches and palm trees. Too sunny. No cold, dark graveyards. Not that I ever go to cold, dark graveyards but I could if I wanted to. I could even go up to the Cloisters and hang out in a castle. I do that sometimes just to feel at home. It's not open at night but I sneak in. Transylvania isn't exactly tropical."

"Well I hope you can deal with Florida weather—for me. I'll book us a night flight. Now what do we do with your coffin? Do you want to travel in it?"

"Not really. What if it gets lost? What if the airline loses it? We'll leave late and I'll ship it separately."

"Maybe you don't really need it."

"I don't want to take that chance."

"Let's experiment before you go. See what you can tolerate. Maybe you just need the dirt from a graveyard nearby and you could sleep in a bed with blackout curtains?"

Sheldon looked terrified. "Sleep without my coffin? It's my security blanket, I'd have insomnia anywhere else. Goldie reads me to sleep when I'm in it."

"What a mama's boy you are!" I laughed.

"Will you read me to sleep?"

"Sure. What the hell. As long as it's not nursery rhymes."

"I prefer Isaac Bashevis Singer's stories."

"You're on. While we're talking about it, what about Goldie. Where is she? I thought she lived with you?'

"She does. She's right over there." He pointed at the statue.

I shrieked in terror. "That thing is a golem? It comes to life?"

"Only when I want her to. There's nothing to be afraid of. She's a pussycat. She's inanimate except when I animate her. There's an ancient spell I use. She can stay there forever when I'm away."

I walked over to Goldie and looked at her more closely. She looked like a terra cotta sculpture of a stout *balabusta*—a Jewish housewife from the old country. The statue had a large bosom and big hips, wore a long, shapeless dress and old-fashioned buttoned-up boots. She was so realistically carved that you could see the individual strands of her hair, which was drawn up into a bun. Her face was plain, with wrinkles, a large nose and sagging jowls; her mouth was puckered and her eyebrows contracted as if she were frowning. I felt she was looking at me, and not in a good way. The weirdest thing was the Hebrew word inscribed on her forehead.

"What's that?" I pointed at it.

"That's how I control Goldie—by changing the word on her forehead. She was brought to life when emet meaning 'truth' was written in Hebrew on her forehead. Now, when I want to deactivate her I remove the first letter, the *aleph*, in emet, which changes the word to met, meaning death."

"Where did you get her? Did you sculpt her?"

"No, my father did. He was a talented sculptor but religious Jews aren't supposed to make representations of human beings. Making a golem is different. When he was our rabbi, he created her to protect the Jews in our shetl from pogroms which is why Jews create golem in the first place. She wasn't much use though, she insisted on cooking and cleaning rather than protecting, so my father just allowed her to be our servant. When he died and I became the rabbi, I inherited her from him. I took her with me when I came to America."

"How convenient, a servant you don't have to pay or feed, and who stays in the corner until you need her," I said sarcastically. "Better than a wife for sure."

"It's not quite that simple," Sheldon said. "Goldie has a strong personality and she's very controlling. When she's animated she's very possessive and likes to order me around. I go along with it to please her. It's nice to have someone who cares."

"What happens when you want to de-animate her?"

"She doesn't like it, but I tell her she needs to rest so she goes along with it."

"I could swear she's glaring at me." I turned away from her, feeling as if I was being watched. "I think she disapproves of me."

"C'mon Rhoda, you're imagining things. That's just the way she looks." He stared at Goldie disapprovingly, as if he believed me and was warning her to knock it off.

"Vampires, golems, what other supernatural creatures are there?" I changed the subject, sensing that Goldie was a sensitive area for him.

"Well as far as I know there are no werewolves, or at least I haven't met one, which is a good thing because the

100

thought of a wolf, much less a were one, gives me shpilkis."

"You didn't tell me you were such a wuss."

"Just because I'm a vampire doesn't mean I'm not still a Jewish boy from the shtetl. We Jews were fair game for anti-Semitic peasants when I was a kid. I learned to be plenty scared of everything. In this country you Jews don't know from fear."

He was right. I'd never thought about it that way. If I were worried about Cossacks showing up to mow down my family I might not be so brazen either.

"I guess I'll have to be your protector," I laughed.

"Not so fast, I'm the one who chased off those muggers in the Park. I'm just not fond of wolves."

"When is the last time you met a wolf?"

"I heard them howling in the woods when I was a kid. The sound terrified me."

"Let's hope there aren't any werewolves," I shivered. "I prefer my mythical creatures to look human, even if they aren't."

Sheldon wanted to make love again but we were still on the pullout couch in his living room, with Goldie across the room. There was no bed in the bedroom, just his coffin, so we couldn't go in there. I insisted he turn her towards the wall so she couldn't see us, and hopefully she couldn't hear when she was de-animated. I didn't believe for a minute that Goldie wasn't aware of what was going on in the room. Maybe she couldn't move, but the eternal vigilance of the Jewish mother never rests. However, eventually I had to rest. I fell asleep totally worn out. Sheldon was inexhaustible. I'd never had multiple orgasms before, but with him I just kept coming. I was amazed by my own capacity for pleasure—who knew I was such a sexpot? I was overflowing with oxytocin—the bonding hormone that floods females after great sex. I was in love and I was also horny as hell. When I woke up ready to go at it again, Sheldon wasn't there. I panicked, immediately having fantasies of being left yet again. I called his name—no response. Then I parted the dark curtains and the room flooded with sunlight. It really looked shabby in daylight—with peeling wallpaper, worn-out oriental carpets and a battered claw-foot table. Goldie remained in her corner, immobile. I closed the curtains and then I remembered the coffin. I walked into the bedroom and cracked the lid a tiny bit. There was Sheldon with a beatific smile on his face, sleeping as peacefully as the dead. Actually he was dead. He certainly wasn't breathing. That was kind of scary—what if he never rose again? What if he stayed dead? I found myself panicking again. Waking up with a vampire wasn't as easy as Sookie Stackhouse made it look.

I knew I'd feel better with some coffee in my system, so I got dressed quickly, and was almost out the door before I remembered that I still didn't have Sheldon's phone number. I started rummaging around for his cell phone—no way he was escaping from me again—and found it on the dresser in the bedroom. I put the number into my phone and let myself out, leaving the door unlocked, not a good idea in Brooklyn but I had no choice, I didn't have the key. I remembered Sheldon telling me the building was inhabited by other Jewish vampires, so hopefully he'd be safe. I walked to the subway, picking up coffee and a bagel with cream cheese and lox on the way. It was delicious. Despite the lousy deli on the Hasidic tour, it was possible to get good Jewish food in Crown Heights. I ordered a dozen bagels and half a pound of lox to take home. I'd need sustenance for my trip to Florida. While I was at it I grabbed a pound of pastrami and a half-pound of chopped liver. Who knew when I'd be near a Jewish deli again? There weren't any on the Upper East Side and I was rarely downtown. As I walked to the subway I started regretting my purchase. I felt guilty about eating all that food when Sheldon had to subsist on rat blood. Plus I still wanted to lose weight. No matter how much Sheldon said he loved my body, I didn't want to be stuck at this size forever.

Chapter Thirteen

I was next to the window and Sheldon sat in the middle on Delta flight 304 to Fort Lauderdale. It was the latest flight we could get, leaving at 9 pm, non-stop, arriving at midnight. We'd rented a hearse to go the airport so we could take Sheldon's coffin. We tried to discreetly check it at the baggage counter but it created quite a stir. A security official in a black suit raced up to us.

"Are you shipping a body, sir? There are procedures for that. You fill out a form and the baggage handlers pick it up at the curb."

"It's empty," I told him.

"Please open the coffin, ma'am," he said menacingly.

Maybe he thought there was a suicide bomber inside, or contraband.

When I opened it he gazed at the well-worn satin lining, totally mystified. The coffin definitely looked lived in.

"Why are you taking this coffin to Fort Lauderdale? And why isn't it going to a funeral home? What do you intend to do with it?"

In the past I would have said, "None of your business," but now, with all the tightened security, any mysterious baggage was the airline's business.

"It's an antique. I'm contributing it to a museum."

"What museum?"

"The Century Village Museum of the Dead. They have artifacts of death from various eras. It's soothing to the residents who are, you know, on their way there."

I just made that up off the top of my head but it seemed to satisfy the young security guard, who had probably never been to a museum, much less contemplated dying. Before allowing it to go through, he felt around the inside looking for contraband. It was a relief to finally see it traveling down the conveyor belt to the baggage compartment.

We boarded the plane and sat by the window. The man at the end of our row took one look at Sheldon and found another seat. He had that effect on some people. The flight attendant came by and asked if we wanted anything to drink. Sheldon said, "Type A, please," and showed his fangs. He loved to freak people out, especially pretty young women, which really annoyed me.

"Sorry." I made a circular motion next to my head. "He's delusional. Thinks he's a vampire. Humor him. Bring him a glass of red wine. I'll have a Diet Coke please. Thanks."

Sheldon and I had worked out the logistics of the trip, which were pretty complicated. I didn't want to scare Mom by arriving with a coffin, so I decided to stash it— and Sheldon himself during the day—in her storage space, which was a locked cage in a dark room in the back of the building, perfect for a vampire to hide out in during the day. Luckily I already had the key so I didn't have to tell her about the coffin. All that was in there was moldy luggage. I'd introduce Sheldon to Mom when we arrived and he'd be sleeping in his coffin by the time she got up. I'd talk to her about my plan during the day, while he was sleeping, and then he'd join me at night and help me convince her. I'd already told her he was a vampire but she still didn't believe me. I was very nervous about this whole plan. Once we were on the plane I started having second thoughts.

"Sheldon, do you really think this will work?"

"Rhoda, it was your idea, not mine. I think I can do the change. I changed my brother, but he was young, and near death from pneumonia. But Zelda was changed and she's probably your mom's age so it's possible."

"How does it work? Will it be scary for her?"

"Have you read Dracula? It's like that. I suck a little of her blood every night until she grows weaker and weaker and finally dies. Then she rises."

"Yuck."

"It's really pretty painless, unlike in some vampire novels. Nothing like *Twilight*. No pain. Just intense sleepiness."

The aspect that really grossed me out didn't have anything to do with blood. "How about the...sexual thing. I mean when Dracula changed what's her name, Mina, didn't she really get her jollies from it. Or he did. She swooned and all that. He seemed to lust for her too."

"That was just Victorian repression—they were afraid of sex so Stoker turned Dracula into some kind of sexual metaphor. He was a nasty vampire, that's all. He liked sucking the blood of beautiful women because he was a sadistic monster. Sadists love killing beautiful things. OK, maybe Mina and Lucy turned him on, but he loved killing Jews too and I didn't turn him on. Don't get me started. That piece of drek. Believe me your mother isn't going to turn me on or vice versa. It will be very hard for me to change her."

"Why?"

"Because she's still completely living, not like my brother, who was dying. I have to be very careful to suck just the right amount of blood for the right number of nights. It depends on the individual. If she dies too soon I won't have a chance to give her my blood, which is vital to the process. If a vampire just drains a human they die—it's the slow process of draining over time that allows the change to take place—at least I think it is. And I don't know exactly how much blood to give her. I've never done it before to a healthy person. I think I'm going to call the Talamasca. They know everything."

"I read about them somewhere."

"They're a secret society, or they were, until Anne Rice outed them. They're scholars of the paranormal with motherhouses all over the world. They do workshops at Omega and Esalen and even the Ghost Hunters on TV consult them. I shocked the socks off them when I told them there were Jewish vampires. They thought Lilith was the only one. But she just got a bad rap from patriarchal idiots. But that's a long story."

"OK, I'll leave the details to you."

When we landed at Fort Lauderdale Airport we had to locate Sheldon's coffin on the baggage carousel. It was undoubtedly the strangest piece of luggage any of the staring passengers had ever seen. He and I got it onto one of those luggage carts and into our hired limo. It wasn't too heavy since Sheldon wasn't in it. We'd hired our own limo for the trip to Century Village since sitting in a group limo with a coffin in the middle of the floor was not something either of us wanted to face.

When we drove into Century I was wondering what Sheldon thought of it. When I first saw it, I'd thought it looked like man's first settlement on the moon—or a prison--stark and barren, with rows of ugly concrete buildings and very little foliage. Now, fifteen years later, there were trees and flowers everywhere. Florida's tropical weather made it hard for any place to look barren for long.

We got to Mom's section, Grantham A--the buildings all had pretentious waspy names. There should have been a Grand Concourse or an Avenue A to remind the residents of home. We stashed the coffin in Mom's storage space before going to her apartment.

Mom was waiting up for us, just the way she always waited up for me. She opened the door with a big grin on her face, excited to meet Sheldon. It surprised me how happy I felt to see her, but then I always felt happy when I saw her—like I was a little girl again who missed her mommy.

"Rhoda has told me so much about you, Sheldon. She didn't exaggerate about you. You do look like Jeff Goldblum."

Sheldon smiled shyly, obviously embarrassed. He probably he would have blushed if he could. "Can I get you something to eat? How about a nice bagel and coffee? That was a long flight."

"Mom, I told you Sheldon doesn't eat."

"That's ridiculous, Rhoda, everybody eats."

I took a deep breath and figured I'd better get this over with as quickly as possible. It wasn't going to be easy.

"Mom, I told you about Sheldon, that he's a vampire. Don't you remember? Could you please take a close look at him? Sheldon, show her."

"I don't really know how to make this easy for you, Mrs. Ginsburg. I know you were raised in a time when Jews believed in evil spirits, *dybbuks*, and the like."

"Oh please, call me Fanny. And my grandmother believed in evil spirits. My mother was a socialist and so am I. I'm an atheist, always have been. I don't believe in God, angels, devils, *dybbuks*, or any other supernatural being. Karl Marx didn't so why should I?"

Sheldon obediently took a mirror out of his pocket and breathed on it—no fog. In fact, no reflection. He took Mom's hand and put it on his chest—no heartbeat. He smiled and showed her his fangs. The real shocker was when he grabbed a knife and sliced it across the palm of his hand, making a deep cut which healed while we watched. Then he rose off the floor about six inches and glided around the room.

Mom grabbed her chest, gasped and fell on the couch. I was afraid she was going to have a heart attack then and there and it would be too late to save her.

"I'm so sorry, Mrs. Ginsburg. I didn't want to shock you."

"Please call me Fanny," she said, breathing heavily and struggling to sit up. I ran over and sat down next to her, put my arm around her and helped her stay upright on the couch.

"Don't worry, I'll be fine," she said, pushing me away. Mom didn't want anyone helping her, she was still in denial about her health. She was also very sensitive about people's feelings. She didn't want Sheldon to think her collapse was his fault.

"I'm used to being polite to my elders. But I guess I'm actually your elder so I'll call you Fanny." Sheldon laughed in a comforting way, ignoring her distress. He realized that it would make her feel worse if he made a fuss about it. He was trying his best to be charming. Which wasn't hard for him.

We sat down on either side of her on the couch so she wouldn't feel that she had to get up.

"Rhoda, what is this creature?"

"I told you, Mom, he's a vampire. He's also a diamond cutter—for a living that is."

"You couldn't have found a vampire doctor?" She tried to make a weak joke. "I guess if you love him I can deal with him not being human. At least he's Jewish," she laughed. At that point I knew she was OK, she'd cope.

"He's also not a Republican," I added. Mom always said she'd rather I marry anyone but a Republican. She hated Republicans more than she hated...well, anyone, except maybe Orthodox Jews. She hated them too. Lucky Sheldon wasn't really a Hasidic rabbi, he was just using that identity for a cover. She wanted me to find a nice Jewish

109

guy—but not too Jewish—any more religious than Reform would be too religious. I felt the same way. The way the ultra-Orthodox treated women as baby-making machines creeped me out.

"Vampires always vote democratic," I reassured her, not telling her that Sheldon couldn't vote. "In fact Sheldon was in the Russian Revolution. He knew Trotsky really well." My mom was a Trotskyite in her youth, but I'd made that up. For all I knew Sheldon was a buddy of the Czar, or more likely Rasputin.

"Leon Trotsky and I were very close at one time," Sheldon chimed in. "I was with him in Mexico before he was murdered. Unfortunately, I was asleep when the Stalinists came for him or I could have saved him. Such a shame. What a brilliant man."

I could tell he was winning Mom over. Sheldon either was really in Mexico at the time, or he knew his history. I'd have to ask him later.

"How old are you, young man?" Mom asked.

"Well, older than you, but not that old. I come from the time of Dracula. Late Nineteenth Century."

"Maybe you knew my grandmother. She came from Vitebsk, a *shtetl* in Russia. The same *shtetl* as Chagall actually. You know our family is probably related to Chagall—everyone in Vitebsk was related to everyone else. That's probably why my Rhoda has such an artistic streak. Did you ever see her paintings? She's so talented."

My mom worshipped art. She always bragged about her family's tenuous connection to Chagall. "That's hers." She pointed to a pastel still life on her wall that I'd done a long time ago when I studied at the Art Students League.

"Rhoda, how could you hide your talent from me? Why haven't I seen your paintings?" Sheldon chided.

"They don't look that great at night, so you probably didn't notice them. I have to get better lighting."

He turned back to Mom. "Fanny, I'm not exactly Russian though I spent some time there. I'm Romanian. I've never been to Vitebsk, but I just adore Chagall."

"Let me show you my Chagall prints," she said, trying to get up but failing. Finally she held out her hand and allowed Sheldon to help her to her feet. Once she was off the couch she stopped to catch her breath before leading him into the living room. Now I knew we were home free. He might be a vampire, but he was also a cultured vampire with the right politics. A Trotskyite who loved Chagall couldn't be all bad.

We sat down again, chatted some more, and then Sheldon kissed her hand in an old-world gesture, said goodnight, and explained that he was planning to stay at a hotel. He wouldn't want to put Mom out.

"I know you only have one extra bedroom and wouldn't want Rhoda sleeping with a boyfriend she wasn't married to," Sheldon announced as his reason for leaving.

"Do you think I'm that old fashioned?" Mom sounded slightly miffed "You're welcome to stay here with Rhoda anytime. The bed pulls out into a double."

"Maybe tomorrow," he said. "But I've booked a room for tonight."

"I'll drive you there," I offered. "Mom, lend me your car keys." I didn't want to explain the entire truth to her yet—that Sheldon didn't sleep at night, slept in a coffin during the day and sucked the blood of small animals to survive. I wanted to break the more shocking news to her slowly.

When we left I asked Sheldon, "Are you hungry? There are still a few hours till daylight. There's always a pile of garbage outside the Winn Dixie. Maybe you could find a few rats."

"I could use a bite, Rhoda." So I drove him to the supermarket and parked in the front while he hunted rats in the back, near the Dumpsters. I really couldn't face the rat hunt. I'd have to come up with other, less disgusting food sources for him while we were here. Alligators? Nah, too cold blooded. There were all kinds of animals in the Everglades including deer. We'd have to take a drive another night so he could go hunting. I took a snooze in the car until he was ready to leave.

"Full now?" I asked.

"Fine," he said without elaborating, not wanting to gross me out.

I showed him where his coffin was and gave him a key to the storage room. I threw a tarp over it to divert suspicion. I didn't want anyone to think Mom was hiding bodies. Sheldon was planning to sit quietly by the pool and listen to a book till daybreak. I'd warned him not to wander around because he'd attract unwanted attention. I'd given him an iPod with the audiobook of one of my favorite novels, Cynthia Ozick's The Puttermesser Papers, so he could listen to it in his coffin if he got insomnia. It was about a brilliant Jewish lawyer and scholar, Ruth Puttermesser, who manages to get elected mayor with the help of her golem, whom she'd created inadvertently out of the soil from her flowerpots. Like most golems, Ruth's eventually runs amok and destroys her life. This was a cautionary tale for Sheldon since Goldie seemed as if she might be on the same path. I knew a rival when I saw one. Then I went back to Mom's apartment, crawled into the sofa bed in her spare room and fell asleep instantly. She was already sleeping so I didn't have to make conversation. It had been one of the more exhausting days of my life.

Chapter Fourteen

Mom woke me up the next morning with her signature pancakes and bacon accompanied by fresh-squeezed orange juice. The smell wafting through the apartment was irresistible. I was happy Sheldon was asleep or it might have made him crazy, either because he was kosher and disapproved of eating trafe or because he still craved real food although he denied it.

"These are great, Mom," I raved as I dug in. "I didn't know you were still cooking. You always tell me how you're too tired to cook."

"For you I make breakfast. Dinner, we go out with the girls. If that's OK with you." She looked at me expectantly. She didn't seem to want to bring up Sheldon but couldn't resist being curious. "Just don't eat too much, you don't want to gain more weight."

I let that pass although it stung. She was right, I had gained a few pounds and shouldn't be eating pancakes and bacon. So why did she make them for me? My guess was that she wanted to have it both ways--to fulfill her role as an old-fashioned Jewish mother who admonishes her daughter to "eat, eat," and as a modern one who says, "Why so fat?"

"Where is that boyfriend of yours?" she asked me.

"Sleeping in his coffin in the storage room."

"What!!! Someone will notice a coffin in there."

"I covered it up with a tarp."

"I hope Tessie Levine doesn't decide to visit her husband's ashes. She sits in there for hours keeping him company."

That was alarming. What if Sheldon turned over in his sleep. Did vampires move while they slept, like humans? I'd just have to hope he slept like the dead.

"I know meeting Sheldon must have been a shock, Mom. He's not what you had in mind as a boyfriend for me."

"That's an understatement, Rhoda. But if he makes you happy, who am I to judge? Does he make you happy?"

"Yeah Ma, he does, but that's not why I brought him to meet you. I never would have subjected you to the shock unless I had a good reason."

"Reason? What kind of reason would you need to introduce the man you love to your mother?"

"A damned good reason, if the man you love is a vampire. It's hard to explain this, mom. I'm working myself up to it." I was wracking my brain about how to bring up that I wanted to turn her into a vampire. I didn't want to freak her out. I was never any good at being subtle or diplomatic so I just blurted it out.

"Mom, I brought Sheldon down here to turn you into a vampire."

She stared at me for what must have been an entire minute, long enough to make me really nervous. "Rhoda, that's the craziest thing I ever heard," she said, looking really upset.

Then she turned it into a joke. "I don't want to live forever. Not in this world that's rapidly going to the dogs—or the Republicans. I don't want to live to see global warming or overpopulation destroy the planet. And your father is up there somewhere waiting for me. What am I saying, I don't want to drink blood! Or have fangs! My God, Rhoda, what can you be thinking?"

"Ma, stop being so political. And you already told me you're an atheist—you can't believe Daddy's in heaven waiting for you if there's no God. You know that you're very sick. You won't agree to another surgery for a valve replacement—which is totally understandable considering what you've been through already--and I can't bear to lose you. So this is the only way out. You're the only family I've got and I love you too much. I don't want to be an orphan." I tactfully ignored the blood drinking and fangs protest.

I went over and gave her a big hug. A tear rolled down my cheek, not entirely unbidden.

"Sweetheart, I'm so sorry you feel this way. I was so happy when you got married because I didn't want you to be all alone when I was gone. Now I don't know what to say." Mom started sobbing. I hugged her some more and we cried together for a while. I was afraid to bring up the vampire thing again.

"Mom, why don't you invite the girls over tonight? I'd like you all to hear what Sheldon has to say about it." I figured with him there we'd think of a way to convince her. And she wouldn't make a decision without the goils anyway.

"That sounds ominous. OK, I'll invite them to dinner."

I knew dinner at Century was always ridiculously early, hours before the sun went down.

"Forget dinner. Make it dessert and coffee. The later the better."

At sundown I tiptoed to the storage room, threw the tarp off Sheldon's coffin and was relieved to see him inside. Somehow I'd thought the Century Village Coffin Police might have removed him overnight. Maybe Century Village residents had been stashing their loved ones surreptitiously in the storage rooms without notifying anyone to save on burial costs. The funeral home everyone

115

used across Century Boulevard was extravagantly expensive.

Sheldon yawned sleepily when he got up, just like a human. It was cute.

"Shel, you have a job tonight and it's not going to be easy. You have to convince Mom to become a vampire. You'll be answering a lot of awkward questions. Her friends will be there and I have no idea how they'll react."

"You sure are good at giving a guy an unpleasant task before he even wakes up. Let me think about this for a while."

"We don't have a while. Mom is waiting for us."

He took me by the hand and walked me out to the pool. We sat and looked at the dark blue sky for a while, and smooched a little. "I have an idea," he said. "I need to make a few calls."

Sheldon got busy on his cell phone. He'd remembered to plug it in somewhere because it was charged. Maybe his coffin had an outlet.

He finally got the person he wanted and walked off to talk. I overheard him say, "If you do that for me, I will be eternally grateful. I know, I know, eternity is a long time for us, but I mean it." Then he said, "Yeah, I'll wait," didn't say anything for a long while, then turned to me and asked if I had some paper and pencil. I handed him the notebook I always carried around. He scribbled something and ripped the page out. He said 'thank you' again and hung up.

"OK, Rhoda, you go and socialize with the girls. I'll meet you at your mom's apartment in an hour or so."

"Where are you going?"

"I don't want to get your hopes up in case my plan doesn't pan out. Just trust me. If it works you'll be really pleased. If not we'll just have to spring vampiredom on your mom somehow."

116

When I got there, the girls were all seated in Mom's living room, arranged on her couch and one easy chair, waiting for Sheldon. Mom had served a pie she'd defrosted and cups of decaf. She'd used her good china. The girls loved coffee but no one dared to drink caffeine after noon. They looked nervous when I walked in.

"What's this vampire thing all about, Rhoda?" Judy asked in her usual cut-to-the-chase manner, as soon as I sat down with my coffee and pie.

"I really don't know, Judy, Or I do know but I'm waiting for Sheldon to get here before I tell you."

Judy was sitting in the only comfortable chair in the living room, an orange armchair with bentwood arms. She wore a plain cotton skirt and blouse and pulled at her skirt awkwardly. I'd never seen her in pants, unlike most of the women at Century who wore pastel polyester stretch pants for all occasions. Her facial features were severe and so was her short gray hair. Judy, unlike Mom, didn't bother much with her appearance.. In fact all the girls had let their hair grow gray. Only Mom still had hers colored dark blonde.

"Is he waiting for the sun to go down?" Judy snickered.

"Judy, could you please be polite," Mom said. "Sheldon is Rhoda's boyfriend and he's a lovely young man. Well, maybe not young but he looks young."

"Oh Fanny," Judy snorted, "you can't possibly believe in vampires. You're an atheist. You don't believe in God much less supernatural beings."

"I believe that he's the real thing," Mom said forcefully, loyal to me. "Remember the stories from the old country, about golem, and *dybbuks*? Well there were legends about vampires too—our grandparents believed in those things. Maybe we're just too rational. We dismiss things Jews believed in for centuries."

"They were ignorant back in the old country," Ellen said emphatically. "Ignorant and superstitious. Now you want to go backwards?" Ellen had gotten dressed up for the occasion in matching gray pants and bolero jacket. She looked quite fashionable.

"Who says it's backwards?" Mom protested. "We Jews were just desperate to assimilate—not to seem weird and foreign. Where did that get us? It got us Hitler, that's where."

"And now even Madonna is studying Kabbalah," I chimed in again, apropos of nothing.

"Don't be ridiculous," Judy sneered. "Who cares what Madonna thinks? How can you take anyone named Madonna seriously in the first place?"

"What about shamans? Jews were healers," I said. "The peasants in Russia came to them for remedies. That's where the whole Jewish doctor thing started."

"My son is a doctor, at Mt. Sinai," Ellen said, "not a shaman. You can't compare them."

"I never said he was a shaman," I sighed. No matter what you said around Ellen she'd bring up her son the doctor.

The bell rang and Sheldon walked in. I introduced him to the girls and he said, "It's nice to meet such lovely ladies," in his most courtly manner, trying to win them over for my sake. I gave him a kitchen chair to sit on, though he rarely had the need to sit. Unlike me, his feet did not get achy.

"What's the deal with this vampire thing?" Judy shot at him immediately. "You look like a regular person to me. You could use some color. A few days at the beach and you won't look so chalky"

"Judy," Mom chided, "please be polite. Sheldon is Rhoda's boyfriend. He may not be the man I had in mind for her, but he's very sweet."

Sheldon gave Judy his best smile, carefully hiding his fangs, and she smiled back. Judy was not immune to male

charms despite her denial of any interest in the opposite sex
. Actually since their husbands died all the girls had sworn
off men. They were determined not to be like Gladys, who
was once part of the group until she married Harold, the
most obnoxious, overbearing, bombastic, single male in
Century. He pursued her, she was flattered, he had money,
she was poor, so she married him. She pretended to be
happy, though how anyone could tolerate Harold was
beyond me. He was a non-stop talker who collared me
every time I saw him and bragged incessantly about the
achievements of his daughters, who he made clear to me
were all more accomplished than I was. We all missed
Gladys, who'd been a lot of fun.

Sheldon looked uncomfortable. "I'm waiting for a
friend to arrive. She should be here any minute."

I couldn't imagine who he was talking about, but just
then the bell rang and Tessie Levine walked in, the very
Tessie who sat with her husband's ashes in the storage
room. She was a short, plump, ordinary-looking elderly
lady, wearing the signature Century matching pastel
ensemble of lavender jogging pants with a white stripe on
the side, a white blouse-style t-shirt with lavender trim and
lavender nylon zippered jacket with white trim. Unlike
most of the ladies she didn't wear sneakers, but sported
white leather flats. She certainly wouldn't have stood out in
a crowd.

"Tessie," Mom said, surprised, but polite as ever. "It's
nice to see you." The other girls greeted her warmly; they
all knew her, though not well.

"I asked Tessie to come over," Sheldon said
mysteriously. I was as bewildered as Mom and her friends
about why she was there. "Tessie is a friend of my friend
Zelda." Now I knew who he was talking to on the phone.
I remembered Zelda from the B.A. meeting. "They're both
members of the Golden Grandmas, which started in New

York and now has a Century Village branch. There are four Golden Grandmas here, and they're all vampires."

You could have heard the proverbial pin drop. I was stunned. The girls were more than stunned, they were stupefied. Judy's eyes widened and for once, she was speechless.

"Yes," Tessie said, "it's true. That's what I am. You know the others too." She named three other women, Hannah, Frances and Letty. The girls nodded in recognition. Everyone knew everyone down here.

"But Tessie, we play mah-jongg together," Miriam protested. "And Hannah and I are in the book club. I've known Frances for years. How is this possible?"

"We don't exactly advertise," Tessie said, "but you may have noticed that none of us are at the pool during the day, and we never go to the early bird. We're just like you except we don't have to spend all our time at the doctor." Her eyes twinkled. "And we can drive at night, and go dancing at night--all night. We feel like kids. No aches and pains, extra sharp vision and hearing. We play tennis, go running, and night scuba diving. We sometimes zip over to the Bahamas for some gambling—without a plane. We've traveled all around the world. It's a nice afterlife."

I noticed my mom staring at her with an expression I interpreted as envy. Mom used to be a super athlete when she was young and missed doing all those things.

"What about drinking blood? Killing people?" Mom asked. "No more bagels and lox? No more bargain matinees. That can't be fun?"

"It's a small price to pay for eternal youth, or eternal old age. You'll see," Tess responded reassuringly.

"Why do you sit with your husband's ashes in the storage room?" Mom asked her.

"I don't want them in the house. Too upsetting. I will never stop mourning him, wishing he were with me,

120

wishing he were a vampire too. Not that I could have made him one—it was too late by the time he died."

"That's pretty ironic," Sheldon said, "I was sleeping in the same place. I could have found you without making a million phone calls."

"I wish you'd found me last night, young man—when we were alone," Tessie said flirtatiously. "You're a handsome devil," she laughed. " I get tired of only female company."

Sheldon laughed. "Rhoda wouldn't have appreciated that."

Mom wasn't interested in Sheldon's charms at the moment. She had too many questions. "It seems my daughter wants me to become a vampire," Mom said "I thought she was kidding, or crazy. I totally dismissed the idea, but here you are, Tess, and you seem fine with this. How did this happen to you? Who changed you into a vampire?"

Ellen joined in the questioning. "Are you glad you did it? What's it like? How do you get turned into one?"

Judy wanted to know, "What do you eat? Can you go out during the day?"

"Slow down, girls," Tessie said. "Give me some time and I'll explain."

"Who made you a vampire, Tess?" was Mom's first question.

"It wasn't my choice, Fanny. I was dying and my daughter changed me. She'd been a vampire for quite a while. I didn't know it, she hadn't told me. I knew she'd become a little eccentric, but then she was a conceptual artist. They're all strange. But I was on hospice at home, I had terminal cancer, so she changed me. She actually didn't ask if I wanted it, I was too far gone. But I was very grateful and neither of us has ever regretted it."

"Does it hurt?" Mom asked plaintively.

"Actually I don't remember. I was in a coma at the time. From what I hear you won't remember either. You will go into a twilight state like when you have a colonoscopy. Oh, you won't need those anymore. Isn't that great? When you wake up you'll be changed."

"If you've read Dracula you know the drill." Sheldon addressed the girls. I will perform the change. She'll die, we'll get a coffin and bury her and then dig her up the next night at which point she will rise as a vampire. No big deal." Sheldon spoke quickly, leaving out the gorier part about sucking mom's blood and giving her his blood, trying to lessen the shock.

"No big deal," Judy shrieked. "My friend will become some kind of monster and you say it's no big deal."

"I get buried alive?" Mom looked terrified.

"You won't be alive at the time, just when we dig you up. You won't remember a thing." Sheldon reassured her. "I didn't know what hit me until I got dug up."

"Rhoda only wants to keep me alive, Judy. She has no intention of having me turned into a monster as far as I can tell," Mom said. "Look at Tess. Is she a monster? Is Sheldon a monster?"

Sheldon looked totally harmless. His hair was mussed, he was wearing jeans and sneakers and smiling widely, showing his gleaming white teeth, which were un-fanged at the moment. He could retract his fangs when he wanted to. He'd even put on a little instant tanning spray at my request so he wouldn't look so deadly white.

"By the way I don't have all the answers," Sheldon said, "neither does Tess. The change affects people differently. Some vampires develop all kinds of amazing powers, like flying, others, like me, can only glide a little. You tend to develop powers that you want to develop. But you have to work at it, like lifting weights."

122

"I've developed the ability to glamour," Tess said. "That means I can mesmerize people and bend them to my will."

"Why would you want to do that?" Mom asked.

"Have you ever had to wait on line at Wal-Mart? Let's just say that I never have to wait for anything."

"Can Fanny go out during the day?" Miriam asked. "We'd miss her at the beach and the early bird."

"Actually she can," Tess responded, "but only if she has a good reason. Her powers will disappear during the day. She'll feel sickly and weak. She'll only be strong at night. Plus vampires need to sleep twelve hours a day, so that pretty much eliminates most daytime activities. She won't wake up until sunset naturally, and will become so sleepy before dawn she'll head right off to bed."

"You don't have to sleep in a coffin?" I asked her. "Sheldon shlepped his coffin all the way down here."

Tess laughed. "Get some blackout curtains for him and he'll be fine. That's an old wives' tale."

"You never told me you could go out during the day, Sheldon," I said.

"You never asked. I don't like to do it because I feel too vulnerable. I could be hit by a car and that would be it for me. If there were any vampire hunters around that's when they'd go after me. I'm mortal during the day. Plus I need my beauty sleep."

"So I could have a heart attack during the day?" Mom asked.

"No you couldn't, vampires don't have human ailments, but you could be killed in an accident, or by a vampire hunter. Just like you naturally want to sleep at night now, you'll want to sleep during the day. You'll see. It's different for everyone. But you're not going to burst into flames in daylight. That's a myth. Florida sunlight, however, will not feel good."

"It doesn't sound so bad," Mom said. "Except for vampire hunters. Who are they? Would they be after me?"

"They won't be after you. You'd have the perfect cover," Sheldon said, avoiding the question. "You're a little old lady."

"Fanny, you forgot to ask what you're going to eat," Miriam chimed in. "How are you going to give up bagels and lox?"

"Food is a problem," Sheldon admitted. "My diet is not something Fanny would enjoy, so I'd rather not talk about it until after her change. Then we'll work it out. Suffice it to say I do not drink human blood like some vampires. We try very hard to stick to animal blood, though human blood is a big temptation."

"We have an animal farm, sheep, goats, chickens," Tess said cheerily, as if she was talking about cooking brisket for dinner. "It's not bagels and lox but I've always loved chicken. Vampires need blood from live creatures, unless they get live blood from a blood bank, so we keep farm animals. We suck the blood out and then we get a rabbi to approve them for kosher consumption. You know kosher means all the blood has to be drained from an animal. It's very convenient and we make money from it. Even vampires can't live on Social Security."

Sheldon stared at her in awe. "Why didn't I think of that. I've never heard of vampires who didn't hunt. I hunt rats. It's disgusting, but I didn't think I had a choice."

"That doesn't mean we don't sometimes lust after human blood," Tess said. "But we manage to resist. It's kind of like being on a diet. Think of it as the Atkins Vampire Diet since it's all protein. I'll take you out to the farm for dinner, Sheldon. We have a Haitian couple who runs it. They don't question us at all—after all, they're believers in voodoo; they believe in zombies, so we're not a big deal to them."

124

"Where do you get the rabbi?" I asked.

"Do you think Sheldon is the only vampire rabbi? Let's just say there are others."

"I don't want to find out too much," Mom said, "or I'll chicken out. If it's what Rhoda wants I'll just do it. How bad can it be? Sheldon here looks pretty happy. So do you, Tess."

"That's because I found Rhoda," Sheldon said. "I used to be very lonely. I was a rabbi before I became a vampire. Not too many nice Jewish girls go for vampires."

"A rabbi! I'm not sure I approve of my daughter marrying a rabbi," Mom said, in perfect seriousness.

"A vampire is OK but not a rabbi," Judy said sarcastically. "Your sense of values is pretty twisted, Fanny."

"He's not a rabbi anymore, Mom. He still lives in Crown Heights with the Hasidic Jews because it's a good cover."

"Maybe you two will move to Florida," she said.

"Oh, Mom. You know I don't like Florida. Too flat, too boring. Maybe you'll move to New York when you're not sick anymore."

"I'm not going to like the cold weather no matter how dead I am."

"You could be wrong about that, Fanny," Sheldon chimed in. "I love the cold and dark. It's a vampire thing."

"Fanny," Miriam interrupted, "I'm not going to let you do this alone. I want to go with you. I'm eighty-five, I've got diabetes and a bad heart. My daughter never visits. What do I have to stay alive for? I'd rather feel good and be able to have an active life again. I don't care about food, I never did." Miriam was teary-eyed. The most delicate of the girls, she was tiny, soft-spoken, with a wispy gray bun on her head. She always dressed in sweater sets and straight skirts which looked like she'd acquired in the 1950s.

125

"Could we play tennis, Tess?" Mom asked. She used to love playing tennis.

"I don't see why not, as long as you schedule it at night. There's no wait at the courts, that's for sure."

"They have tennis courts here that are lit up at night," Miriam said. "Fanny, just imagine it, we can play tennis again."

"OK, I'm in too," Ellen said. "I'm not being stuck by myself here."

"How about me?" Judy did not sound happy. "I don't want to do this. It sounds nuts to me. I'm in pretty good shape. My grandchildren would be really upset."

"Judy, you don't have to do anything. You can always change your mind down the road when you see how it works out for your friends," Tess said reassuringly.

"Are you going to change us all at the same time?" Mom asked.

"Sure," Sheldon said. "It will be easier for the girls to go through the change together. What do you think, Tess."

"I really don't know," she said. "I never changed anyone and never saw it done. None of us knows much about the change—we all went through it when we were dying. You'll have to do some research, Sheldon. You've been a vampire the longest. I hear it's easier for the oldest vampires to do the change."

"I can't believe I'm agreeing to do this, Rhoda," Mom said. "I must be crazy."

"We're all crazy," Miriam said. "But haven't we always been the Century Village crazy girl gang? Everyone already thinks we're nuts because we drive at night and travel to Europe on our own, not on a tour."

"Gee, that is pretty gutsy," Sheldon said.

"Maybe I should do it too," I said. "How can I get old when Mom stays the same? And when you stay young,

126

Sheldon. You'll get tired of me. You'll start going after younger women."

"No, Rhoda. I love you because you're human. I don't know how I would feel if you were a vampire like me. I love that you're so sweet and soft and juicy and zaftig."

"Shame on you, Sheldon. I thought you loved me for myself, not because I'm human."

"C'mon, that is part of yourself. It's no rush anyway. You can become a vampire when you get a few more wrinkles."

"But you look thirty-five and I'm already forty-one."

"Rhoda, I have enough to deal with changing your mom and her two friends. I've only changed one other person in my whole un-death, my brother Herschel. That was easy. He was young and dying already. Your mom and her friends are relatively healthy so it will be harder. Let's see how that goes."

"OK, I'll wait. But not for too long. I'm going on a diet so I won't be so zaftig when I go through the change. I don't want to be zaftig for eternity."

"That's a good idea, Rhoda," Mom said. "You really need to lose some weight anyway."

"Mom, just because I mentioned losing weight doesn't give you permission to chime in."

I'd long ago threatened her that the next time she mentioned my weight I'd stop talking to her, and she'd managed to keep her mouth shut. Until now.

"I like you the way you are, Rhoda," Sheldon reassured me. "Zaftig suits me just fine."

Chapter Fifteen

Changing three old ladies into vampires wasn't going to be a picnic for Sheldon—or maybe it was. He'd get to drink some human blood for a change instead of the usual animal variety which might or might not compromise his abstinence. Before facing it, we decided to take a night out together. Who knew when we could relax together again without worrying about how we were going to manage changing three harmless old Jewish ladies into three dangerous creatures of the night?

Leaving the girls at Mom's house, we borrowed her car and decided to cruise down to South Beach, just to escape the claustrophobic, elderly atmosphere of Century Village. I wanted to take a romantic walk on the beach with Sheldon and maybe a little midnight swim. By the time we got to South Beach it was midnight and the streets were loud--crowded with Eurotrash types wearing as little as they could get away with without being arrested. . I wished Sheldon could eat and drink because the Cuban food and Mojitos were calling to me, but I didn't want him to think I was a glutton. I wondered if he resented me because I could eat food and he couldn't. I tried to resist stuffing myself when he was around but it wasn't easy.

"C'mon, Sheldon, how about we hit some clubs?" I suggested.

"Clubs? What kind of clubs? I've never been to a club."

"You certainly led a sheltered life before you met me. Didn't you ever get wild and crazy, dance all night, feel like you were one with the music?"

"Rhoda, the last time I danced it was the waltz. I have never felt at one with Strauss, but I doubt that's what you're talking about anyway."

I led Sheldon to the News Café on the South Beach strip. The strip was almost as light as day since the art deco hotels were brightly lit with neon signs. The restaurants all had outdoor café and scantily glad girls enticing passersby to come in, but I doubt they would have appreciated just one for dinner. This café seemed to tolerate people watching without ordering. I decided to just have coffee so Sheldon wouldn't feel deprived.

The outfits on the girls were even skimpier than the last time I'd visited, if that was possible. Latina models probably. Heels were so high that I would have fallen over in them instantly. The girls wore low-cut tops with their cleavage hanging out and shimmery tights in day-glo colors that started below their belly buttons. They flaunted their sexuality with an abandon unknown to uptight New York girls like me, who mostly wore black from head to toe.

"So what do you think, Sheldon? Have you ever seen girls like these?"

"I think I should look the other way. I'm a nice Jewish boy remember?" he gave me a shy smile with a hint of mock innocence.

He wasn't looking the other way. He was like any other boy; Jewish or not, he liked to ogle beautiful women.

Just then a tall blonde masculine-looking woman with strong features, a huge head of hair that had to be a wig, heavy makeup, a purple mini-dress and sinewy muscled arms and legs, plunked herself down next to us. I realized quickly that she was a drag queen, but wasn't sure Sheldon would know. In his day even women weren't supposed to dress like that, much less men.

"Hi there." She smiled broadly, exposing a very expensive set of capped teeth. I could always spot caps since

129

I had so many of them in my own mouth. "I'm Hedwig. Can I join you? "

I wondered what she was selling, or what hustle she was running. South Beach is like Times Square that way. Strangers who befriend you usually have a hidden agenda.

"Would you two be interested in going to the Vampire Ball at Saints and Sinners with me?" Hedwig asked. "Here's a flyer."

"What?" Sheldon said. "Why us?"

"You remind me of a vampire lover I had once," she said flashing her choppers at Sheldon. "Tall, dark, handsome, cold as ice with pasty skin. I begged him to change me but he ran off with one of my girlfriends instead. You men are all the same, dead or alive." Hedwig tossed her long blond curls and smiled. "He sucked some of my blood, though. It was divine."

"Sheldon, why didn't you ever do that to me?"

"I'm not one of those fuck and suck vampires." He sounded horrified. "I've been clean and sober for fifty years now. One drop of human blood and I could go off the wagon and turn into a killing machine."

I wondered how he was going to suck Mom's blood without turning into a killing machine. I'd ask him that later when Hedwig wasn't around.

"Come with me." She looked at us seductively and raised her heavily penciled eyebrows. "Show me some fang, honey."

Sheldon obliged, brandishing his incisors with a theatrical hiss.

"I am so psyched!" Hedwig shrieked. "I'm bringing a real vampire to the Vampire Ball. I will be the belle. The drinks are on me. That's if you drink, Mr. Sheldon."

"I never drink wine and I never smoke shit," Sheldon drawled, imitating George Hamilton in Love at First Bite. I was surprised he watched vampire movies, but then again, why wouldn't he?

"Here's the address, Mr. Sexy," Hedwig giggled. "I'll meet you two there."

She gave us a black postcard with a big Vampire Ball in elaborate white calligraphy, and an address on Washington Avenue, not far from where we'd parked.

"Do you want to go, Shel?"

"Why not, honey, we're on vacation. I've always wanted to go to a Vampire Ball. The vampires I know are not exactly a fun bunch. They're more likely to sit around and discuss the fine points of Talmud."

Saints and Sinners was a huge, two-story establishment with seven bars. In a town with hundreds of clubs all vying for tourist dollars, this one advertised that you could go bar hopping without ever leaving the premises. The Vampire Ball was in a room so dark I stumbled on my way in and had to grab Sheldon so I wouldn't fall down. Hedwig saw us, though. As soon as we walked in she gave another piercing shriek and ran towards us so fast I was afraid she'd knock me over. She managed to stop abruptly on her six-inch platform heels, grabbed both of our hands and started pulling.

"Sheldon, Rhoda, please come and meet my friends."

Hedwig's friends were, like her, huge drag queens in a variety of flamboyant outfits, from skintight pants to cocktail dresses. They all wore platform heels, heavy makeup and wigs. I liked them all immediately since they fussed over Sheldon and me like mother hens.

"You two are so adorable," one of Hedwig's girlfriends gushed. "I want to dance with Sheldon, can I borrow him? It's not every day you get to dance with a real vampire at the Vampire Ball."

"Sure." I waved Sheldon towards her, as a tan, shirtless, extremely handsome man in a mask and cape whom

Hedwig introduced as Anibal grabbed me and dragged me towards the dance floor.

"Your boyfriend is a real vampire?" Anibal whispered in a Latin accent. "I know a few vampires, but they real dangerous. I wouldn't invite them to a ball."

"Why not?"

"Some of the dancers might not make it home," Anibal leered at me. "They like blood and they like it hot."

"Sheldon's not like that. He doesn't drink human blood."

"A vampire who don't drink human blood? I think he's funnin' you girlie, girl. You gonna wake up dead one of these days."

"You've got it all wrong." I pulled away from him and walked back to the tiny round table Hedwig had gotten for us on the side of the dance floor. The laser lights were making me dizzy and the loud hip-hop music was giving me a headache. I searched the floor for Sheldon and Hedwig but all I saw were extravagantly dressed drag queens in a variety of Elvira outfits and half-naked caped men who I assumed were gay. On the stage a person of non-specific gender was stripping seductively, showing phony fangs as he took it all off. His white skin looked powdered, not like Sheldon's marble-smooth limbs. So where was Sheldon? I was getting nervous as I looked around. I wended my way to the ladies room and there he was near the bar, doing some kind of bump and grind with Hedwig and a gay boy dressed as a girl vampire. They were both having a lot of fun slithering up and down his body and he seemed to be enjoying the attention.

"Sheldon, enough already, let's get out of here."

"But Rhoda, I can't disappoint these ladies."

I grabbed his hand and started dragging him across the dance floor. He looked back at the girls and waved goodbye regretfully. Hedwig said, "OK, OK, I understand you want your man back. But he is the cutest little vampire I've ever met. If you two ever need anything, or just want to get in touch, here's my card."

She shoved a pink business card at me, which had silver stars all over it, and a phone number. That's all, no name, no email address, just a phone number. Very classy. I wondered if she was an escort or provided sexual services as well as dope. Sheldon looked at the card and raised his eyebrows.

"You know the ultra-Orthodox guys go for girls like that," he told me as soon as we left. "They're always looking for kinky sex. Or any sex. That's what happens when you can't have sex with your wife for two weeks every month until she goes to the mikvah, and she's always pregnant. It's strange because in Judaism you're supposed to enjoy sex, but somehow black hats never pay attention to that particular part of the Talmud."

I was determined enjoy a little kinky sex myself that night, preferably on the beach, so after we left we walked on Collins Avenue until we spotted a deserted stretch of sand. The beach in Miami is really flat and wide so there's a long distance from the street to the water, providing a bit of distance from the bright lights and people. We ducked under one of those blue cabanas that provide shelter from the sun. I supposed we weren't the first ones who'd used them for shelter from prying eyes, but they seemed to be made for that. I grabbed Sheldon and dragged him down onto the sand.

"Rhoda, are you sure this is a good idea? Sand might get into some sensitive areas."

"Stop being a wuss. We'll cope with it," I told him as I unzipped his jeans. I was wearing a skirt and sandals, perfect lovemaking-on-the-beach-garb. Luckily the beach in Miami is hard packed so the sand more or less stayed put. His skin felt cool in the heat of night. He cooled me off and heated me up as we moved against each other. The sensation was extra exciting. After we'd both collapsed on the sand, me panting, him looking like he would pant if he could, Sheldon suggested a midnight swim.

"We don't have our suits."

"Who needs suits?" Sheldon picked me up and ran to the water. He was so fast that if anyone was watching they wouldn't have seen much. Once we were in the ocean we started making love again. I had never had sex under water, and reveled in the feeling of weightlessness while I wrapped my legs around him. Both Sheldon and the warm Florida ocean caressed me softly. He could have lifted me up without the help of the water, but the water made me feel unselfconscious, like a sexy mermaid. It turned out Sheldon could not only fly a bit, but he could also skim the water like a dolphin. As I held onto his back he gamboled in the waves, going under and over and zipping out far from shore, then coming back. He carried me back to the little cabana quickly, but no one was around anyway. I was so giddy and exhilarated that I could barely find my clothes so Sheldon dressed me. It was completely thrilling—and exhausting. I took a nap on the beach while he relaxed.

"Maybe we should move to Florida," I said as we drove back to Century Village.

"Not a chance. Too sunny. Give me cold, dark, gloomy weather anytime. New York reminds me of Transylvania. It's home to me."

"Guess you're right. I wouldn't want to move away from Charlene anyway. And my clients are there. I do like to visit editors now and then. By the way I have about three deadlines that I've totally ignored. I better get on the laptop when I get back to Mom's."

"You can work tomorrow while I sleep in the storage room."

"I hate to send you back there again."

"It is pretty dreary. Maybe your Mom would let me put the coffin in the spare room where you're sleeping."

"We can ask her. After all she'll be sleeping in one herself soon."

Chapter Sixteen

Walking into the funeral home from the Florida sun was like walking into a dark, chilled coffin with fluorescent lighting. Maybe that was the point. Windowless, carpeted, oppressively quiet, with some new agey music playing so low you could hardly hear it. Fleisher's Funeral Home, despite its Jewish identity, looked like it could have buried any religion. There was a small Star of David on the wall, but that was it. Everything was beige, except for maroon drapery over what may have been windows but it was hard to tell, not a crack of light came in. The funeral director fit the part as well. Middle aged, portly, with a five o'clock shadow, he wore a conservative gray suit, white shirt and tie that squeezed his fleshy neck. He was sweating despite the chilled air. He gave me an anemic smile that I knew was supposed to project sympathy, but just made me uneasy.

He held out his hand. "I'm Mr. Fleisher, your grief counselor. Please come into my office. How can I help you?" he said unctuously, seating me in front of his huge mahogany desk after he finished giving my hand a quick shake.

"Well, I need to make plans for my mother's burial. She's eighty, in poor health, and I don't want to wait until after....after....you know what."

"Of course, Ms. Ginsburg, I understand," he said with the kind of phony sympathy all salespeople use. It got on my nerves. "We have a number of pre-planning options. I'm sure we can find one that's suitable."

Sheldon and I had figured out the details of the change the night before.

"I think a newly made vampire needs to be buried a coffin in order to rise," he said. "After that maybe they can sleep without them, but they do need to be buried first."

"That is going to make it very complicated. How can we smuggle coffins out of Century Village after you finish the change on the girls? There are too many busybodies around here waiting to pounce on the good apartments as soon as someone dies. Mom's is between the pool and the lagoon; someone will be calling the real estate agent on the least suspicion. Why don't you call the Talamasca or someone from B.A. on that one? Maybe there's another way."

"You're right, I may be living in the past century, vampire-wise. There may have been technological improvements in the change. After all I haven't done it since, well, the last century."

"Can you email the Talamasca? I don't want to run up Mom's phone bill."

"Email? I guess so. If I knew their address."

"Let's Google them."

I brought my laptop out to the pool, Googled Talamasca, and sure enough a website came up with Talamasca.uk.org. You needed to register to get on the site, and I registered with my email address. Once on I looked for the FAQ and there it was, very detailed information on everything a vampire or aspiring vampire needed to know, including how to change someone into one. Sheldon just wanted to know about coffins and burial. He said he knew the rest.

- *On the night following death, bury the human in a graveyard or a crypt. The next night coffin can be opened and human will be a fledgling vampire. Make sure human has a source of fresh blood immediately. Animal blood will suffice, though fledgling vampire may crave human blood. Discourage this. The more human blood fledgling drinks, the more he will crave.*

• *Fledgling will want his coffin to sleep in for comfort although it is not necessary. Totally dark room will suffice.*

"Sheldon, where are we going to get coffins for three old ladies? And how are we going to bury them and come back when they rise?"

Suddenly the solution came to me. "We're going to use your coffin."

"But I will have insomnia without my coffin. I sometimes have insomnia with it—that's why Goldie reads to me."

"You're going to have to deal with insomnia. I'll get you some pot. It will put you to sleep. We're going to use that coffin for the girls."

"One coffin for three women? Are we going to stack them like cordwood?"

"Sheldon, you are not funny. No, you're going to change them one at a time. In fact, that will be even better. Each one will be there to reassure the others. Mom will be first."

"Where are we going to bury them?"

"You're a big, strong boy. You can do it."

"I don't do manual labor. I'm a rabbi."

"You were a rabbi, Shel. You're branching out."

"That doesn't answer the question. Where? I doubt we can bury them by the pool without anyone noticing."

"Maybe we need to find a crypt—it's above ground. Easier to go back and get them the next night."

"Providing we don't run into anyone."

"We need to talk to the funeral director." There was a funeral home conveniently located on Century Boulevard right across the street from Century Village. No need to travel for the funeral.

"What do you mean "we?" Sheldon said raising his eyebrows. I think you mean you. I don't believe funeral homes are open at night, plus I'd probably spook a funeral director. He's seen too many corpses. A walking one would probably really confuse him."

"OK, I'll do it. I'll make an appointment tomorrow."

"What are you going to ask?"

"I guess I'll find out how to buy a crypt? Ask him to show me a few. Then I'll pick a likely spot for Mom and the girls. Someplace quiet."

"No loud corpses, eh?"

"Sheldon, for a vampire, you have a sick sense of humor."

"I want a crypt," I informed Mr. Fleischer. "In a mausoleum. Mom has a horror of being underground. And I want to have access to it before she dies. So I can show it to her, you know. I want to take her there myself."

"What kind of crypt are you interested in?"

"What kinds are there?"

"Oh, dear, we have a huge range. Some are in cemeteries in upscale areas like Boca. The mausoleums range from Baroque to Classical to Gothic to the type that's built into a hill, with waterfalls, grottos, meditation gardens, palm trees. Those are more expensive. Others are plainer."

When he gave me the price range I gasped. I picked plainer. Much plainer. Mom wasn't going to spend much time there after all.

"I can take you to see a mausoleum in Everglades Eternal Rest Cemetery, in Tamarac. Not the most elegant, but it is reasonably priced."

"Uh-huh. I don't think Mom would want to spend my inheritance on her final resting place. Can I see it?"

"Do you want to drive with me?"

"Would it be OK if I followed you. I need to do some shopping and I love the Wal-Mart over there."

He shrugged. "Your choice."

The truth was that the thought of sitting in a car with this guy gave me the willies. I followed him to a cemetery that was unrelievedly bleak. No trees, scrubby grass, no actual gravestones, just flat plaques in the ground. There was one big concrete building that I assumed was the mausoleum.

"Why are all the graves marked with flat stones?" I asked as soon as we parked and started walking towards the concrete building.

"Upright gravestones tend to fall over—Florida is all one big swamp. Flat ones are more stable." He chuckled. He'd come to life a bit in the cemetery. "Here's the mausoleum."

"It looks like a bomb shelter."

"Well actually it was one. They sold it to the cemetery. A bomb shelter was pretty stable on this ground."

"Geez, that is weird. Anyway, let's get this over with."

He showed me the interior, which was basically a wall of niches with drawers, like a morgue. The only decoration was another Star of David on the wall.

"After the coffin goes in, the niche is sealed with material that inhibits the odor of decay, of course. Anyway, once the person is entombed in their crypt, no one really wants to go inside the mausoleum. There are plaques outside to commemorate the inhabitants."

"Listen, can I get access to the mausoleum. I mean the key to the door."

"We don't usually do that. Why would you want the key? Once your mom goes to her eternal rest, the door will be opened for the burial, and then closed."

"I want to take Mom to visit. She wants to make sure where she'll be buried."

"I could come out here with you again, I suppose." He sighed. "I have the key. There's no one on site to let you in."

"I need the key. Mom is very self-conscious. She would not come out here with you. I can't pay you without the key."

He sighed again. I guessed he was used to strange requests from the soon-to-be- bereaved. "I guess no one would mind. There's no caretaker on the site and to tell you the truth, hardly anyone ever visits. It's not very pretty."

Hearing that visitors were rare was a real relief.

"Well, that's it then. Let's go back to your office and I'll give you a check. You can give me the key."

"You can drop by later. After you go to Wal-Mart."

"What? Oh yes, Wal-Mart," He'd dropped the hard sell and was being nice. I'd totally forgotten about Wal-Mart. "I'll skip shopping. Now that I've settled on the crypt, I'd prefer to get the arrangements over with."

When we got back to his office he handed me the key. I gave him a hefty check for the crypt and for perpetual care. I would need it again for the other girls after Sheldon changed Mom.

"Do you want to see our casket selection? We have a large range of lovely final resting containers in all materials from teak to lead. If you pre-order the casket when you pay for the plot, or crypt in your case, you get a big discount.. If you don't take advantage of the discount today you lose the opportunity for a really good deal."

"I don't need a casket. I have one actually. In the storage room at Century Village."

"You have one? What are you doing with a casket?"

"Don't ask! You don't want to know."

"I suppose not," he said, taking my check and pocketing it. "It's your funeral."

Chapter Seventeen

Mom had spent a great deal of time deciding what to wear for her death.

"What do you think, Rhoda, should I just wear a nightgown, or pajamas?"

"I have no idea mom, pick what you're most comfortable in."

" I don't want to wake up and look shlumpy, but on the other hand I do want to be comfortable. I know, I have the perfect dress."

She settled on something festive—a long, loose Mexican dress with a day of the dead motif—little skeletons dancing on a yellow and red background.

"So apropos, don't you think?"

The first night Sheldon was very tentative about sucking Mom's blood. He sat by her bed on one side and sunk his fangs into her neck while I held her hand on the other side.

"That hurts," mom whined. At least she wasn't shrieking.

"Let me get some EMLA cream for her."

"What's that?" Sheldon asked.

"It's a numbing cream. She has some in her kitchen drawer. It's handy stuff." I got the tube and rubbed some of the ointment on mom's neck. Then we had to wait another hour until it took effect. I turned on *True Blood* on HBO in the meantime to give mom some idea of the vampire life.

"Turn that off," she said after the first episode. Watching Bill get drained in the parking lot of Merlotte's was too much for her.

Sheldon went back to mom's neck, but this time he looked like he was enjoying himself a little too much. He kept glancing at me guiltily. I knew that look. It was the one I had when I ate ice cream when I was supposed to be on a diet.

"How does this feel, Fanny?" he asked, his fangs dripping with a few drops of blood.

"It looks disgusting, I'll tell you that much," I said.

"Rhoda, shhhh, you'll freak out your mom," Sheldon warned me.

"I can't feel a thing Sheldon, just go ahead." Mom, as usual, was being brave.

After a little more sucking, however, she fell asleep.

"I'm going to stop now, Rhoda. I don't want to hurt her." Sheldon looked miserable. He drew away from Mom reluctantly.

"You're supposed to hurt her Sheldon. In fact you're supposed to kill her." I was determined to be matter-of-fact."

"I wish you wouldn't be so blunt, Rhoda. This is your mother we're talking about."

"You're the vampire, why are you such a sissy?

"I have a reverence for mothers, especially the Jewish mother of the woman I love. It goes against my instincts to hurt her, although her blood is pretty tasty."

"Yuck," I guess I'm a wuss too. Let's go to bed.

We spent the night watching the first season of *True Blood.*

"If I looked like Sookie would you love me more?" I asked Sheldon wistfully. I'd always fantasized about having a body like Anna Paquin that would look great in shorts and a tight t-shirt. I reassured myself that I had a vampire as hot as Bill Compton so I had no need to be jealous.

"I'd like you to dress more like Sookie," he said, "but I like your body the way it is."

I determined to buy some sexy outfits, even if there was no way I'd be caught dead—or even undead--in shorts.

The changing process didn't go as smoothly as we had hoped. Night after night Sheldon sucked blood from Mom, and day after day she'd wake up feeling fine.

"What's going on, Rhoda," she asked on the third morning. "Aren't I supposed to die and change into a vampire? Maybe we should just give the whole thing up and go shopping."

"No, Mom, please be patient, we're still working out the process."

"You better figure it out quick or I'm going to die of boredom."

At least mom hadn't lost her sense of humor. But Sheldon and I were quickly losing ours.

Despite the fact that I knew Mom was going to rise as one of the undead, I felt guilty about wanting her to die—and terrified as well. There was no way to avoid those primal feelings. I just wanted it all to be over and was getting stressed by hanging around and waiting for it to happen. The girls were stressed out about it too. Every day they'd come over expecting to hear that Mom had died in the night and every day she'd be chipper as ever.

"I love your outfit, Fanny. Perfect for the occasion," Miriam told her.

"This is taking so long I've had to wash it twice. I may be losing my life but I'm not losing my fashion sense."

"I'm doing something wrong, Rhoda." Sheldon said that night. I'd never seen him look so upset. Usually even-tempered and smiling, he sat glumly with his head cocked thoughtfully, brows knitted, trying to figure out the answer.

"I don't know what it is. I have to do some more research."

We went back to the Talamasca website and followed the FORUM link. We hit the subject *Changing Human to Vampire*. There were some questions that seemed relevant.

Deadgurl asked:

I don't know how much blood to suck from the human?
The vampire should use his fangs to suck a moderate amount of blood from the human each night until the human weakens. The vampire must not take too much, or the human will die ... for good.

"I probably haven't been taking enough," Sheldon said when he read this passage. "I was afraid of killing Mom too soon."

What is a moderate amount?
A mouthful is moderate.

What if the human refuses to die?
Try two mouthfuls.

What about the vampire giving the human his blood? Is that necessary?
Yes, humans can't change into vampires without drinking some vampire blood. Actually when the human becomes faint, the vampire must offer the human a substantial amount of his own blood—preferably from a vein. If the vampire has medical equipment he can use an IV and collect it in a blood bag to offer the human.

How long does the change take?
It can happen in one night to one week, depending on how vigorous the human is and how old the vampire is. It's

quickest with sick humans, slowest with healthy young humans.

"Omigod, Sheldon," I said. "You haven't been giving Mom any of your blood have you?"

"No, I couldn't." He looked embarrassed.

"Sucking blood from my poor sweet Mom is OK by you, but you can't give her any back. What kind of stingy vampire are you?"

"I have to admit it, Rhoda, I faint at the sight of blood. I don't mind when I'm sucking it because I don't actually see it, but if it's my own blood I get nauseous. As you saw when I cut my hand it's not easy for me to bleed. I have to make a really deep puncture wound. Don't you know any nurses who could run an IV for me?" he asked plaintively.

"Oh sure, there must be plenty of nurses with IV equipment who would take blood from a vampire," I said. "You changed Herschel. Didn't you have to give him blood?

"That was a long time ago. I forgot."

"C'mon Sheldon, You never forget anything."

"OK, I did give him a little blood, but it really made me sick, I was hoping I wouldn't have to do that again. I'll call Tess. Maybe one of the Golden Grandmas can help."

The next night Sheldon sucked more of Mom's blood, until she actually felt faint. Then Tess arrived with Hannah, one of the Grandmas who had been a nurse. Hannah was dressed in a nurse's uniform and was carrying medical equipment, including what looked like an intravenous line, a bag, and even a rolling hanger for it.

"Where did you get this?" I asked.

"From Miami-Dade Memorial," Hannah replied. "Dressed like this you can pretty much take whatever you want."

I was kind of shocked because my mom's friends were generally law-abiding, but I guessed that after becoming vampires, Golden Grandmas had to learn to live at least a little bit on the wild side.

"We heard you were having some problems with Fanny," Hannah said. "I'd like to help."

"Have you ever changed anyone?" Sheldon asked her.

"No, but I do have some medical background. Of course they didn't teach this kind of thing in nursing school, but I can improvise."

She started setting up the IV equipment, then ordered Sheldon to stick out his arm. He screwed up his face, looked in the other direction and gasped as she stuck in the needle. The blood started flowing into the bag.

"Here, Fanny." She put some of Sheldon's blood in a large medicine dropper—the type used to give medicine to kids-- and said, "Fanny, open your mouth."

Mom did not look happy while Sheldon's blood dripped into her mouth; in fact, she gagged once, but she dutifully accepted the whole dropper-ful. Sure enough after she took it, she started looking pale and fell back onto her bed.

"This is disgusting, can't you add some Burgundy to it, or at least grape juice?" Mom screwed up her face to show how bad it tasted before gasping, "I feel quite faint, Rhoda," and then passed out.

The next morning I went into Mom's room and was horrified to find that she wasn't breathing. It was one thing to talk her into becoming a vampire. Then it was only theoretical. Now it was real. I was sitting with a real, live, undead, not-breathing Mom. Maybe she wouldn't rise? What then? I started sobbing. Sheldon was asleep and I had to wait until sundown until he woke up to bury her. I sat by her bed, sure I'd made a terrible mistake and killed my own mom for good. I cried, wailed actually, and didn't know what to do. I didn't want to call the girls because then they'd get hysterical. I couldn't call the Golden Grandmas because they were asleep. So I called the suicide hotline, 1-800-suicide. I remembered the number. I'd heard they would talk to you even if you weren't suicidal, but just going through an emotional crisis. This was definitely a major emotional crisis. I was smart enough to block my Caller ID. After all I was admitting to homicide, not suicide.

"Suicide hotline," a perky voice answered. "Are you having an emotional crisis?"

"Yes. I am." I didn't know what else to tell her because my story was so bizarre.

"Do you feel as if you can't go on?"

"No, I want to go on. I'm worried about someone else not going on?"

"Aha. You're grieving. What happened? How can I help you?"

"I just killed my mother. Or rather I got my boyfriend to kill her. He's a vampire and we're going to bring her back to life so it's not like I really killed her. But I can't help feeling horribly guilty. What if she stays dead? I'll be a murderer. I may even go to jail, even though they'd probably consider it euthanasia. But you can go to jail for that too. And even if she comes back to life she'll still be dead, if you know what I mean. How will I ever live with myself?" I started wailing inconsolably.

"If she's not really dead, you can forgive yourself. You just need to be strong," the voice said softly and sympathetically. "Why did you want her to become a vampire?"

"She's really old and sick and I couldn't bear to live without her."

149

"That is so sweet. Not many daughters would make that kind of sacrifice for their mothers. Now you'll have her forever, or vice versa."

"You believe me?" I realized that this was a ridiculous conversation. The suicide hotline lady was taking me seriously. I hadn't expected that. I just wanted to hear some comforting words.

"Why wouldn't I believe you? Been there, thought about that."

"You turned your mother into a vampire?" That would have been a bit too much of a coincidence.

"No, but I'm desperate to save my grandmother. She is the only person in the world who ever really cared about me and she's in the ICU. I'd do anything. Can you give me some help? How do you go about it? Who does it for you? Where would I find a vampire to change her?"

So instead of the suicide hotline lady helping me I wound up helping her. I told her about the Golden Grandmas, gave her my phone number and Zelda's phone number and the New York address of Bloodaholics Anonymous since she was in New York. She said she'd call Zelda and ask if she could go to their next meeting in New York. She thanked me profusely and told me I'd be fine— I'd done the right thing. By the time I got off the phone I felt much better. Whoever said there's nothing like helping others to help yourself was right.

I called Charlene and told her the whole story too. As usual she was incredibly reassuring.

"Rhoda, you just have to try to relax. This is going to work. I know it will. You had that whole group of old lady vampires tell you so, and Sheldon as well. Try to take a break and go swimming. Go out for breakfast and stuff your face. Have pancakes. Anything distracting."

It was great advice and I tried to take it but I couldn't. I knew I'd feel so guilty swimming in the sun that Mom would never see again that I went into the living room and turned on the TV to wait it out. I watched soap operas which I usually found ridiculous. Today they didn't seem exaggerated at all since my life was turning out to be equally melodramatic. I popped a macaroni and cheese TV dinner in the microwave and ate it, not tasting a bite. After a few hours of more agonizing I drove to the rental car company as Sheldon and I had agreed upon. We had reserved a huge Chevy Suburban with a few rows of seats that could be put down to make room for a coffin. I left Mom's car at the rental place, took the Suburban and wended my way carefully through the streets since I wasn't used to driving a car that was closer to a bus.

By the time I got back to Mom's I was so exhausted I fell asleep. When I woke up it was sunset. Whew! I made it. I woke up Sheldon, who by this time was sleeping in his coffin in Mom's spare room. He still refused to sleep in the bed, but he was going to have to at least for one day because Mom was going to be buried in his coffin.

Chapter Eighteen

When Sheldon woke up we faced the most difficult task. Getting the coffin with Mom in it out of the house and into the SUV without anyone noticing. Century residents were very nosy; since nothing ever happened, gossip was a scarce commodity. There wasn't much chance of not being noticed unless we waited until midnight. OK, we'd wait till midnight. We decided to throw a tarp over the coffin for further camouflage.

We killed some time by going for a swim and making love. I was too distracted to really get into it, but I loved feeling Sheldon hugging and kissing me. I needed the comfort and closeness. We watched a little TV news but murder and mayhem in Miami was not exactly calming so I turned it off.

By midnight Century Village was deserted. I made Sheldon put Mom in the coffin, but I couldn't watch. I couldn't help imagining what it must feel like to be stuffed into a tiny space, unable to breathe or see the light, buried alive. I knew I had to stop thinking about it or I would get a full-fledged panic attack. I couldn't even bear to be stuck in an elevator, I was so claustrophobic. I reminded myself that Mom was dead—or undead--and if she made any noise we would hear her. Luckily Sheldon was strong enough to lift the coffin by himself and put it in the car. With a tarp over it, it looked like—well, a coffin with a tarp over it. But no one was watching anyway.

When we got to the cemetery I felt kind of spooked but Sheldon looked quite happy.

"My people," he said, expansively opening his arms

"Could you please take this seriously, Sheldon, we're burying my mother."

"Haven't you ever heard of graveyard humor, Rhoda?"

"It's gallows humor, dummy." I giggled, which relieved my anxiety a tiny bit.

We drove right up to Mom's mausoleum, found that the key opened it, and slid the coffin easily into the crypt. When we left it there I wanted to open it first and kiss Mom but I was afraid of what I'd find. What if she had her eyes open? What if she looked as terrified as I felt. She was being buried alive, after all. OK, she wasn't underground and if she woke up she could probably open the coffin enough to get out since her space in the crypt was really big. It wasn't like a drawer in the morgue, it was much roomier than that. Actually it looked like it had been converted from one of the pantries in the bomb shelter. There may even have been a little leftover food around. But she'd be terrified finding herself in a mausoleum in the middle of a cemetery. Better not worry about that.

There was no way I could leave, without checking on Mom. I had a flashlight so I asked Sheldon to hold the coffin lid open while I peeked inside. Mom didn't look dead at all. She looked surprisingly peaceful, as though she were just sleeping—and, from the expression on her face, having a good dream at that—although I knew she wasn't breathing and her heart had stopped. There was a subtle difference between her and other bodies I'd seen. Her soul, or whatever animated her—her momness—was clearly still there. She didn't have that waxworks look that normal dead bodies took on shortly after death. But I was still incredibly nervous, not at all sure this scheme would work.

I still had to get through the rest of the night and the next day before going back to the cemetery and seeing if Mom rose properly from the dead. And I had to deal with an insomniac vampire who was going to have an anxiety attack in the morning without his coffin, despite the blackout curtains I'd hung. When we got back to Century he started pacing back and forth in the apartment. I drove him to the beach so he could pace there. Anyone outside at Century after midnight was suspect. He walked back and forth on the beach while I took a nap on the sand. There were a number of other insomniacs doing the same thing so no one noticed.

"Shel, can we go back to the mausoleum to make sure Mom is OK?"

"No, there's no need for that Rhoda, she's fine."

"How do you know that? She could be really dead and not just undead."

"Rhoda, we are bound together now by blood. Your mom is my child." Sheldon gave a stifled laugh.

"What? You're my mom's father? That would make me—what? Your granddaughter? That's ridiculous."

"Sire. I'm her sire since I created her. That makes her my progeny or whatever you want to call it. Sounds silly I know since she's so old, but she's not as old as I am. I now have a connection to your mom. When she's in danger I'll know it. I may not be able to do anything about it, but I'll feel it. Just like most parents somehow know when their kids are in trouble."

"That's handy, mom is pretty unpredictable. She just might get into trouble."

We drove back. He lay down on the pullout bed in the spare room and tried closing his eyes.

"I can't sleep, Rhoda," he whined, wide-eyed.

"It's been about five minutes, Sheldon. You're a big baby. I brought your favorite Singer stories to read to you."

By the time I'd gotten halfway through "Gimpel the Fool," his favorite, he was undead to the world. I breathed a huge sigh of relief. Finally, he didn't have to schlep that *fershtunken* coffin everywhere. He could stay at my apartment. We could actually travel.

While he was sleeping the girls arrived to see how Fanny was doing.

"She's dead and buried," I told them.

Ellen burst into tears and Miriam started sniffling.

"Are you sure this was a good idea," Rhoda?" Miriam asked, wiping her nose. "Maybe she'll stay dead."

"No, we're sure that won't happen," I reassured her. "We checked it out on the Internet. We're going to raise her tonight."

"When can we see her?" Ellen asked.

"As soon as I've got her settled in bed."

" I thought she had to sleep in a coffin?" Judy said.

"No, that was just Sheldon who got into the coffin habit. But you can't wake her. She's going to need her uninterrupted beauty rest for a while."

"She'll be sleeping like the dead, eh?" Judy couldn't resist the bad joke.

Chapter Nineteen

Sheldon was really lucky that he slept through the worst of it. I had to survive the entire day alone, not knowing whether Mom would be really dead or undead when we opened her coffin. Figuring out how to spend my days alone in Century was going to get old fast. The only thing I could think of that would keep me entertained, or at least numbed, was shopping. I got in Mom's car and headed to the nearest Wal-Mart, my favorite distraction. I guiltily took her checkbook, which had my name on it as well. I was on all her accounts so I wouldn't have to worry about probate when she died. That might be handy now that she wouldn't be able to get to a bank during the day, but with ATMs everywhere it might not be a problem.

I wandered around aimlessly, at a loss in a Wal-Mart for the first time in my life. Nothing appealed to me. I tried on a few t-shirts but all I could think of was what Mom was going to wear after her change. What do newly made elderly female vampires wear anyway? Tessie dressed in the usual Century Village pastel polyester. So I shopped for Mom instead of me. I wanted to buy her some snazzy outfits in navy or maroon silk or another classy muted fabric, just in case being a vampire brought out her dark side. I decided against black—too funereal. Somehow vampires and the loud Indian prints Mom favored equaled cognitive dissonance to me. But Wal-Mart had nothing in muted colors, much less silk. I had to go to Saks to find what I was looking for. Their clothes were astronomically expensive—Mom would have a fit if I spent hundreds of dollars for one outfit but I did it anyway. I'd just cross out the price and tell her it was on sale. I got her a pretty dark red dress with a matching burgundy shawl embroidered with little red rosettes that I would have liked if it fit me. I also got her some gorgeous black pumps in size six.

Then I went to Best Buy and got her a cell phone, which I was determined she would somehow learn to use. I wanted to be able to get in touch with her at all times, in case something happened to her. Was I having a premonition of disaster? Maybe, but I put it out of my mind. Before the change Mom's memory had been failing along with her body. She just couldn't remember how to use any modern technology. She loved photography, and had bought herself a digital camera. She couldn't figure out how to use it no matter how many times the photo store guy showed her. Even if she had figured out the camera, what was she going to do without a computer or printer to print or store the pictures? So I bought her a computer and a printer. Email was a must. She had to be able to write to me. Plus Best Buy was open late and she could always confer with the Geek Squad after sunset on how to use the cell phone, the computer, the printer, etc. I sure hoped the change sharpened her mind along with revitalizing her body.

After spending enough of Mom's money to get a big lecture from her, I put away the checkbook and headed for the beach. Bobbing around in the ocean waves was more therapeutic than I'd anticipated. I dove under and rode them back to shore, which exhausted me. Then I sat on the beach and baked in the sun, a luxury I usually never allowed myself due to fear of aging. I'd seen too many Florida women my age with leathery, wrinkled faces. Today I needed to bake—the heat of the sun drained me of anxiety. I refused to worry about how I looked in a bathing suit even though the light of day did not show my thighs to their best advantage.

157

After exhausting myself in the ocean I treated myself to a huge Jewish meal at The Deli Den in Hollywood. Obama had stopped here while he was campaigning in south Florida and Mom had her picture taken with him (it pays to be a little old Jewish lady and live in a swing state). I think he had the brisket and a black and white cookie. I had matzoh ball soup and a huge pastrami sandwich on rye. I was glad neither Sheldon nor Mom was around to observe my gluttonous behavior, but I felt guilty anyway. Poor Mom wouldn't be having pastrami again—ever. I felt so bad I ordered a big slice of cherry cheesecake to cheer myself up.

By the time I got back to the apartment and took a long nap, it was time to wake Sheldon up.

"Sheldon, I am having a major anxiety attack," I said as soon as he opened his eyes. "How do we know Mom will rise like she's supposed to?"

"We don't. But Tess probably does. We'll take her along. She's going to have to help us with the transition, find blood for Mom to drink. She'll be pretty thirsty when she wakes up."

We picked Tess up in the Suburban and I was impressed by how she hopped up into the back. It was pretty high.

"Ready to rock and roll?" Tess said.

"Mom hates rock and roll," I answered.

"That might change," Tess said, "I never liked rock and roll either until I became a vampire back in the 'seventies. Then I became a big disco fan because they were open all night and I could dance. I'm mad for dancing."

"Weren't you worried about looking out of place?"

"Remember Disco Sally?

"Yeah, she hung out at Studio 54 back then. She was a darling of the stars wasn't she?"

"That was me," Tess said proudly. "I was one hot grandma."

"You outlived just about everyone else who hung out there."

"Yeah, and the Studio 54 regulars who are still around, like Mick Jagger, look worse than I do."

"Do you still hit the clubs?"

"Not much anymore. Young people these days are too prejudiced against old people. You have to look like them, act like them, be them. They treat us old people either like we're invisible or garbage. I hate kids today. Back in the 'seventies you could be old and wrinkled as long as you were willing to be outrageous—think about Andy Warhol and all the misfits he picked up. I hung out at The Factory too. Oh, I could tell you some stories."

"Do you ever take revenge on those kids?" I asked. "I know you could."

"I won't answer that question right now. Suffice it to say I go to the local B.A.."

"I go to B.A. meetings in New York. I'm a sponsor." Sheldon eagerly reported.

"I've had some bad moments, where I lost control," Tess said sadly. "But since we bought the farm it's much easier to stay out of trouble. The animals meet our needs. Your mom and her friends will join us at the farm. It will be easier for them since we've paved the way."

We were so busy chatting that I barely noticed when Sheldon turned into the cemetery and drove up to the mausoleum where Mom was entombed.

"This is nice," Tess said admiringly. "I was buried underground. Very messy."

"Who buried you?"

"My daughter, she's the one who turned me. She happened to have a big farm in upstate New York so it was easy. She keeps a burial ground for vampires going through

159

the change. It's not easy here in Florida. Every square foot of space is a condo complex or a swamp. You don't want the coffin to be flooded."

"I wonder if that's where the expression 'bought the farm' came from?"

"Could be," said Tess.

"Here it is," I announced.

We got out of the truck and Sheldon opened the mausoleum with the key. It occurred to me that even if the key didn't work we had two vampires who could break in.

"Does anyone have a flashlight?" I asked. The night before we'd used a flashlight to find our way around inside.

"Damn, I forgot the flashlight," Sheldon said. "I don't need it and neither does Tess. We can see easily in the dark. Unfortunately it's too dark inside for you to see anything."

"That's OK," I said quickly, only too relieved to be off the hook. I was terrified of opening that coffin, having no idea what I'd find inside. "I'll wait outside."

Tess and Sheldon went in together while I sat on a bench. After a half hour I hadn't heard a sound and wondered what was happening.

"What's going on in there?" I yelled.

"Don't worry, Rhoda," Tess yelled back. "Your Mom's OK, she's alive, or rather undead. She's just taking some time to regain consciousness. It's not instantaneous when they rise, especially if they're old. Everything is slower when you're old, vampire or human."

"Rhoda, is that you out there, Honey?" Mom's voice rang out, much louder than I'd heard it for a long time.

"Yes, Mom, I'm out here waiting. Are you OK?"

"I guess so."

She emerged from the mausoleum a few minutes later looking pretty much like herself—her old self. In the moonlight I saw her walking towards me with a determined stride that she hadn't had for a long time. I'd gotten so used to her being frail and hesitant that I'd forgotten the powerhouse she used to be. When she was healthy—in her seventies--she'd visit me in New York City and walk for miles while I took the bus. She'd drag me to museums, window shopping, concerts, plays and any other interesting event she saw in the newspaper. I'd have to beg her to slow down so I could take a rest. That was the mom who emerged from the tomb. Her face had a big grin, her eyes twinkled and had even regained their old green color, her hair was the same bleached blonde but shiny not dull. She was still wrinkled, yes, but the wrinkles looked more superficial, they didn't etch so far into the skin of her face. Her voice was strong and clear again. She looked at least ten years younger. I felt a huge weight lift off my shoulders. I hadn't realized how terrified I'd been. She was brushing off her dress, followed by Sheldon and Tess.

"There's a lot of dirt in that nasty place. How did you find it? Couldn't you have gotten me into a classier cemetery, or at least a mausoleum that doesn't look like a bomb shelter that no one has swept for centuries?"

"Mom, you've only been undead for five minutes and already you're complaining about the accommodations." I laughed in relief.

"I am incredibly hungry," Mom said, sounding somewhat bewildered. "I suppose I can't have any scrambled eggs?"

Both Tess and Sheldon chimed in with a horrified, "NO!"

"We'll take you for some lamb's blood, Fanny. At least it's biblical." Sheldon smiled at his own joke.

"I'd rather be dead than never eat another bagel."

"You are dead, Mom."

161

"I don't feel dead, Honey. I feel like myself, just a little peppier, and hungrier. I haven't actually been hungry for a long time. Since I got sick."

"It will take some time for you to get used to your new diet, Fanny," Sheldon said. "Tess and I will help you adjust."

"Let me walk around a little first and try out my new youth."

She ran away from us, and I mean ran. I hadn't seen her run since I was in my teens.

"This is amazing," she yelled back at us. "I can run and I'm not out of breath." Then she sat down abruptly, eyes wide with terror. "Omigod I'm not breathing,"

"Fanny, take it easy," Sheldon told her. "You have to get used to your new body. It is a totally new body—not the one you had when you were young, but an immortal one. You can breathe if you want to, but you have to practice. There's a lot of adjustment. It took me months. Psychologically it's not easy either. You might need therapy."

"Therapy? Who would believe me?"

"There are vampire therapists, Fanny," Tess told her. "They specialize in vampire problems like SVD."

"Is that a sexually transmitted disease?" Mom asked. "I thought we didn't get sick. That's why I agreed to this meshuganah plan."

"SVD is sociopathic vampire disorder," Tess informed her gravely. "Some vampires lose their consciences after the change and start thinking of humans as lesser beings whom they can murder or manipulate at will. That's when they wind up in vampire rehab."

"Rehab?" Mom sounded even more bewildered.

`"Don't ask! No need to think about that now, Fanny. You have too much to learn about the vampire lifestyle first."

"I'm desperately hungry...and thirsty." Mom whined. "Please, can I get something to eat, or drink I guess it is? How about a glass of water? Can I have water? "

I felt terrible for her. She sounded pitiful. I'd never heard Mom beg for food or water before.

"No, you can't have water, Fanny. It will make you sick. Let's get her to the farm, then" Tess answered, directing us all to the van. "We've got a ways to drive."

Chapter Twenty

We turned out of the cemetery and hit I-95 North.

"Where the hell are we going, Tess?" Mom asked.

"We're going to Volturi Ranch on lake Okechobee, it's about a hundred miles northwest of here."

"Why so far?" I asked.

"Florida is too built up around here. We've got a huge ranch up there with lots of deer and even exotic animals the original owner imported for hunters. Vampires from all over come down here to hunt. Shel, you might enjoy hunting a deer, but Fanny would probably prefer our tamer sheep and goats."

"Don't underestimate me, Tess," Mom almost growled. "I'm feeling predatory tonight."

"I'd like some coffee and a snack. Is there anything for humans to eat?" I was starving.

"We'll find something for you, Rhoda," Tess said. "You can eat at the casino. The Seminoles have a big one nearby. Did you know that some vampires are really good gamblers? That's how they get rich. They develop photographic memories and card count. We have to be careful not to get thrown out."

"Sheldon, it might be a lot easier to gamble than to cut diamonds for a living?" I suggested.

"Rhoda, I have a terrible memory and I hate to gamble. I hate games. I can't even win at Checkers."

We stopped at the first gas station we saw. Tess got out to pump.

"Shouldn't I do that?" Sheldon asked. .

"I'm a vampire, not a little old lady. I can pump gas," Tess huffily replied, grabbing the hose and stuffing it into the tank.

"Hurry up, why dontcha," a beefy man with a ponytail yelled from his pickup behind us. There was only one pump and we were at it. He turned to the blonde next to him and sneered, "This old broad is going to take all week to finish pumping gas."

I heard a growling from the back and then the door opened and Mom flew at the man, yanking open the door of his truck and instantly latching onto his neck with her teeth. She clung to him and I heard a sucking sound.

"Mom!" I yelled. "Get back in the car."

Sheldon looked horrified and went after her and grabbed her so quickly I barely saw him move. The man held his neck with an expression of horror and disbelief, staring at Mom. I'm sure he had no idea what hit him.

"Tess, let's get out of here quick," Sheldon yelled.

Tess moved fast, pulling the hose out of the tank and jumping back into the van. Luckily she'd used a credit card.

We zipped back onto the road and Sheldon turned to Mom. "Fanny, what were you thinking?

"I wasn't thinking. I'm so tired of being put down by young people. They think we're dirt. It was automatic. Plus I'm hungry."

"Geez, Mom, you have to control yourself. You could get into a lot of trouble." I said.

"You could get us all into trouble, Fanny," Tess said. "We try to fly under the radar, metaphorically that is."

"I'm so sorry," Mom said, sounding truly remorseful. "I'll try to control myself from now on. It's just so strange being in this body. I have impulses I never knew existed."

"You'll learn, Sweetie," Tess smiled at her. "Just follow what I do."

"Mom, give me your dentures. That should make you pretty harmless."

She obediently handed them over. I asked Tess, "Do dentures grow fangs? What if you're a toothless vampire?" I'd noticed that Sheldon's incisors turned into fangs when he was excited. He hadn't plunged them into me ... yet.

"We have vampire dentists who make retractable fangs for dentures. When they're in the vampire's mouth dentures act like real teeth, but they're removable. It's very handy."

"Live and learn." I grimaced. "Or rather die and learn."

Mom settled down but still looked pretty unhappy. I held her hand, which seemed to help.

"Hope you're not going to go after me, Mom," I said, trying to make a lame joke.

"Rhoda, don't be ridiculous. You're my daughter. I would never hurt you. I didn't know what I was doing back there. It was like there was a monster inside me. I wasn't myself at all. This whole vampire thing isn't going to be easy."

There *was* a monster inside her. I should have known it, I'd heard the stories at the B.A. meeting. I just assumed she'd be like Sheldon, or Tess. But then both Mom and I had always been compulsive eaters. We'd struggled with our weight our entire lives, except recently because Mom was so sick she'd started losing. I guess human compulsive eaters become vampire compulsive bloodsuckers. I hoped Mom wasn't going to attack anyone she knew, just strangers. But that was bad enough.

Eventually we pulled up into a long driveway with a lot of scrubby tress and vegetation and a long low structure that looked like a lodge . No houses were in sight.

166

A tall, very handsome, very black man with a Haitian accent came up to the car. "Yo, Miss Tess, I see you got a new lady here? She one of you?"

I was surprised to see Tess touch and stroke his arm and look up at him flirtatiously. It wasn't an old lady gesture.

"This is Fanny, Jean. She's going to be visiting with me. A couple of her friends are changing soon and they'll be coming too."

"That's good, Miss Tess. We'll buy more animals with the money from selling these."

"Fanny, do you want to feed now?" Tess asked Mom.

Mom looked ravenous. We followed Jean to a large barn filled with a variety of animals, from sheep to goats to chickens. A young man in a T-shirt, jeans and sandals, with a yarmulke, side curls and fringes hanging out from under his shirt, was standing there waiting for us. Jean introduced him as Rabbi Izzy and told him Sheldon was a former rabbi.

"Great to meet you, Sheldon," Izzy said, asking him a lot of questions about what he did and what living in New York was like.

"I wish you'd come down here and join me. I always have to be here to certify that the animals are kosher. Sometimes I want to go on vacation."

I couldn't do this kind of work. Too bloody." Sheldon wrinkled his nose and quickly changed the subject. "How did you manage to become a vampire rabbi? Do the local rabbinical authorities know about it?"

"Of course they don't, and I certainly wouldn't tell them, I'd lose my job and possibly worse. They don't check up on me. Even though there's nothing non-kosher about what I do. Did you know that for an animal being slaughtered by a vampire is totally humane. They don't feel a thing."

167

"If you say so," Sheldon said. "The rats I capture don't seem too happy about it."

"Rats! That's disgusting. How about a goat?"

"I'd love one." Sheldon patted his stomach with enthusiasm.

"Can I leave please?" I backed away. "I don't think I could watch you all suck the blood out of these poor little animals."

Jean gestured me to follow him. "I'll get you some real food, Miss Rhoda, I'm famous for my jerk stew. Let's leave these bloodaholics to their evil ways."

I was taken aback by the "evil" word, but he said it so good-naturedly that I let it pass.

Jean fed me some fabulous spicy stew in his little house, down the walkway from the lodge, which was decorated with colorful Haitian folk art and squishy, comfortable furniture. I'd bought a few paintings from Haitians on the street in New York City and treasured them. His wife Yasmin, a statuesque pretty black woman with straightened, neatly coifed hair and a peasant skirt, came in and sat down with us. She had a lilting accent that sounded Jamaican.

"How did you two get involved with a bunch of vampires?"

Yasmin laughed. "It was that or live in with white folks. I get to live with my husband and kids here and have my own house and a nice life. I used to have to leave my kids with my sister in Jamaica so I could take care of white ladies. Plus we like these vampires. They're the good ones, they don't hurt anyone and they pay for the animals, which we get to sell to a kosher butcher after Izzy certifies them. Very profitable."

"Who are the bad ones?" I asked.

"You don't want to know!" Yasmin said, making the sign of the cross. "They're dangerous."

By the time Mom came back from her dinner, if you can call it dinner, with Sheldon, I was napping on Yasmin's couch. I woke up abruptly when they came in. Sheldon had his arm around Mom's shoulders in a paternal gesture and was herding her towards me. Tess was nowhere in sight. Mom was acting strange although the strangeness was hard to define. It was as if she were herself but herself on speed. She'd always been speedy, but now she was all over the place,

"What an adorable painting," she said to Yasmin, pointing at one of the Haitian artworks on the wall, a colorful oil of a woman with a bundle on her head. "Wherever did you get it?"

Before Yasmin could answer Mom lifted some flowers out of a vase and breathed them in deeply. "Ah, what a scent. I don't believe I've ever smelled flowers like these before. What are they?"

Before Yasmin could answer that question she zipped over to where I was sitting, plunked herself down and effused, "Rhoda I have no idea what you and Sheldon did to me but I feel reborn. Why didn't you do this to me years ago? Why have I been so old for so long?"

"Mom, how could I have done it years ago? I needed Sheldon. I'm not a vampire."

"Oh, that's right. Well you'll just have to become one. It's an incredible experience. I wonder how long it will last?"

"Forever," Sheldon chimed in.

"There's no such thing as forever," Mom said sternly in her schoolteacher voice. "Everyone knows that." Not waiting for a response, she got up and zoomed over to a corner where there were a few modern sculptures that seemed to be assembled out of odd bits of junkyard refuse

169

and rubber tires. I thought they were odd looking, but Mom picked one up and started gazing at it raptly.

"This is the most beautiful thing I have ever seen. It looks like a woman bending over her baby."

She was tripping out-- acting like I did after my first hit of LSD—as if everything in the world were new and wondrous. I found it disconcerting to say the least to see my practical, no-nonsense mom transformed into a hippie on an acid trip.

Yasmin proudly announced, "That's the work of Jean Camille Nasson, a famous Haitian sculptor."

I would have been impressed if I weren't so worried. "Sheldon, what's going on? She is not acting like herself."

"Don't worry, bubeleh, it's just the effect of first blood. After that first feeding a new vampire sees everything as if it were brand new. It won't last. By tomorrow she'll be her cynical self again."

In the meantime mom was scaring me.

"How come she thinks she's not going to live forever?"

"That concept takes some time to get used to, Rhoda. You can't wrap your mind around it right away. It took me a long time to realize I was immortal. It was frightening—and not pleasant. When you have all the time in the world, it's hard to figure out what to do with yourself."

"Mom has never had a problem keeping busy. I'm sure she'll just go on doing what she's always done—movies, concerts, walks on the beach, sewing."

"I wouldn't bet on that," Sheldon said. "Some vampires change. They get hungry for excitement along with blood. Your mom may be that type."

"Why are you talking about me as if I'm not here," Mom said. "I am not going to change. I'm still a socialist and always will be."

Chapter Twenty-One

Mom was really irritating on the way back. She sat behind us and kept pointing out landscape features. The worst thing was that it was night and I couldn't see them.

"Rhoda, look at that gorgeous lake. Let's stop and take a swim."

"You must be nuts, Ma. I can't see a lake. And if I could I sure wouldn't want to take a swim at four a.m."

"Really. It's four a.m. I can see everything like it's, well, daytime."

"Look up ma, no sun."

"I won't have trouble driving at night anymore."

"Stay out of the sun, Fanny," Tess admonished her. "You're a newbie and you might get a bad burn. Plus it will hurt your eyes really badly, even with sunglasses."

"I'm going to miss the sun," Mom said sadly. It was her first real expression of dismay at her new state. It suddenly hit me that bad things could happen to good vampires. Anything that hurt Mom from now on would be my fault—and would make me feel guilty. She could blame me for anything that went wrong with her new life. Mom, like all Jewish mothers, was an expert at pushing guilt. She'd pretty much given it up in her old age but I wasn't sure why. Maybe she realized I really was a good daughter and she started feeling guilty about depending on me so much. Guilt was a double-edged Jewish sword, and we both wielded it expertly.

I was driving since Sheldon didn't have a license and Tess was in back with mom. I didn't trust her to drive quite yet. She might start ignoring the speed limit.

"Shel." I turned to him, talking in a low voice so Mom wouldn't hear. "Do you think we did the right thing? All kinds of things could go wrong. You saw her attack that truck driver."

"Rhoda, do you think I'm deaf?" Mom piped up from the back seat. "I can hear every word you say. I did not attack a truck driver."

Sheldon laughed. "You may not know this, Rhoda, but along with night vision she now has vampire hearing. You can't whisper behind her back anymore."

"Your hearing may have improved, Mom, but your memory is still a bit dim." I automatically turned around to talk to her, almost swerving off the road before remembering that I didn't have to turn around for her to hear me. "You sure did attack a truck driver and you better not do that again."

"You really don't have to worry, dear," Tess said reassuringly. "I will keep an eye on her and make sure she doesn't get into trouble. We Century Village Golden Grandmas do a lot of fun things that will keep her busy."

"Like what?" Mom asked.

"We travel. I never mentioned vampire cruises, did I?"

"Vampire cruises? You've got to be kidding." I was stunned. It seems vampires had their own nighttime world that existed right beside the human world. How was it possible no one knew it about it?

"Aristotle Onassis started a cruise line for us. It's so convenient. We can board at night, explore at night, and he even serves real, perfectly preserved blood. It's not as tasty as live blood, but good enough. That's what billions can do, even after death." Tess hugged Mom. "Fanny you are going to have a great time."

"What?" I shrieked. "Aristotle Onassis is a vampire?"

"Quite a few fabulously rich men are," Tess said matter-of-factly, leaning forward to talk in my ear. "If you had all the money in the world and you were getting really old wouldn't you look into eternal life? He had enough resources to hire investigators to find us. Now he's one of us. And there are more. I won't out them, though. Most of them are very secretive. Onassis only goes out in disguise."

"Did you know about this, Shel?"

"No. I've led a very sheltered afterlife, Rhoda. I've been studying Torah and *davvening* all these years," Sheldon grinned at me lasciviously. " But now that we're together why don't we go on one of these cruises? As long as we can spend a lot of time in the cabin." He did a double eyebrow raise that reminded me of Groucho.

"They're only for vampires, no humans." Tess sounded apologetic. "But maybe Rhoda will decide to become one of us."

"That is not a possibility. Not yet," Sheldon said. "I like her just the way she is."

"I admit it sounds like fun," Mom chimed in, sounding very enthusiastic. I knew how much she loved foreign travel. "But how do you get into museums. I couldn't imagine traveling to Europe, let's say, and missing the Louvre."

"That's just like you Mom. You have eternal life, you can travel the world and you're worried about museums." I was relieved, though, that she was still a culture vulture, still the same mom.

"Rhoda, you just are not sufficiently interested in culture," Mom chided me from the back seat in her schoolteacher voice. "I can't imagine how that happened when I dragged you to every museum in New York when you were a child."

"The operative word is 'dragged,' Mom. No wonder my feet hurt every time I pass the Met."

Ignoring me, Tess answered Mom's question. "Onassis can unlock doors, Fanny. He gets us in everywhere. And we have the museums to ourselves. No gawking tourists to get in your way."

"So what do we do at Century? Not much nightlife there?" Mom asked.

"Midnight swims in the ocean are a treat," Tess replied. "I know how much you like to swim, Fanny. And we go clubbing."

"Clubbing? What's that?"

"Mom." Now it was my chance to chide. "How can you not know what clubbing is? It means going to nightclubs."

"Like the Copa?"

"Fanny, there hasn't been a Copa for fifty years. And you were too young to go there when there was," Tess informed her stiffly. "No, we go to Miami. South Beach. Lots of nightclubs and dancing."

"Isn't that just for young people?" Mom sounded incredulous. "I can't imagine they'd even let you in."

"We're a novelty to them," Tess laughed. "Remember, I was Disco Sally, I know the ropes. The kids think we're cute. And when they see we can out-dance them they go nuts."

"Clubbing.....mm mm." Mom said, bewildered. "It's a whole different world. I can't imagine wanting to socialize with kids. I don't even like kids today—with all those tattoos and pierced bodies. But dancing sounds like fun."

"Dancing with old folks isn't much fun for us, Fanny, we're too spry for them. We can keep up with kids so why not dance with kids?"

"I'll give it a try. Why not? I'm game."

That's what I love about my mom. She's always been game for anything. I took her snorkeling in Key Largo for her seventy-fifth birthday. She was terrified but had a ball. Maybe I'd done the right thing by her in turning her into a vampire. I breathed a relieved sigh inwardly. It was going to be alright. She was going to start enjoying her life again, and I could enjoy mine—with Sheldon.

Chapter Twenty-Two

By the time we got back to Century it was almost daylight. Mom was worried about sleeping. "I don't know how I'm going to fall asleep Rhoda, I'm still wide awake," she said when we got back to the apartment.

"You're on vampire time now, Fanny," Sheldon told her. "Your vampire body clock will put you to sleep at sunrise automatically. In the meantime just read a book or watch TV. You need some extra rest—the change takes a lot of energy."

"Do vampires get insomnia, Sheldon?" she sounded worried. "I've been plagued with insomnia my entire life, ever since I was a kid. It would be worth missing daylight just to get a good night's, or day's, sleep."

"No, Fanny, we sleep like babies, dead babies, for twelve hours. You'll have a wonderful, deep sleep. When you wake up you'll feel refreshed, and you won't remember your dreams."

He must have seen a hypnotist on TV; he knew the lingo. I knew it wasn't true--that Sheldon had insomnia-- but maybe the power of suggestion would keep Mom from having it.

"OK, g'nite you two," she said, giving us a little wave and heading for her bedroom. "I'll use ear plugs so I can't hear you."

I wondered what had come over her. She'd never been particularly considerate before. Maybe becoming a vampire had improved her manners. "That's sweet of you Mom, thanks," I said.

As Mom adjusted to vampire hours, I was slowly adjusting too. I didn't want to miss any time with Sheldon.

I was ready to make love before the sun came up but he looked totally exhausted.

"Is there something wrong, Sheldon? I've never seen you this tired, or tired at all actually. You're either raring to go or sleeping, nothing in between."

"Changing your mom took it out of me, Rhoda. I lost some blood you know." He lay down on the bed and yawned, ready to snooze.

I sat down next to him, stroking his face gently. I loved his features, they were so aristocratic, so old-world handsome, like a renaissance painting. He didn't look like anyone I'd ever dated. Well, there was that one time I'd had a fling with a model, but he was so taken with himself that he barely paid any attention to me.

"What are you staring at, Rhoda," he asked me, looking bewildered. "Do I have blood on my face or something?"

"You have no idea how adorable you are."

"No one has ever called me adorable before. I like it." He started kissing me passionately, not tired anymore.

"How about a quickie?" I asked.

"I don't do quickies. I'm going to live forever. I want to stretch it out." He pulled me down on top of him and pulled off my T-shirt. I stayed on top this time, a position we hadn't tried before. I could barely keep up with him-- he was so hard and moved me up and down on him so fast.

"Don't throw me off, Shel. I feel like I'm on a bucking bronco." I managed to stay in the saddle somehow and got totally lost looking in his gorgeous green eyes. I liked looking down at him, feeling in control of this powerful, supernatural creature. It lent an extra thrill to lovemaking. The bed we were on was creaking loudly. I hoped Mom had fallen asleep already.

By the time we finished about an hour later we were both exhausted. Sheldon pulled me down next to him, leaned on his elbow and looked at me. "I may be immortal, Rhoda, but I'm not eighteen anymore."

"What? I thought you were just as peppy as an eighteen-year-old."

"No one is that peppy, you should have met me at that age. Thank goodness I didn't become a vampire as a teenager. can't imagine being horny all the time for eternity."

"C'mon, let's take a shower together." I took his hand and pulled him towards the bathroom with the stall shower, which was the bathroom we used. Actually only I used the toilet. It seems vampires absorb all their food directly into their bodies and don't eliminate anything. Very efficient and easy on the plumbing.

"What temperature do you prefer?" I asked Sheldon, pushing the lever.

"I like it hot, of course," he told me, "since I'm so cold. Hot water feels delicious. But I have to be careful not to make it too hot because I'll burn myself without realizing it. I don't actually feel hot and cold the way you do."

"While soaping me up, Sheldon mentioned the fact that we had two more old ladies to turn into vampires. "I don't know how I'm going to survive that," he told me as he soaped my right thigh. I started wishing dawn weren't so close. I was definitely interested in another round.

"First of all I don't want to lose my abstinence. Sucking blood from your mom was a serious breach of B.A. rules."

I hadn't asked him how it had affected him because I was trying to be sensitive and not hurt his feelings, so I was glad he'd brought that up himself.

"Are you OK with it now?"

"Actually the blood of the very old isn't all that tasty. Your mom wasn't anywhere near as delicious as you would be," he laughed. "Nowhere near as tasty as some of the young ones I had when I was first changed. I wasn't all that tempted to finish her off. But I was…a little tempted."

"Don't tell me, I don't want to know," the idea was pretty revolting. Actually it was a big turn off.

"I had no idea you used to suck blood from humans."

"Many, many years ago. I killed them, often accidentally. B.A. saved me. Why don't I take your mom to a B.A. meeting before we leave Florida. That should keep both of us in line."

"Sure, great idea. How about Miriam and Ellen? You still have to change them."

"Rhoda, I'm going to ask Tess and one of her friends to change Ellen and Miriam. I can't do it. It's not good for my mental or physical health. Drinking human blood is a *shanda* and giving my blood makes me weak. I can't possibly change two more people,"

It was my turn to soap. Sheldon was always clean because he didn't sweat. He didn't need to shower really, but his hair and face got dirty just like mine. I didn't care about his hair and face, however, and went to work on his muscular arms and armpits which smelled of apricots for some reason, working my way to the line of fine hair down the middle of his chest. I started stroking his smooth back. Thank goodness he wasn't all hairy. There was something repulsive about the idea of a hairy back on a vampire—or on anyone.

"Shel, do you think Tess can find anyone else willing to do it. It's very draining, literally, and they're old—yes vampires—but old. Plus Ellen and Miriam aren't their friends."

"They're Golden Grandmas and committed to helping other old folks, vampire or human, or human *to* vampire. I think they will."

Toweling off when we got out was almost as exciting as soaping, but by that time both of us were too exhausted to do anything about it, plus it was Sheldon's bedtime. I realized I was hungry since I'd been driving all night without anything to eat. I tucked him in and then went off to the kitchen to make myself some scrambled eggs.

Before I went back to bed I sat in the kitchen, shoveling eggs and toast into my mouth, figuring out what was next. I realized I was totally stressed out from all the upheaval in my life, and all the arrangements and plans I'd had to make. Sheldon could hardly help much—he wasn't familiar with making travel reservations, visiting funeral directors, Florida roads, Google research, hiding coffins in storage areas, on and on. In the space of two months I'd met a vampire, fallen in love with him, lost him, found him again, been introduced to an entire vampire other world, turned my mother into a vampire. I was kind of fried.

I took the frozen waffles out of the freezer, popped them in the toaster oven, smothered them with maple syrup and wolfed them down. The downside of Mom living forever started sinking in. I loved her, yes, but she was also an obnoxious Jewish mother who wanted to intrude into every aspect of my life. Now there would be no respite, she could stalk me forever. I thought about a story I'd heard on TV by a gay comic about his mother's funeral. A friend came up to him at the funeral and said, "Congratulations." He was bewildered and asked, "What for?" "You have a partner, you just bought a house, adopted a child, your career is taking off, and your mother's dead." At the time I thought it was funny. . Mothers are supposed to die and now mine never would and I had no one but myself to blame.

I rummaged in the cabinets and found a box of matzo and made matzo brie. I had a great recipe. It was Mom's recipe and she'd never eat it again. I started bawling while loading the dishwasher and wiping off the counters. I doubted that becoming a vampire would make her any less of a neat freak. She always gave me such a hard time if I left dishes in the sink. "Rhoda, the ants will take over if you don't get every crumb." I supposed she had a point, this was Florida after all. At least there were no roaches. After cleaning the counters I hit the ice cream in the freezer. I'd consumed at least 1,500 calories and it wasn't even 9 a.m. I resolved to go on Weight Watchers again as soon as I got back home.

Finally I staggered off to join Sheldon in our room, which we'd made dark as night with blackout curtains. He was snoring. I'd never suspected that vampires snored.

Chapter Twenty-Three

Florida B.A. meetings were in a much more comfortable environment than New York meetings. No damp, chilly church basements. Tess had arranged for B.A. to meet right there in Century Village in the clubhouse. How she had managed this was beyond me, because if anyone knew what was going on she would have lost her condo, but Century Villagers weren't likely to guess. Most of them had never heard of vampires, they didn't read *Twilight* or watch *True Blood*, although a few must know about Anne Rice.

One reason Tess managed to get space for meetings was that they took place at 10 p.m.

After most Century-ites were long asleep and the clubhouse was actually closed for the night. She had access to the yoga room, which meant everyone had to sit on mats on the floor. This wasn't a problem for vampires, who were pretty limber, even old ones, but I was going to have a hell of a time getting up from one of those mats. I had insisted on going with Mom and Sheldon. I wanted to see how the meeting affected her.

Another problem for Tess was getting B.A. members from the outside into Century. There was a security guard at the gate who checked everyone's passes. If you didn't have a pass, the guard would call the person you were visiting to get permission to enter. Tess would vouch for people she knew were coming and then get them passes somehow. For the ones she didn't know there was a forgery ring in Fort Lauderdale that got papers of all kinds for vamps who needed them, whether they needed to get into Century Village or through U.S. Customs. Most B.A.

meetings were open to all, but this one was like a speakeasy. You had to do the equivalent of knocking three times before you could get in.

I brought the meeting up with Mom the next night while we took a midnight swim in the pool. Being a vampire wasn't such a bad thing for an avid swimmer like her, the pool was always empty after dark. It was hard to talk because Mom now swam so fast I couldn't keep up with her.

"Slow down, will ya, Mom, I have to tell you something, or ask you something."

"It's hard to slow down, Rhoda, I'm like a regular dolphin these days." She kicked water in my face as I struggled to reach her.

"You can do it, Mom, try the sidestroke with one arm." I watched her flip on her side. "That's it. No kicking."

"Sheldon and I want you to go to a B.A. meeting," I gurgled, swallowing some water as I spoke. "It's at the clubhouse and Tess runs it."

"Is that some kind of degree program?"

"No, it's like AA, except for vampires. Bloodaholics Anonymous. It's a 12-step program for vampires who are having trouble keeping their bloodlust under control. I went to a New York meeting with Sheldon. Very nice people."

"I'm no addict. At least I don't think I am. Plus those 12-step programs are always talking about God, aren't they? You know I'm an atheist." Mom started kicking and swam to the other end of the pool. I'd have had to yell to keep talking to her.

"Slow down goddamnit."

"I forgot. Sorry." She swam back in my direction, cutting through the water like Mark Spitz.

"Do it for me Mom. Otherwise I'll be too worried about you when I go back to New York. If you go I'll feel that you're, well, taken care of."

"Are there any cute young men there?" She winked.

"What? I thought you had no interest in men?"

"Since I died and became a vampire I've come back to life in more ways than one. And what do I see, a bunch of old farts like me. I know I don't have hormones but I feel like I do and I want handsome."

"What makes you think handsome would want you, Ma. You're eighty years old forgodsakes."

"I don't feel eighty. How about this cougar thing I've read about—where younger men go for older women?" Mom batted her lashes flirtatiously at me, then had to wipe the chlorine out of her eyes. It seemed vampires didn't like chlorine any better than I did.

"By older women they mean forty, Mom. Not eighty."

"How about a forty-year-old man? I'd even go up to fifty?"

"I have no idea who's coming to the meeting. It's later tonight. You'll find out when we get there."

"I have to look through my closet for something really nice. Maybe that pretty dress with the African print. And my platform wedge heels. What do you think?"

"You'll look gorgeous Mom," I said but she was already out of the pool and halfway back to her condo before I finished the sentence.

It took her an hour to get dressed and put on makeup. She wasn't any faster at getting ready to go out now than she'd been when she was human. Actually, it took even longer because she had more energy to try on clothes. When she finally exited her bedroom she looked pretty good, I had to admit.

"Fanny, you're a vision," Sheldon looked at her admiringly and smiled. Mom's face lit up.

184

"If you weren't my daughter's boyfriend I'd snap you up, young man."

"Don't mess wit my man, or I mess wit you." I gave her a menacing look and she laughed.

We got to the meeting a little late, but it hadn't started yet and there were plenty of yoga mats left. I looked around and instead of the black and gray outfits everyone wore in New York's B.A. meeting, there were a plethora of pastels, women in slacks and matching T-shirts, men in nylon jackets and leisure suits. I looked around and didn't see a male face under age seventy-five. Mom looked disappointed. I was relieved. I wasn't looking forward to seeing her come on to some hapless young male vampire. I was also glad that there were some elderly male vampires. I wondered if they called themselves the Golden Grandpas.

Tess stood up and read from a pamphlet: "We're working Steps One and Two at this meeting. We admitted we were powerless over our addiction; that our lives had become unmanageable. We came to believe that a Power greater than ourselves could restore us to sanity. I'll talk about my own experiences. Everyone thinks I'm long past Step One, that I've got it all together, that the vampire life was always easy for me, but that's far from the truth. I still struggle with my desire for human blood. When I go to Wal-Mart and see all those juicy young housewives I get so hungry that sometimes I have to leave without buying what I came for. I haven't fallen off the wagon—well maybe once at Marshall's—but I still come to meetings every week to stay abstinent."

"I'm not powerless over anything," Mom whispered to me. "And my life isn't unmanageable. All these men are *alta cocker*s, let's go."

"Mom, shh. This meeting is for Sheldon too. You need to stay and just listen. Go sit down." I pointed out an empty mat next to me.

Mom obediently sat where I told her, and I managed to lower myself onto a mat, with the help of Sheldon. I really need to do some yoga, I thought, I'm about as flexible as a corpse with rigor mortis. Ick. I've got to stop thinking about death.

An old guy in a sweat suit with a lot of gold jewelry and a deep tan got up next. He looked like my deceased Uncle Manny who always had a tan. I wondered where he got the tan considering vampires couldn't get one naturally.

"Isn't that Manny?" Mom whispered.

"I sure hope not," I said. "We went to his funeral."

"My name is Sal and I'm a bloodaholic." the man announced with a distinct Brooklyn accent.

"I guess it's not Manny," Mom said.

"Sometimes I DO go after one of the juicy housewives," Sal continued. "I can't go shopping anymore at all, it's too tempting. I give my shopping list to one of the Golden Grandmas. I stay home and go with Tess to the ranch once a week, that's the only trip I trust myself to take. Life is getting pretty boring. I was an alcoholic before I became a vampire. Actually I died of cirrhosis and came back a bloodaholic. I guess addiction continues after death."

I wondered if that meant Mom was destined to be a bloodaholic since she struggled with her addiction to sweets her entire life and was always on one diet or another. Maybe non- addictive personalities have an easier time with their post-mortem hunger.

Sheldon got up next. I told Mom to sit still and be quiet while he was talking.

"My name is Sheldon and I'm a bloodaholic. I came down to Florida with my girlfriend to turn her mother into a vampire. To do that I had to suck her blood for a number of nights, which compromised my abstinence. I haven't actually drunk any human blood for many years and this awakened my taste for it. I don't know how to deal with that. I'm trying to resist but now old people actually awake my hunger when it used to only be young people. Luckily I'm fine around my human girlfriend, and people I know, but strangers look damned appealing. I think I can control myself, but I'm not sure."

Everyone clapped and thanked Sheldon.

"Now can we go?" Mom whispered fiercely to me

"No," I whispered back in a firm tone. "You need to hear what these people have to say. They're your friends now, whether you know them or not. You may have to come to these meetings someday. Like every night from now on."

Mom sat down and dutifully listened to the rest of the speakers. Most of their stories were pretty tame compared to the New York B.A. meeting. These folks had been turned into vampires in old age, usually by their vampire children. Mom and I weren't the norm because I was still human. They talked mostly about missing real food. I heard tales of yearning for pastrami, pickles, lasagna, gnocchi, matzo ball soup, even corned beef and cabbage from an Irish lady. Mom listened intently, then got up to speak.

"My name is Fanny and I'm the mom who was just turned into a vampire by Sheldon here. I would kill for a coffee ice cream cone right now. I'm hungry and I know I'll get sick if I try to eat regular food anymore but I haven't accepted that. Tess took me to the farm in Okeechobee and I killed a little lamb and felt terrible about it. It was such a cute little thing. I accidentally attacked a truck driver on the way there. I'm afraid I might lose control in the future and attack a store clerk. I hate those kids, they're so rude. I'm not fond of truck drivers either. They're always trying to run us older drivers off the road." I saw some nods of agreement. "Thank you for listening."

More applause and a group "Thank you Fanny."

187

Mom was nothing if not charming and socially adept; she caught on immediately to what was expected of her in any situation. Plus she loved to talk. I knew she couldn't resist chiming in after everyone had shared. I was terribly relieved after the meeting. Mom was in good hands.

On the walk back to her condo she turned to Sheldon. "What's with this higher power thing they're pushing at these groups? I'm an atheist and that's the way I raised Rhoda. We don't believe in God.

"Not God, Fanny," Sheldon said patiently, immediately assuming his rabbinical air of authority. "A higher power as you understand him."

"I don't understand why there's a need for a higher power. Or a God. Even I know vampires sell their souls to the devil for eternal life. Luckily I don't believe in the devil either."

"There's quite a lot of disagreement among vampire religious scholars whether or not we have immortal souls. Personally, I say we do, especially those who have given up killing humans."

"I don't believe in souls either. We live, we die, *fatik*, that's it," Mom said.

"You didn't die Mom," I said, running to keep up with the two of them. Trying to stay abreast of two vampires when you're an out-of-shape human is not easy.

"Well, I might as well have. I don't understand all this so I'll just ignore it at meetings. Is that OK, Sheldon?"

"That's fine, Fanny. You can go to B.A. without believing in anything. Some people see the group itself as their higher power because it helps them stay abstinent."

"I'll do that," Mom said, having resolved the issue to her satisfaction. "Now I'll race you two to the door?"

Was she kidding? She and Sheldon took off, leaving me standing there. I ambled back slowly, relieved that I didn't have to try to keep up with the Century Village vampire track team.

Chapter Twenty-Four

We took a night flight back to New York a few days later after making all the necessary arrangements for Tess to change Ellen and Miriam. She took over effortlessly—she was a take-charge type and had all the necessary equipment. Getting through customs was easy this time since we weren't checking through the coffin. Actually that coffin had almost derailed our whole plan. I wanted Sheldon to leave it with Mom so Tess could use it for the other girls but he flatly refused.

"I can't possibly return home without my coffin, Rhoda," he sputtered angrily as we hauled it into the storage room. I'd never seen him so angry. "For one thing Goldie would be extremely upset. She's used to it. She depends on predictability—when anything in the apartment changes I never hear the end of it. And how could you ask me to give up my coffin! That's my history, my family heirloom, the only thing I have left from the old country. I've slept in it for a hundred years."

I wanted to get rid of it so he'd get used to sleeping at my apartment in my bed, but that was clearly not an option. We compromised. He would ship it back UPS to Crown Heights, but agreed to stay at my apartment without it if I bought blackout curtains.

"But what is Tess going to use for Ellen and Miriam?" I asked him.

"Look on the Internet for a coffin. I'm sure you'll find something," Sheldon suggested helpfully.

Sure enough at www.coffintables.com I found a casket kit for only $800. The ad read: Traditional Austrian casket design. Approximate set-up time - 1/2 hour. Tools required - universal screwdriver set, hammer, wood glue. All pieces cut to length and sanded. Made With Solid Pine and Rope Handles - Bedding is an option.

"Are you handy, Sheldon?"

"C'mon Rhoda, I'm Jewish. I can barely hammer a nail into the wall."

My ex-husband couldn't screw in a light bulb and I never knew a Jewish guy who could fix anything, so I had to look elsewhere. Mom knew Tony, a handyman who worked for Encore, the Century Village maintenance company. She called and told him she was ordering a pre-fab coffin to use as a coffee table until she passed on, at which time it would bear her remains. "I don't want to trouble my daughter to buy one," I overheard her telling him on the phone. "They're so expensive at funeral parlors. I thought it was a good idea to pre-plan."

Tony was used to strange requests from Century Villagers, many of whom were suffering from dementia, so he agreed to assemble it. I called and had the coffin Fed Ex'd overnight and the next day Tony knocked it together in about an hour including a teak-stained finish. Voila! Instant coffin coffee table. It was a handsome piece, actually. Mom had a huge Spanish shawl with fringes and embroidered flowers that she threw over it, and with a few artfully placed chachkas it looked quite stylish. The girls loved it. In fact both Miriam and Ellen decided to buy one for themselves before Tess changed them. Tess agreed that it was always a good idea to have a coffin as a backup sleeping place in case she or the girls got insomnia. In the bright Florida sun even blackout curtains didn't block all the light. She thought the coffin coffee table idea was brilliant because it also served as a hiding place should vampire hunters start looking for the Golden Grandmas.

It was hard for me to leave Mom and go back to New York, even though she repeatedly reassured me that she'd be fine. When she woke up at sundown I took her hand, sat on her bed and stroked her face, which felt smooth and not soft anymore the way it used to. It wasn't hard exactly, but more like plasticine, the clay they give kids to play with. I was used to the feel of that skin on Sheldon's face, but it felt very strange on mom, who used to have the soft, wrinkled skin of the very old.

"Mom, how can I leave you alone and go back to New York? How do I know you'll be OK?" I was nervous about what might happen to her without me around to monitor her behavior. How did I know Tess and the other Grandmas would look out for her the way I would?

"You don't. So why don't you stick around? I've always dreamed of you moving down here. I'll get you and Sheldon a nice condo in Century and we can all be together."

"Sheldon hates Florida, mom. He can't tolerate the heat, plus his brother and his golem are in Crown Heights?"

"He has a golem? What kind of mishegas is that. There's no such thing as golems. They're mythical creatures."

"So are you mom."

"I give up," she threw her hands up, her lips curling in a smile. "It's a whole new world. I guess I'll have to get used to it."

"Me too, this is all very strange. Will you really be OK?"

"Rhoda, I've managed on my own since your father died. What's so different now? I just have to change my diet, that's all. I've been on Weight Watchers, Jenny Craig, the grapefruit diet, the Atkins diet, the Zone diet, the

South Beach diet and a juice fast. So now I'll be on the blood diet. It's not so different really."

I guess I wanted to believe her so I did.

By the time Sheldon and I boarded a 10 p.m. Delta flight to La Guardia my anxiety level had dropped from a nine (need Ativan NOW) to my usual five (worried about everything but managing to cope). Mom was settled with a feeding schedule at the ranch with Tess providing transportation, and had agreed to go to regular B.A. meetings. It wasn't difficult to get her to agree once we had settled the God issue. She loved the social aspect and actually didn't seem to mind the stale blood that came out of the coffee carafe. After the meetings she invited the group back to her condo and they schmoozed all night.

As soon as we got into our seats I dropped off to sleep. I hadn't realized how exhausted I was. Sheldon, of course, was wide-awake since it was nighttime. When I woke up three hours later we were taxiing into the airport.

"Sheldon, maybe you can discreetly carry me. I am incredibly exhausted."

"No problem, Honey. Just lean back and I'll give you a little ride." He put his arm around my waist and zipped me out of the airplane, through the airport and down to baggage claim. After we got our bags we stood outside the terminal waiting for a cab. Sheldon turned to me looking somewhat abashed and said, "I have to go back to Crown Heights Rhoda, do you want to come with me?"

There were no cabs in sight so we didn't have to make an instant decision. "But your coffin won't be back yet, you don't have a bed, where are we going to sleep? I'm ready to pass out." Sleep was all I was concerned with at the moment. "Why don't you come home with me?"

193

"You don't have curtains either, I have a big closet I can sleep in. Actually it's my hiding place just in case."

"Just in case of what?"

"Vampire hunters, SS, I don't know. All Jews should have a couple of hiding places and a valid passport."

"I don't have either," I admitted. I kept meaning to get my passport renewed but never remembered.

"Why don't we both go home to our own places?" Sheldon suggested. "I don't want you to get upset, but I'm feeling the need for some space."

The word "space" triggered panic. Every time a guy had told me he needed "space" it meant bye-bye Rhoda. I felt nervous because the last time he'd gone home he'd disappeared. But I didn't want to seem too possessive. That was not an attractive quality in a woman, or man for that matter.

"OK, Shel. Just give me your phone number this time." I grimaced, trying to be casual. "And don't lose your phone."

I brought out my cell phone and selected "new contact." OK, what's the number?

We traded cell numbers—Sheldon didn't have mine either in his contact list. Actually he didn't have a contact list, he remembered numbers by heart. A good memory is another vampire trait, one that I sure could use. I wonder if I'm getting premature senility because I'm so forgetful.

A cab pulled up. "Age before beauty," I said to Sheldon, opening the door for him. "I'm going to visit you in Crown Heights tomorrow," I told him, ignoring his request for "space." I went on. "Give me your window dimensions and I'll hang blackout curtains. And I'll bring a blow-up bed for us."

"Rhoda, I already have a Jewish mother. I get all the mothering I need from Goldie. She shops for me, remember?" He looked amused.

"Oh, I forgot. Well, I'll take care of the bedroom stuff OK."

"You get a good night's sleep," he said, avoiding the issue. He grabbed me and gave me a long wet kiss and squeezed my behind before he stepped into the cab. "I'll call you. I do want you to meet my *mishpuchah*—Goldie, Herschel, and my *minyan*."

That was reassuring. He did want me to meet his family so he couldn't want that much space. Or maybe he was just conflicted. I felt a bit apprehensive about meeting so many Hasidic vampires and a golem, but if I was going to be with Sheldon I had to be part of his world as well as vice versa. I decided to dress very modestly and arrive on his stoop looking demure. I waved goodbye to him as his cab pulled out.

Chapter Twenty-Five

My apartment looked lonely and barren without Sheldon. I started missing him desperately and almost picked up the phone to call. Luckily the sun was coming up so I knew he wouldn't answer. Then I realized how dependent I was on him, how attached, how hurt I was going to be if he left me. I thought about Bella in *Eclipse*, how she became suicidal when Edward left her. I loved that book. I cried all the way through it, related to every bit of angst that Bella felt. What was wrong with me? I was forty-one years old, why couldn't I grow up already. I knew what was wrong with me. I'd been abandoned by my husband, Sheldon had already taken a powder on me once and now he wanted "space." I was insecure about him for a reason. I didn't know anything about him really, how he spent his time, whom he spent his time with, what was important to him. I'd just incorporated him into my life without really paying attention to his needs. What did I expect? I knew I'd gotten into trouble with guys before by trying to run their lives. Was I doing it again? Was I too needy, too desperate for love?

I decided to give him some space even though it rankled that he'd used that hated word. I'd read *He's Just Not Into You*. I'd read *The Rules*. I knew what men wanted. But vampires? Were they different? Being a self-help and an Internet junkie I started surfing Amazon for a book that would help me. Amazingly I found one. *So You Want to Marry a Vampire: The Rules for Capturing the Heart of a Creature of the Night*. So I immediately downloaded it onto my Kindle and started reading.

Based on *The Rules*, it was absolutely fascinating. A lot of what was in the book wasn't relevant to my situation—but the authors made it clear that vampires were men first and foremost and I'd have to do the hard-to-get number or I might lose Sheldon. I hated, hated, hated playing hard to get but after reading the first part of the book I realized it was crucial, and made a pledge to myself to try. I decided not to call him, but wait until he called me. Here's as far as I got before I conked out:

SO YOU WANT TO MARRY A VAMPIRE

The Rules For Capturing The Heart Of A
Creature Of The Night

A Rules Sampler:

•Don't let him know how fascinated you are with vampires.
•Don't let him taste even one drop of your blood
•Don't assume that it's easy to keep him interested.
•Don't let him turn you into a vampire too soon.

Sound familiar? You may have heard these rules in some of the vampire novels, movies and TV shows you've read and seen. We, your fellow female, though undead, advisors, understand what it is like to be totally besotted with a vampire. After all we were once human too. Unfortunately, now that we are one of the undead like them, they're just not into us anymore. They much prefer human girls, who are still able to eat cheesecake. Why they would find eating attractive is beyond us since they can't eat anything but you-know-what, but there must be something about watching a girl bite and swallow something besides human flesh that turns them on. They much prefer girls like you who are still vulnerable, trembling, juicy, brimming over with blood, rather than us--their bloodless female brethren—which is why we go for human guys, but that's another book.

We have been where you are now and we know how to capture the heart of Mr. Hunky Vampire because we once did. Ultimately we succumbed to the lure of becoming a member of the undead fraternity, something you must do only after you have that ring on your finger if you want to keep him around. We all know men are attracted to mystery, to a woman who they desperately want but can't have. Remember, The Rules are not about getting just any man to adore you and propose, they're about marrying the vampire of your dreams. Marriage to a vampire is incredibly risky because changing into one is dangerous, and because timeless, undying love is extremely rare. We can't imagine loving anyone for centuries—or even for one human lifetime. Neither can most vampires. You, of course, want to find a vampire who is capable of eternal love, such as a member of the Cullen family. We will show how to find and capture the heart of such a rare and precious creature of the night.

You may say this approach is frustrating. You lust after the vampire of your dreams and want him now—marriage be damned. Well, doing what you want to do is not always a good idea, especially when it comes to loving a vampire. It's certainly not a picnic to have to murder your fellow humans for food for all eternity. After all, you were brought up with ethics and morals despite your sexual lust for a creature of the night. Killing people is simply not nice. We know, you've heard all those stories of "vegetarian" vampires a la *Twilight*. Balderdash (old vampire expression). Yes, we vampires can resist killing a particular human with whom we're sexually and otherwise besotted (another old vampire expression) but we can't resist killing humans in general. Trust me, when you fall asleep, and eventually you will fall asleep, your handsome, soulful vampire lover will be out draining the blood of some homeless drug addict whom no one will miss. If you marry him eventually you will be doing the same thing. No, the Japanese have not invented synthetic blood. That's a vampire fantasy. How we wish they had. Marriage to a vampire is a commitment to a heinous lifestyle, one that you may regret. That is why you must be absolutely sure HE is the one before you commit.

Our best advice is forget marriage to a vampire, have a fling with your sexy forever-young Mr. Wrong and then marry boring Mr. Right, have kids, and check out before the world gets really sucky. Will you listen to us? Probably not, but we must make the effort.

Since you insist on ignoring our advice and marrying a vampire, we want you to be happy. This is why we have written our time-tested (centuries of time) rules to success.

Rule #1:
Be A "Creature Unlike Any Other"

Actually, your vampire is the creature, you're the creature feature. To attract the vampire of your dreams you don't have to be rich, beautiful or exceptionally smart, but you do have to….

•Change your body clock. Girls who can hang out all night and not fall asleep will be much more appealing to a creature of the night.

•Not wear perfume. Vampires hate perfume. They want to inhale the heady aroma of blood pulsing through your veins.

•Be aloof. It's not that vampires aren't attracted to girls who pursue them—it's just that they are more likely to kill them than to fall in love with them. After all, if you're an easy lay, you're also easy prey.

•Radiate confidence. Remember, you are girl who can handle a supernatural being who could kill you at the drop of a drop of blood. Act as if you are a combination of Buffy and Bella—a woman who knows how to run really fast and wield a wooden stake—strong yet vulnerable.

•Get a life. Vampires are attracted to girls who do things and don't just sit around reading the *Vampire Diaries* or *Twilight* for the tenth time. You have to get out of the house. You will meet a vampire when you least expect it—in a dark alley, in a biker bar, even on the subway at midnight. Put yourself in danger, who knows, he might rescue you. Worst-case scenario—you're his dinner. It's a thrilling way to go.

Rule #2
Don't Talk to a Vampire First (And Never Pursue Him)

Vampires came of age in an era when women wore corsets, fanned themselves seductively and cast sidelong glances at attractive men. Therefore, you don't want to throw yourself at a vampire. He will take it the wrong way and see you as dinner rather than relationship material.

Feel free to cast him a few come-hither glances, but no more than a few. Let him talk to you first. When he does, at all costs don't be too witty—vampires do not like smart alecky girls. There is not a vampire alive, or undead, who would date Whoopi Goldberg. Barbara Walters yes, Whoopi no. Vampires do appreciate class and intelligence, not wisecracks.

Avoid these typical conversational gaffes:

"What century do you come from?"

"Do you sleep in a coffin?"

"What was it like to die and then come back to life?"

"What blood type do you prefer?"

"Know any cool graveyards to hang out in?"

"Do you have any superpowers?"

"Can you take me for a ride on your back?"

"Do you tan in the sun, or burst into flames?"

Do talk about current events, and politics. Vampires love to talk about politics. They have been around long enough to see kings, presidents, and evil regimes come and go and take the long view of history. Vampires are very impressed by girls who have actually heard of the Weimar Republic and who know there were two World Wars, not three. If you don't know anything about history ask him a lot of questions and look fascinated by the answers. One yawn and you're toast, or worse. A lot worse.

Don't be afraid to be boring. Vampires go for boring. They need relief from the adrenaline rush of looking for victims and killing them.

When a vampire starts the conversation take your cues from him. If you hear growling, or see fangs descending, cross to the other side of the room quickly. Let him get his appetite under control before you allow him to approach you again.

Rule #3
Don't Meet Him Halfway or go Dutch on a Date

There is no reason to ever meet a vampire at some bar in Manhattan if you live in New Jersey. You will have to take the bus and the subway while he can fly. Any vampire who is too lazy to fly to your place is not marriage material. He was made in the wrong century and he's been spoiled by women's libbers.

Never go Dutch. Most vampires have had a couple of hundred years to watch their investments increase in value and can afford to treat you.

When a vampire asks you out, let him suggest where to go. He will probably not ask you to dinner because he'll be afraid of making you uncomfortable while he watches you eat. If he does ask you to dinner order rare meat. It will show you're not squeamish about blood.

Be cool and don't ask who Beethoven is when he asks you to a concert. Many vampires have cultural tastes that run to the old fashioned, such as classical music and ballet Certainly don't protest that you hate that boring dreck and would much rather go to see Lady Gaga. Be aware that like most old people vampires hate rap music.

Rule #4
Don't Call him And Rarely Return His Call

Sadly, times have changed and even vampires have cell phones these days. This is no excuse for calling, however. If you're following the rules he should be calling you, or at least flying over and knocking on your window at midnight to ask for a date.

Don't call him during the day when you know he's sleeping. Yes, we know you think this is a clever way to evade the rules and leave a message that won't count, but vampires are not stupid. They know you know they can't answer the phone during the daytime so why would you call them? To make a fool of yourself, that's why.

If he calls you, don't make small talk. Vampires don't do small talk, mostly because so much of it involves food, e.g. what did you have for lunch? You do not want to know what he had for lunch.

If he leaves a message for you feel free to call back—in a week. Vampires have a long view of time and a week for them is like a day for you. If you call back too soon you will seem overly desperate.

Don't be upset if you don't hear from him for weeks after a great first date. He is busy sucking the blood of other girls. He will get around to you eventually.

Do not leave a personal message on his Facebook or MySpace page. Vampires actually come from an era where people did not broadcast their intimate thoughts to everyone on the Internet. Be discreet.

If you text a vampire spell out complete words. You are dealing with a being from another time who has no idea what BCNU means, much less : -). Do not insult his intelligence.

No tweeting about him—EVER.

Chapter Twenty-Six

I was already on Sheldon's body clock as the book recommended so I fell asleep and woke up after dark because my phone was ringing. YES! It was Sheldon. I didn't have to play hard to get. He asked me to come to Crown Heights to visit him. I pretended to be outraged.

"Sheldon, you want me to get on the subway after dark and go to Brooklyn alone? Aren't you picking me up?"

"Sorry, darling, of course I'll pick you up. I'll be there in about an hour—the trains are really slow this time of night."

Not for the first time, I wished that Sheldon knew how to fly like vampires are supposed to, but I didn't say anything. I was trying to change my bossy ways. I also didn't ask if he wanted me to sleep over with him, or if he even had gotten a bed. I didn't want to sound pushy. I was proud of myself.

Before he arrived I called mom on the new cell phone that I'd bought her before I left. She'd picked up the basics of using it really quickly, unlike her pre-vampire self who was getting somewhat senile and couldn't fathom new technology.

"Rhoda … how nice to hear from you."

She sounded a bit formal, like she'd been rehearsing her lines.

"What's wrong mom, you sound strange."

"It's been very hectic around here. Tess and Hannah are in the process of changing Ellen and Miriam and I'm helping. So far it's going fine but you never know what's going to happen. I'm nervous about someone seeing us leave here with the coffins."

"I'm sure it will be fine, Mom, it worked out OK with you."

"And then I'm kind of hungry all the time. It's not like being on Weight Watchers either. I'd love to be back on the point system." She sounded plaintive.

"Haven't you been to the ranch?"

"Once, after we changed Ellen. But I'm always hungry anyway. Rhoda, I have to admit it--I lust after human blood, and other things."

"Are you going to the meetings?" I didn't ask her what things. I didn't want to know.

"Yes, but they're not very exciting."

"Mom, you're not supposed to be seeking excitement. You're supposed to be adjusting to your new lifestyle. You're getting me worried.

"No need to worry, Honey. I'm fine. Never better, actually. I go swimming every night and Tess and I have gotten to be great friends. She's going to take us all clubbing soon—as soon as Miriam and Ellen are ready. I'm really looking forward to it."

I wasn't sure it was such a great idea, but I didn't want discourage her. "Fine. As long as you call me every day and let me know how you're doing, OK?"

When Sheldon arrived and suggested we take a train back I wasn't pleased, but I didn't say anything. I tactfully asked, "Sheldon, can't you afford a cab?"

He looked abashed, like he would have blushed, if vampires could blush. He turned away and said softly. "I'm sorry Rhoda. I can't. I lost my job because I've been out so much. I'm pretty broke."

"What? You lost your job? I had no idea." I felt terrible. Here he was out of work because he'd been helping me turn mom into a vampire. I didn't have any money either. I hadn't done any work lately because of all the tumult with Mom, and the inheritance I'd expected wasn't arriving any time soon. In fact I had no idea how she was going to support herself for eternity. Her teacher's pension and Social Security would run out eventually. There must be some way they were notified when people passed one hundred or more. She'd have to pretend to die at some point. Unless there was Social Security for vampires. I'd have to ask Tess how the Golden Grandmas supported themselves.

"That makes two of us, Shel. We're both broke. We have to come up with a way to make money."

"I won't be broke for long Honey. I never told you but I have a cache of huge antique diamonds I've squirreled away over the years. I'm going to start selling them, but it has to be done very discreetly, one by one. You can't dump a bunch of antique diamonds on the market without anyone noticing." Sheldon looked a little shifty when talking about his diamonds. They probably weren't all completely kosher in origin.

"So you really don't have to work?" I wanted to know if he had enough for both of us, but that really was too brazen a question, even for my pre-Rules self.

"Not really. I worked to keep myself busy, but now you'll keep me busy. I can help you out too, Honey, once I get some of them sold."

He answered my question before I asked. What a gentleman.

The train was freezing and we had to wait a half hour for it. He helped me up the three flights to his apartment, though, which was basically the same dump I saw the first time I visited, except now I didn't see a coffin, probably because it hadn't arrived yet. However, he opened the door to the bedroom and showed me there was an actual queen-size bed and heavy curtains, which were pulled back since it was nighttime.

"Sheldon, you got these for me. I am so pleased."

"Actually Goldie ordered them while we were in Florida."

"Goldie, I thought she became a statue when you weren't around."

"Well I animated her while I was away so she could do some chores. I want you to meet her. She's hiding in the kitchen. She's a bit afraid to meet you."

"Why?"

"She's shy. She actually doesn't know any humans personally. Only the ones in stores."

He shouted, "Goldieeee!" and she came into the living room.

Goldie looked like one of the those stout Russian peasant women you see in old photos of Moscow. She was short, wore all black with a babushka on her head. There was no way to tell she wasn't human unless you looked closely at her complexion which had a pebbly texture, kind of like stone, but it could also have just been acne scars. The letters on her forehead were barely visible when she was animated. Her arms and legs were huge—they looked a lot bigger than I remembered--and she lumbered rather than walked. She glared at me unsmilingly when Sheldon introduced us.

"Goldie, this is Rhoda. You said you wanted to meet her." Sheldon sounded uncomfortable.

"We never have a woman in the house, it's forbidden to a Jew unless he's married. Sheldon is not supposed to even look at a woman, especially a human woman," Goldie glared at me. Her voice was gravely, like her face, and she spoke with a really thick Yiddish accent. I had to resist the urge to turn and run out of the apartment. Goldie was more than intimidating—she was frightening.

"Goldie." Sheldon addressed her sternly, seemingly unintimidated by her. "You never brought this up before. There have been women over. Remember Tzeitl?"

"Vampires and golems don't count, they're not real women. No human women, especially not ones dressed like her." She emphasized the "her" scornfully. "What happened to Tzeitl, she was such a sweet, modest girl from the old country, one of our kind, I thought you were going to marry her."

Sheldon never mentioned women of any kind., much less a "Tzeitl" who he planned to marry. Who the hell was she? I wanted to start interrogating him immediately but zippered my mouth mentally. These goddamned Rules were hell to follow.

"Goldie, you are my golem, not my mother. You do my bidding not the other way around." He didn't sound like he believed it, more like he was saying the words for my benefit.

Goldie was not impressed. She made a loud "harrumph" wheeled around and walked back to the kitchen.

"What's her problem?" I was bewildered. "I thought she wanted to meet me?"

"Well she did, but probably just to find out if you were the hussy she suspected you were. She's very old-fashioned, I'm really sorry. She acts like my mother." Sheldon said apologetically, but not that apologetically, He sounded faintly proud that Goldie was so overprotective. He probably missed having a mother like all Jewish boys do.

"Why don't you de-animate her like you did the first time I visited?"

"Shhh," Sheldon whispered loudly. " I don't want her to hear you, she'll be furious. De-animating Goldie is like throwing your mom out of the house, she gets extremely insulted and never lets me hear the end of it. I only do it when I really have to."

"Oh," I said, disappointed. I was determined not to pressure him anymore, so I just stood there, waiting for him to make the next move. I wished he'd explain Tzeitl. I was desperate to grab him and drag him into the bedroom but I wasn't anxious to have sex with Goldie glowering in the next room.

"Why don't we go back to your apartment, Rhoda."

I wasn't about to argue with this—it was what I wanted him to do in the first place, but I did also want to meet the rest of his *mishpucah* like he promised.

"How about Herschel? Doesn't he live upstairs? You were going to introduce me? And how about the rest of your *minyan*, the Hasidic scholars you study with? Where are they?"

"Let's just go, Rhoda. I don't want to push my luck. I need to talk to them first, tell them about you. I thought Goldie would help me out with that but she's being impossible. I have to talk to her alone about it, but not now."

"But I promised Charlene I'd fix her up with a vampire."

Sheldon gave a very long sigh. "The chance of any vampires in my *minyan* dating a *shiksa* is remote. You're going to have to find her a *goyishe* vampire. Let's get out of here."

I was relieved to leave—we'd be a lot more comfortable at my apartment, or at least I'd be more comfortable—but I was still uneasy. How were we going to combine our worlds? The Upper East Side secular Jewish world and the Crown Heights Hasidic vampire world. Could any two milieus be more different? Well, it could be a lot worse—what if I were a devout Catholic? At least we were both Jewish.

Sheldon marched into the kitchen and I heard him say coldly, "Goldie, I'm disappointed with you. We're leaving. I will let you remain animated because you have chores to do, but unless you change your attitude you will lose your shopping privileges. Do you understand?"

"You should be so lucky, you shmuck," she barked from the kitchen. "You couldn't get near enough to erase my *Aleph*." She marched past me out the front door, slamming it on her way out.

"I don't seem to have much control over the women in my life." Sheldon shrugged helplessly. "You are all a strong-willed bunch."

"Now that she's gone, why don't we try out the new bed in your bedroom."

"You have a one-track mind, my little *knaydlach*."

"Is that how you think of me, as a dumpling? Short, round and what else?"

"Soft and juicy of course," he added, holding out my coat. "I think we need to leave. Goldie will be back any minute. Golems have no innate inhibitions. They'll say or do anything. She will walk right in on us and start lecturing me when I have my pants down. If anything could ruin the mood, she could."

The last thing I wanted to do was face the cold winter night again, but I didn't argue—again, obeying the Rules—and I followed him out the door.

Chapter Twenty-Seven

When we got back to my place it was still early—for us that is. It was only midnight. Despite all the traveling I was glad Sheldon had come back with me. I felt so much more comfortable in my own apartment with my own bed, plus I had a stocked refrigerator, or I did before I went to Florida. I surprised him with the blackout curtains that I'd asked Charlene to buy and hang while we were in Florida. She had terrific taste—they were gorgeous faux suede in a subtle rose that matched the tea roses on the rug. Sheldon couldn't have cared less about the color of curtains or the rug.

"I'd like to get back home tonight, Rhoda," he said almost as soon as we walked in the door." I hope you don't mind. I have a lot to do after being away for so long." He sounded distant, as if he was thinking of other things, like maybe Tzeitl. A wave of jealousy and disappointment came over me, but I kept my mouth shut.

"We still have time before I need to leave, though," he grabbed me. "It's been a while."

It had only been two days but for us that was a long time. Sheldon seemed distracted. Instead of being gentle and taking his time like he usually did, he actually got rough with me, throwing me down on the bed, stripping off my jeans and entering me from behind. It was quite thrilling actually—kind of kinky. I wondered if he ever did kinky stuff like spanking or bondage. I decided to get some velvet ropes and discreetly tie them to the bedposts. Maybe he'd ask what they were for and I could make a subtle suggestion that he tie me up. Being ravaged by a vampire while totally helpless to resist was a vivid feature of my fantasy life.

"Do you like it this way?" he whispered in my ear.

I wished he hadn't asked me. That kind of took the thrill out of being taken against my will.

"Do me baby," I whispered back huskily.

"What? What does 'do me' mean?"

"Geez, Sheldon, forget about it. Just don't stop."

He didn't stop until I finally collapsed on the bed. I just loved that he could last long enough to make me come over and over. I rolled over on my back and hugged him to me. "I love you, darling."

He didn't say anything back, just stroked my hair. That was nerve-wracking. No, I did not ask. But I wondered what happened to the effusive lover he had been in Florida.

"Rhoda, I need to go soon. I need to feed before dawn. I'm really hungry. I miss the farm in Florida. I'm stuck hunting rats in the subway again. Or homeless people. "

At my expression of alarm he laughed and said he was kidding.

"Maybe we can buy a farm in upstate New York someday," I'd always wanted to move to Woodstock.

"I can't leave the City. But we'll figure something out. I'm thinking of keeping live animals at the Dominican Market in Brooklyn. There are some Santeria practitioners who might keep them for me. I might have to participate in a ceremony or two, but it would be worth it."

He'd traveled to Florida, so he had left the City before. It wasn't Goldie, he could de-animate her. Or could he? Maybe he could give her to Herschel for safekeeping. Maybe he was still seeing Tzeitl. I was burning to ask. I remembered the sob stories he'd given me about being so lonely he wanted to kill himself. Was he making that up?

Sheldon gave me a peck on the cheek when he left and didn't seem to notice that I just stood there, not responding. "Don't slam the outside door on your way out, you don't want to wake the neighbors," I warned

"Ok, bye."

Not an "I'll call you," or when he wanted to see me again, or what our plans were for the future, our next date. After he left I flung myself on the sofa and started weeping. That's the problem with the Rules, you wind up weeping on sofas. I made myself a vodka martini and continued weeping, turned on HBO and caught up on episodes of *True Blood*. I wished I had a vampire boyfriend like Bill who was so faithful and adoring—the only thing that kept him and Sookie apart was that he kept getting kidnapped by werewolves or other vampires. Oh, and he almost killed her. Little things. . Every time poor Bill turned around someone was cutting him up or draining his blood. *True Blood* made me feel grateful my vampire and his *minyan* were too religious for those kinds of shenanigans. Or at least I hoped they were.

Someone knocked on the door and then walked in. Charlene; She heard the TV and figured I was home.

"Rhoda, why didn't you call to tell me you were back? I've called your cell a million times but you never answered. I was getting really worried. What happened in Florida? C'mon, give."

She saw what I was watching and knew better than to turn off the TV in the middle of *True Blood* so she sat down and waited for it to be over.

Then I told her the entire story. I hadn't realized how crazy it all was until I actually described the details. Then I told her what had just happened with Sheldon and that I was following the Rules because I didn't want to lose him.

"About time, Rhoda."

"What do you mean by that?" I was insulted.

214

"Well, I never wanted to say anything but now that you've come to the conclusion yourself, I will tell you that you have run off a few guys with the Rhoda Training Program."

"What?"

"You know, you want to make them over, uncover their hidden potential, turn them into suitable mates. I think you've finally found someone you can't change. He's more likely to change you—into a vampire."

I sulked for a while but finally admitted she had a point. "So now what do I do?"

"Nothing."

"I can't do nothing. It's not in my nature. That's why I hate the goddamned Rules."

"OK, if you don't hear from him soon I'll take you to Emma, the most powerful witch I know. She will cast a spell for you. Her spells just about always work, so you do have to be careful what you ask for."

Chapter Twenty-Eight

I held out for about twenty-four hours and was about to pick up my cell phone when I saw Sheldon's number on my caller id. He'd actually tried to get me the night before and I'd missed his call. Dammit. Or maybe it was a good thing. I was being fetchingly unavailable for a change even if it was only by accident, or by AT&T's bad coverage. I wanted to call back immediately but it was only 4 p.m. and he wasn't up yet. I couldn't call Mom either. I'd been worrying about her too. It was getting to the point that all my significant others were vampires and couldn't be contacted during the day. Except for Charlene who was at work. Which was what I should be doing. I hadn't pitched any stories since getting back from Florida three days ago and my bank balance was pitifully low. I decided to capitalize on my real life vampire experience and pitch a story to—whom? Who would publish a story about real life vampires? I thought for a while. I'd pitched an editor I knew at *Cosmo* on "Are Vampires Better in Bed?" and had the assignment immediately. I could write about fictional vampires as well as my own experiences. I started by researching S&M for the intro and before I knew it, it was dark.

"Rhoda, I'm so glad you called back. Where were you last night?"

Aha, a little anxiety on his part for a change. "Oh, here and there. Nowhere in particular."

"Why didn't you answer my call?"

"Guess I was just too busy."

"I hope you're not too busy to go out with me tomorrow night. I have a special date planned for you.

Wear your warm boots, a down coat and a warm hat—it's an outdoor thing."

"Are we going ice skating again?"

"Nope, much more exciting than that. It's a surprise."

After we hung up I called Mom, who answered immediately. "Why haven't you called me, Mom, we agreed to talk every day."

"I've been busy."

"There are an awful lot of busy vampires in my life it seems. What have you been up to? Are you going to meetings? What are you eating?" I didn't have to have to play by the Rules about grilling Mom. She wouldn't mind.

"Please don't interrogate me Rhoda, you make me feel like a naughty child. You never cared before what I was doing. What's the big deal now?"

I thought about that. Actually I hadn't cared before about what she did with her time, only about her health. Now her activities were related to her health in new and frightening ways.

"What happened with Ellen and Miriam?" I changed the subject, trying to be tactful. . "Did they go through the change already?"

"Just Miriam. Ellen is being buried in the crypt tonight and tomorrow night we'll raise her and take her to the ranch. I'm looking forward to that. Then we girls will be together again. Except for Judy of course."

"What's going on with Judy?"

"She's not speaking to me anymore." Mom sighed. "I feel bad about that but what can I do?"

"No big loss, ma. She was always a terrible pill. She kvetched about everything."

"True, but she knew all the gossip and she wasn't one of those do-gooder types." She gave a wicked laugh. "I've always liked that quote, 'If you have anything bad to say about anyone, come sit by me.' Who said that anyway."

"I'll look it up on the Internet for you. I see you may have lost your life but not your sense of humor."

By the time we hung up I felt relieved, reassured that mom was still herself—she hadn't turned into some out-of-control monster. I realized that was my worst fear, especially after the truck driver incident. Of course I still didn't know what she was eating, but I decided not to press it. I didn't want her to start avoiding my calls.

I was dressed for the arctic by the time Sheldon arrived, looking stunning in a bomber jacket instead of a black coat for a change.

"You look scrumptious," I told him.

"You look warm, which is good. Let's go."

We took a cab downtown to Thirty-Fourth and Fifth and he took my hand and led me to the Empire State Building.

"When was the last time you were at the top?" he asked.

"When I was a kid. I haven't been up there since."

"Let's go. It's a clear night and we'll have a great view."

I wanted to make some sarcastic comment about this being *some* special date. The Empire State Building wasn't exactly a thrill for a jaded New Yorker like me. I'd been to the top of the Twin Towers when they were there. Now that was a thrill. However, even I felt a sense of wonder when we got out of the elevator. The lights of the City were laid out below us with incredible clarity. I could see lines of light up and down the streets and little matchbox cars. When I was a kid the observation deck was totally open, and I remember my father picking me up so I could see everything, asking him where all the people were, and him laughing. I didn't understand the concept of being too far away to see them. Now there was a huge spiked fence

218

with bars that curved over towards us. I doubted anyone could climb over that, but I suppose with enough determination it was possible.

It was cold and windy, but at least it wasn't crowded. Actually, there was hardly anyone up there, which wasn't surprising considering it was January. I guess it wasn't a wintertime attraction for tourists but it must be a vampire favorite because it's open all year round until 2 a.m., and vampires are immune to weather. I was gazing raptly at the view with my hand in Sheldon's when I felt myself being lifted up by the waist. I shrieked but he held onto me tightly as we rose above the fence and started flying over the City. He held on to me tightly, one hand around my middle and the other under my arms.

"Hang on tight."

I gasped. I had nothing to hang on to, nor did I have the strength to answer. I was terrified because I thought Sheldon didn't know how to fly and now we were soaring a hundred stories over Manhattan. I had my eyes closed so I can't say I was enjoying the view. Finally I cracked open one eye and was stunned. I'd flown over the City in a plane but this was much better. I had a bird's eye view of a sparkling wonderland. No dirty streets, no car exhaust, just a glorious enchanted city, like Oz. I was on a magic carpet ride, something I'd fantasized about as a child. Back then I'd wished I'd had a magic carpet so I could escape my lonely life and fly anywhere I wanted. Sheldon was fulfilling that dream.

"I thought you didn't know how to fly," I turned and yelled into his ear.

"I've been practicing. I wanted to surprise you."

"You succeeded."

"Are you cold?"

"I think the adrenaline is taking care of the cold." Actually I couldn't feel my feet, but since I didn't need them at the moment it didn't matter.

"Look, the George Washington Bridge!" I yelled. We were flying uptown, then over the Hudson to New Jersey. Sheldon gently alighted on a narrow street and led me into a cute little hotel on the waterfront. He had a key to a quaintly decorated cubbyhole of a room. It had a double bed with an old-fashioned chenille cover, flowered wallpaper, and couple of nineteenth-century landscape prints in the wall. The room was lit with candles and there was a basket of fruit and chocolates for me on the dresser. The smell of hot coffee drifted out of a coffeemaker next to the fruit basket.

"How did you manage this?" I was awed.

"Friend of mine owns it. Hasidic guy."

"What's the occasion?"

"Do I need an occasion? Let's say it's a celebration of me learning how to fly. I wanted to surprise you and I thought it would be fun to stay here. We've never stayed at a hotel."

I couldn't stop grinning and gave him a huge hug. "This is the most incredible night of my life. OK, the second most incredible. The first was the night I met you."

Our flight that night was not only over Manhattan, but in that charming room. I think I entered into an altered state during lovemaking. Sheldon started kissing me, and kissing me and kissing me. Softly but intensely. He seemed to be in a dreamlike state. Time slowed down to a crawl, and I went there with him. When I tried to get him to touch me he said, "What's the rush?" Those words were thrilling. He made love as if sex were new to him, like he didn't want any part of the experience to end, like he wanted it all to last forever, each kiss, each touch. When I did come -- after I can't remember how many hours--it was unbelievable.

As daylight was approaching Sheldon sweetly ushered me out. I thought I was in for another flight, which I wasn't looking forward to. After all we'd just spent the night in bed and I was all warm and glowy from sex. The last thing I wanted was a windy, cold ride home. But yet again Sheldon had anticipated my desires and there was a white limousine waiting for us outside the door.

"Your coach and four, m'dear," he said gallantly, bowing and ushering me into the limo. I was thrilled, but it wore off quickly when we got to my house and I invited him to sleep there for the day.

"I'd like to, Rhoda, but I have to get back to Brooklyn. Too many things going on."

What the hell were all those things?

Chapter Twenty-Nine

I thought that night might be the turning point for us, that Sheldon would finally propose, or want to move in with me, but instead he got more and more cagey and less romantic. He not only didn't take me back to his apartment again, but he only came to see me a couple of nights a week, and never on weekends. When I'd asked him what he was doing he deflected my questions. I would have had to go into full interrogation mode to find anything out and I didn't want to antagonize him. Every once in a while we'd go to dinner but I hated sitting there stuffing myself while he ate nothing. It felt rude somehow even though he said he didn't mind. I had no idea how he was feeding himself these days. I asked if he'd set up anything with the Dominican live chicken sellers but he didn't give me a straight answer. He did fill me in on the diamond sales—which were going well on Ebay and to diamond dealers on Canal Street. He was slowly amassing a fortune again but didn't tell me what exactly he was doing with the money. I hoped he hadn't found another Bernie Madoff to invest it with. He stopped telling me how much he loved me and would only have sex occasionally. I was distraught. Sheldon may have been different from other men when it came to eternal life, or what he had for dinner, but relationship-wise he was the same as the unavailable men I'd been pursuing since my teens. Maybe he just wasn't into me. But how could that be, he was a vampire and he'd sired my mother—he'd flown me over New York City--he couldn't just be another player.

Mom was also becoming more and more elusive. When I called I often heard loud rock music in the background and she sounded like she was still on speed. Mom had always been hyperactive and busy, at least before she got heart disease, but this was a new phenomenon. Sometimes she talked so fast I could barely understand her.

"What exactly are you doing, Mom," I'd asked her the last time I called.

"I am having an incredible time, Rhoda. Being young again when you're old is like having a new lease on life. OK that sounds clichéd but it really is true."

"What do you do with your time?"

"Well I swim at night a lot, I go to concerts and theatre, movies, rollerblading, tennis, hang gliding, bungee jumping, clubbing. I go to the farm twice a week to feed."

"Hold on mom. Hang gliding? Bungee jumping? Where the hell did you do that?

"Oh there's a guy in Boca who takes me out after dark. It's a real thrill. I'm even thinking of taking a trip somewhere. I just have to figure out the logistics, you know, what with traveling at night and eating and all. Maybe I'll come to New York and visit you. We could all go out together."

Putting a hyper Mom in my studio apartment where I was hoping Sheldon would visit more often was not my idea of fun. And what would she eat? I couldn't see her hunting for rats. She might get tempted to go after humans. There were so many of them crowded together in New York, some of whom wouldn't be missed if they disappeared.

"OK, Mom, I'm glad you're having fun. Just call me occasionally. I'm feeling neglected."

"Sorry dear, I'm just too busy sometimes."

I started spending more and more time with Charlene, who was patient enough to listen to me obsess about Sheldon.

"I thought we were on our way to a commitment but he's become less and less available," I whined one Saturday when I had nothing to do and no date with Sheldon that night. "I barely see him. Maybe he's gone off the wagon and is killing people, or maybe, God forbid, even has another woman. It seems impossible for any man, dead or alive, to be faithful."

"Why don't we go to Soho?" Charlene suggested. "You need a change of scenery. There's an art exhibit at the Satanic Gallery—with pictures of vampires I believe."

Soho was a refreshing change from my apartment. It was a sunny winter day for a change. The perennial gloom of winter had lifted and the streets were filled with fashionably dressed New Yorkers strolling around, most of them couples, which made me feel lonely. I comforted myself with the thought that I couldn't do this with Sheldon anyway—it was daytime. When we stopped at a sushi place for lunch I reminded myself again that I hated to eat in front of him. I kept trying to think of things I couldn't do with him to cheer myself up. It worked a little.

At the Satanic Gallery Charlene pointed out a picture of a vampire with a Dracula look, dark cloak, and fangs. "Doesn't this one remind you of Sheldon, Rhoda?" He had his teeth sunk into the neck of a blonde damsel.

"The only thing he has in common with Sheldon is the hooked nose. I don't understand why pictures of vampires always portray them as these horrible monsters. How about nice vampires, who don't kill people? Sheldon is ridding the subway system of vermin. He's helping the New York health department." .

The walls were filled with monsters—many of them dripping blood from their fangs. I couldn't wait to get out of there but Charlene was closely examining the pictures.

"That one has sure got the dark, mysterious thing going." Charlene was still staring at the picture.

"Oh, please. That looks like some kind of hideous creature, not my dear Sheldon, who I haven't seen or heard from in a week by the way."

"Why don't you just come out with it and ask him what's going on?"

"He might just say it's over."

"I know you're trying to follow the Rules, but there's such a thing as going overboard in the other direction from not pressuring—it's called letting a vampire fly all over you."

"Lame joke." I giggled a little, grateful that Charlene was at least trying to cheer me up. "Do you have any suggestions? What should I do?"

"Call him. Insist on the truth. At least you'll find out what's going on."

"I'm no stalker," I protested. "I'm trying to give him space."

"Give me a break, Rhoda. You love the guy, he loves you, maybe he's in some kind of trouble. Why not try to find out.

Chapter Thirty

I didn't have time to call him. As soon as I got home after our Soho expedition the phone rang. It was Sheldon.

"Rhoda, your mother is in danger," he said urgently, with no small talk preamble. "You have to call and find out what's going on. We may have to go down there again."

I felt like I was going to faint and fall off my chair. Waves of guilt washed over me. I'd been going along blithely assuming that everything was OK because Mom said so, even though my intuition had told me otherwise. I didn't want to find out too much.

"How do you know? Who told you?"

"She has my blood that means I'm part of her and I'll know when she's in danger. Right now she's in a lot of trouble."

"But I haven't heard a word from anyone. I talk to mom just about every night. She says everything is fine. She's been sounding pretty hyper, but nothing alarming. Or maybe I'm in denial. What kind of trouble is she in?"

"I have no idea. I just know it's bad. Try to call her," Sheldon ordered. "If you don't get her, call Tess, start calling all her girlfriends. See if you can find out what's going on."

"Why don't you call Tess?" I really wanted to get off the hook on this one. I was terrified.

"Rhoda, she's your mother and you need to deal with this. I will help but you have to call her."

"OK," I said in a whisper. "I'll call."

"Don't worry Honey. We'll take care of whatever it is. She'll be fine." He was reassuring all of a sudden. I guess he realized how much he'd scared me.

226

"Can you come over?" I pleaded. "I really need you to be here when I call." I didn't tell him what I'd done, that it was all my fault. I just knew I couldn't deal with whatever I found out alone.

"I'll be there in fifteen minutes."

"Are you taking a cab? You can't get here that fast even by cab."

"You forget, I can fly."

"Isn't that dangerous? Won't you be seen?"

"Hey, we flew from the Empire State Building and no one noticed. People don't see what they think is impossible. They just tell themselves I must be something else, like a large bird."

"OK. Thank you for coming. I really appreciate it."

"You sound pitiful. Just hang on, I'll be there."

I bent over with my face in my hands and started crying hysterically, totally unable to stop. I tried calling Mom but for the first time there was no answer on her cell.

When Sheldon walked in the door (he had the key) I didn't even hear him. He gave me a big hug and a bewildered look,

"Rhoda, what's wrong? This news doesn't call for tears—yet."

"It's all my fault, I'm the one who made you change her. Now she's in trouble and I did it to her."

"Well get over the Jewish guilt and get on the phone."

"Why can't you call?"

"Rhoda, what is wrong with you?" he asked in a curious, but not blaming tone. "She's your mother, you need to do the inquiring. You're usually so in control of everything. It wouldn't look right for me to call. And remember, don't tell anyone you suspect she's in danger. You're just calling because you haven't heard from her lately."

"Why can't I tell the truth?"

"I don't want you causing the girls to get all upset just in case I'm wrong."

"Are you ever wrong?"

"I've never been wrong about Herschel. I always knew when he was in trouble, and in the early days he was always in trouble."

"Why?"

"I'll tell you about it some other time. Now pick up that phone."

I called Tess first, no answer. I left a message. Same story with Miriam and Ellen. Judy answered on the first ring.

"I have no idea where your mother is, Rhoda, or Miriam or Ellen for that matter, and it's your fault for coming up with such an irresponsible crackpot scheme. All the girls now think they're vampires. You've somehow convinced them they can only drink blood. I never believed it for a minute but they sure do. What were you thinking anyway?"

"Just tell her to call me if you hear from her," I said and hung up. Judy was obviously not going to be any help. She just made me feel even more guilty.

"Call Tess's friend Hannah, you remember her. She's the nurse who ran the IV for me. Here's her cell number."

"I got an answer right away.

"Hannah, this is Fanny's daughter. Do you know where my mom is?"

There was a long silence. "I don't think Tess wanted me to tell anyone because she thought she could solve the problem before anyone notified you, but things aren't going so well."

"Things? What things?" I started pacing around my apartment, twisting strands of my hair, a nervous habit I had that I thought I'd managed to break.

"Rhoda, your mom has gone rogue."

"Rogue. What the hell does that mean?"

"She's disappeared and bodies have been turning up in Miami. The police are very suspicious. Of course they don't know about vampires but your mom, or whoever is doing this, has been very sloppy. The bodies have puncture marks in the neck and such."

"Where is Tess? And Ellen and Miriam?" I looked down and realized I had torn out a handful of hair, which I was now holding. I stopped pacing, sat down and tried to be calmer, at least a little bit.

"Tess and Ellen are in Miami looking for Mom and Miriam. They disappeared together. That's really all I know. I'm sorry I can't tell you more," she said, sounding upset herself.

"I'm going to come down there and help look for her. If Tess or Ellen turn up ask them to call me on my cell." I gave her the number.

"I'll do that. Calm down, Honey. Tess will find her."

"By then she may have been arrested for murder. That's worse than dying of a heart attack."

"Call me when you get in." Hannah hung up.

Sheldon put his arm around me. I curled up into him, put my head on his shoulder and cried some more.

"Let it all out. Then get a tissue and make reservations for the next flight to Fort Lauderdale. I'll come with you."

"Oh Sheldon, thank you, thank you."

"No need for thanks. I'm fifty percent of the problem. I'm the one who turned her into a vampire in the first place. Obviously I didn't do much of a job of teaching her how to feed safely."

"Yes you did, Sheldon. You took her to the ranch, took her to Century B.A., we thought she'd settled in and everything was fine. We were wrong. Mom has always been strong willed. She's the original 'I did it my way' Jewish mother."

"Can we get down there tonight, Rhoda? Once dead bodies start turning up we're talking a B.A. red alert."

"How are we going to find out where she is?" I asked.

"I'm sure Tess has some clues. If the girls were 'clubbing' she probably went along too. Tess adores dancing."

I opened my computer and searched for flights, booking us on the red eye to Fort Lauderdale with a credit card I couldn't pay off, but I'd worry about that later. I printed out our tickets so we could board quickly. At least this time we wouldn't have to check in a coffin.

Chapter Thirty-One

On the plane I decided that it was time to throw the Rules out the window. I was too dependent on Sheldon now. I loved him but I also had to be able to trust him. His recent evasiveness had eroded my confidence in his feelings for me—and by extension, for Mom-- even though he was her sire.

"What's going on between us Shel?" I asked after shoring up my courage with two vodka martinis. "You've been very distant recently. You've pulled way back from me emotionally. I haven't wanted to press you about it, but now I feel I have to know?" I realized it wasn't only the Rules that had stopped me from asking Sheldon what he was up to. It was dread about what his answer might be. I'd completely lost my confidence in my feminine charms after my husband dumped me—not that I'd had a whole lot of it before.

"Rhoda, I've been waiting to apologize for what I've put you through these last months," he said, leaning over to give me a tender kiss. "I know it's been very hard on you never knowing when I was going to show up. Don't think I didn't appreciate your patience. Actually I wasn't expecting it, knowing you."

"I've been following The Rules," I told him, after I'd asked the flight attendant for yet another vodka martini.

"Rules? What rules?"

"I don't think you want to know. They're from a book-- too silly. Anyway what's been keeping you away? Was it Tzeitl?" I held my breath.

"Geez, that Goldie, she loves to make trouble. Tzeitl is Herschel's fiancée, she's a nice Jewish vampire girl. When I introduced her to Goldie she just ignored the fact that Tzeitl was Herschel's girl, and decided I should marry her, but that would never happen.

"You mean I've spent all these months sure that you're cheating on me with Hershel's fiancée. I still haven't met Herschel by the way. Or Tzeitl. Why is that?"

"That's what I was going to tell you. Herschel and the rest of the Hasidic vampires in Crown Heights don't want to let me go—they insist that I stay in the building and come to their services. There are only ten of us vampire Hasids and I'm the rabbi. Without me there's no *minyan*. This means they can't pray. It's a disaster for them. Where will they find a replacement for me?"

"Rabbi? You told me you were a former rabbi. Is that why I never saw you on weekends?"

"Yup, it's Shabbat. But they pray twice a day and were always pressuring me to be there when I wanted to visit you. I felt guilty. I was trying to please all of you but just wound up getting everyone pissed off. And that's not all. Goldie was pushing guilt as well. She wanted me to stay home and keep her company."

"Goldie? She's a golem, not your mother."

"Tell her that. She thinks she's my mother. She keeps reminding me that I created her and I have to be there so she can take care of me."

"Can't you de-animate her?"

"She won't let me. In fact she won't let me near her because she knows that's what I want to do. Every time I de-animate her she lays a ton of guilt on me when I bring her back to life. She doesn't like you and doesn't want me to live with you—or marry you. I can't take the guilt-pushing. She's the only mother I've had since I became a vampire and I do love her. What with Herschel and my friends and Goldie pulling me in one direction and you pulling me in another, I felt like I was being drawn and quartered. I didn't know what to do."

"Marry? Who said marry?" I was stunned that he even mentioned the "M" word. We'd never spoken about marriage.

"That would seem to be the natural thing eventually, don't you think?"

"If I become a vampire that is?"

"Yes, if you become a vampire. Marrying a human would not work." Sheldon, looking uncomfortable, quickly changed the subject,

"Why didn't you tell me about all this? Why keep it to yourself?"

"I was afraid you'd leave me. I never told you I was still religious; that I was still a rabbi. You're an atheist, like your mother. I thought she'd hate me and you would drop me."

"That's ridiculous," a great wave of relief washed over me. If it wasn't another woman we could work it out. "I don't care if you're a rabbi. I don't care if you're the Baal Shem Tov. I'm not an atheist, I'm actually very spiritual. I just don't know what kind of spiritual."

"You are?" Sheldon sounded relieved as well. "That's wonderful."

"Just don't tell my mother, she thinks God is a four letter word."

We hadn't solved anything though. How could Sheldon leave his *minyan*—or Goldie—to be with me? He'd never be able to live with himself. Should I become a vampire? I certainly wasn't about to become a Hasidic *balabusta*. How could we reconcile our two different worlds? Vampire and human, kosher and non-kosher, religious and secular, bloodlust and compulsive eating.

"What do we do?" I asked him.

"I have no idea," Sheldon said, throwing his hands up. "I was trying to have it both ways."

"We can't resolve this now, darling," I reassured him. At least now I knew it wasn't another woman, or it *was* another woman, but she was made out of clay. "We can figure it out when we get back, if we ever get back. We still have to find Mom."

Chapter Thirty-Two

Despite Sheldon's newfound ability to fly we still had to take a limo from the airport. It seems he couldn't fly with luggage. I had the key to Mom's condo so we went straight there although we knew she was in Miami somewhere. Her condo would give us a base, plus I was hoping we'd find some clues there to her whereabouts.

Mom's apartment was dark and her bed hadn't been slept in. The place had an air of having been empty for a while. I got really bad vibes from being there without her. I'd never without her greeting me with a big hug, a huge grin and a "do you want something to eat?"

I put my bag in the spare room, sat down on the bed and asked Sheldon, "What do we do now?"

"Look through her drawers and closets, Rhoda. Maybe you'll find something that will give us a clue."

I went into her room and started rummaging through her stuff. I didn't find anything strange until I got to her makeup. There was a black lipstick, black eye shadow and hair gel. Mom never wore black lipstick or black eye shadow or used hair gel. I went through her closet and noticed black clothing—a few long skirts with uneven hems, a black fitted jacket with lace at the ends of the sleeves, and a few ruffled black scarves. Mom never wore black. No one in Century Village ever wore black. It was considered a major fashion faux pas in a town where no one wanted to be reminded of funerals or death.

"I have no idea what all this black stuff means, Sheldon. Do you?"

He shook his head and raised his eyebrows quizzically. "The only vampires I know who wear black are Hasids."

"Well I doubt Mom has become an Orthodox Jew all of a sudden. That would be more of a stretch than becoming a vampire," I laughed, which broke the tension somewhat.

"Try to get Miriam or Ellen again," he told me. "I'll try Tess."

Ellen answered this time on the fourth ring. "Oh Rhoda, I've been meaning to call you," she said in a falsely chirpy tone, as if I were a collection agency.

"I tried calling you a few times, and Miriam and Tess. I haven't gotten anywhere. No one returns my calls." I was angry by this time. "Where is my mother? I can't seem to get her on her cell phone. Why hasn't anyone called me?"

"We didn't want to alarm you, Rhoda. We knew you'd get hysterical. We figured we'd find her before you noticed you hadn't heard from her. But that didn't work out did it?"

"No, Sheldon felt she was in danger so we came down here. What the hell happened to her? How could you lose her? Is Miriam with her?"

"They're both gone and it's my entire fault." Ellen dropped the chirpiness and started crying, a piercing wail that was so loud I had to hold the phone away from my ear. She didn't sound as if she could talk coherently on the phone so I suggested we come over and talk to her. I didn't wait for her agreement, just put down the phone and had Sheldon fly us over there. It was only a short distance away but I was too impatient to walk and there was no one around in Century at night to see us, and even if they were around they probably wouldn't look up. Old people get vertigo when they look up, Mom told me.

Ellen's apartment was in Queensgate, another ersatz-sounding British name even though it was unlikely that one actual British person resided in any building in Century.

I was surprised when she opened the door. There was actually some disorder in her apartment. The last time I'd been there it was pristinely clean like all of mom's friend's places. This time the white rug looked like it could use a vacuuming, the couch pillows were in disarray and there were clothes hanging over some of the chairs. The only pristine area was the kitchen, which was visible from the front door. That wasn't surprising considering it was a vampire's least used room.

"Rhoda, Rhoda, please come in. Sorry for the mess. I haven't been myself lately. I don't seem to care about neatness like I used to. I'm hardly ever home. When I am home, I'm sleeping—during the day of course." She had stopped crying, but her face still had some red lines on it. I supposed it was true that vampires' tears are bloody. Ick! When Sheldon sobbed it was tearlessly, thank goodness.

"You want to know about your mom of course. I don't know much but I'll tell you what I do know." Ellen herself looked pretty disheveled. Her usually helmet-like blonde hair was stringy and looked like she hadn't washed it for a week, and her blue polyester pantsuit was as wrinkled as polyester gets.

"Just tell me how this happened? What were you all doing in Miami anyway and how did she disappear there?"

"Well, we were in the habit of going dancing in South Beach. You know there's not much to do in Century at night and the clubs in South Beach are open pretty much all night."

"I can't imagine any of you dancing to rock, or whatever kids listen to these days, or going into a club where everyone is under thirty," I said. "How did you get in? How did you learn to dance?"

"We glamoured the bouncers and from there it was pretty easy."

"You did what?"

"Glamoured," Ellen said as if I should know what she was talking about. "Sheldon explain it to her."

"Vampires can hypnotize humans into thinking whatever we want them to think. I don't use that power because I think it's unethical, but obviously Ellen here and her friends don't feel the same way."

"Sheldon, don't get all Hasidic high and mighty with me. I know you're not exactly Mr. Clean Vampire," Ellen retorted, obviously insulted. "Tess has told me some stories about you."

"Can we please stop bickering here. I need to find my mother. Where was she last seen?"

"Tess and I left her and Miriam at Club Dread, a Jamaican place on Washington Avenue. They play reggae. Your mom loved it. She said it reminded her of the days when she and your dad danced Calypso to Harry Belafonte."

"How did you lose her?"

"Tess and I went to another club that played salsa, which we like better. We were supposed to meet up with Fanny and Miriam after the clubs closed at 5 a.m. but they weren't where we'd agreed to meet. We went back to Club Dread and looked for them but the bouncer said he hadn't seen them leave."

"Maybe they glamoured him so he'd forget that he saw them."

"I have no idea."

"And where is Tess?"

"She stayed in Miami with a friend. She's still looking for them, but I spoke to her recently and she wasn't having any luck." Ellen sounded miserable. "I've lost my friends. All I have left is Judy and she doesn't even believe I'm a vampire. I don't talk to her anymore."

I was having a hard time feeling sorry for her since she'd lost my mother. I was not looking forward to playing

Anita Blake, vampire hunter, in South Beach, but I supposed I would have to try.

Chapter Thirty-Three

Sheldon and I arrived at Club Dread the next night, when
the club opened. We borrowed Mom's car since she'd left
an extra set of keys hanging by the door. I couldn't
understand why she hadn't taken it—usually she was the
designated driver when the girls went out, but I guess now
they all could see in the dark.

Club Dread was on the main strip in South Beach,
glittery Collins Avenue with all the Art Deco hotels and
neon signs. It actually was in one of the hotels, a rather
seedy one. The bouncer at the door, if that's what he was,
was a large Jamaican guy with, of course, dreadlocks,
dressed in jeans and a tight white t-shirt that displayed his
bulging muscles, obviously the result of some serious body-
building. He had ear buds and was dancing to the music on
his I-Pod, oblivious to us, and to the other patrons who
were just strolling in The place could have burned down
for all he'd have noticed.

"It's no wonder he didn't notice Mom and Miriam
coming or going," I said.

"I doubt they had to do a whole lot of glamouring to
get in," Sheldon added.

"He's probably just around in case there's a fight." I
took his hand. "Let's go in then. Maybe there's someone in
the club we can ask."

The music inside was so loud I couldn't imagine how
we could ask anybody anything, but it was still early and
the dance floor was almost deserted. The bartender was just
lounging around waiting for customers. Sheldon whispered
in my ear that he'd do the questioning because he'd be able
to hear the answers. I gratefully agreed.

There were no barstools. Actually there didn't seem to be any place to sit, just an enormous dance floor, a balcony with huge floodlights shining down, and a stage with sound equipment. I supposed the band would show up later. There were some perfunctory island-y looking decorations on the wall, but I doubt anyone ever looked at them.

Sheldon leaned over the bar and shouted in the bartender's ear. I couldn't hear a word he said or anything the bartender said back. I really had to have my hearing tested. I'd visited one too many of these clubs in my twenties and probably ruined my hearing.

Sheldon took my hand and led me back into the lobby, which was quieter.

"He did see your mom and her friends come in a couple of times about two weeks ago—but he can't remember which days."

"What did he say?"

"He laughed about the three crazy old ladies on the dance floor...mon. He said there were a bunch of kids surrounding them and yelling something like, 'You go girls.' They wouldn't have needed to glamour anyone to get in. He said they were really entertaining and kids kept coming back hoping they'd show up again."

"That's not much help."

"No, it's not."

"Let's go to a café and have a drink. Or I'll have a drink. We need to think of something else."

We walked to the News Café, where we had sat last time. The place reminded me of Hedwig, whom we'd met there.

"Hedwig!" I shouted. "She said if we ever needed anything to call her. Now is the time. But I don't have that little pink card she gave us. Dammit. You don't have it by any long stretch of the imagination, do you?"

"No, I don't, but I remember the number. We vampires have superior memories along with our other attributes. You know what those are, don't you?"

"This is no time for joking. I'll take care of your attributes after we find Mom. What's the number?"

Hedwig answered immediately. I'd noticed that half of the passersby on Ocean Avenue were talking on a cell phone, the other half were taking pictures with one. Miami was, like New York, a connected City. I told her the whole story.

" No problem, you just wait there with your adorable vampire man and I'll be by soon. Old ladies clubbing are not exactly the norm. They won't be hard to find in this town. I'll put the word out on the tranny network."

"Tranny network?"

"Transvestite, transsexual and transgender, dahling."

"So how do you find things out?"

"Ve haf our vays."

I had to laugh despite my mood. "We'll wait."

For the first time since Mom disappeared I relaxed a little. Hedwig was so reassuring. I knew she'd come through, and sure enough when she showed up about an hour later she did have some solid information.

First she gave Sheldon a big smack on the lips, leaving a neat red lip outline that I wiped off with a tissue. She sat down gracefully, crossing her long, long muscular legs and adjusting her miniskirt.

"I asked around and sure enough, they've been seen, at The Morgue, with a couple of Goth boys."

"Omigod, the morgue. What are you talking about? They're not dead. Or they are dead, but you know…"

"It's a Goth nightclub."

"Pardon my ignorance, Hedwig," Sheldon said, "but what is Goth?"

242

"They're misfit kids who wear all black and have a lot of tattoos and piercings and listen to punk music."

"I can't imagine Mom hanging out with kids like that or listening to punk music. Reggae I can understand, she's always liked ethnic culture, but punk, no way?"

"Maybe they couldn't resist. They would be heroes to the Goth kids who fantasize about being vampires. After all, who wears all black and is really dangerous—vampires of course. Goths adore vampires."

"But they're little old ladies."

"Wouldn't matter a bit to Goths. Actually it might make them even more glamorous—what could be more cool than a little old lady vampire? A totally new type of killer—someone no one would suspect."

"This keeps getting worse," I said, feeling shaky, "Who were those boys, and what about the bodies?"

"I know about the boys." Hedwig raised her eyebrows. "But I haven't heard anything about bodies."

"The vampire grapevine has heard tell of bodies turning up in Miami, with puncture wounds," Sheldon said. "The victims were drug dealers, according to my sources. No one paid a lot of attention--it seems drug dealers turn up dead every day in this town."

I asked Sheldon where he heard this and why he hadn't told me. Somehow he'd managed to get in touch with Tess who gave him the scoop about the bodies. It seems vampires keep very close track of police blotters, noting any killings that might be vampire related. He hadn't wanted to alarm me although he knew he'd have to eventually.

"Geez, that is not good," Hedwig said, crossing her arms, which I noticed were shaved. "These boys are a nasty bunch according to my friend Faye, who hangs in the Goth clubs. They sell heavy drugs and have rap sheets a mile long."

"Does anyone know exactly who these boys are? Do they have names? Where do they live?"

"I didn't get anything that specific, Rhoda. Sorry. We'll have to stake out The Morgue to find them. Assuming they're still going there." Hedwig's mouth turned down apologetically. Her eyebrows should have gone along but they didn't. Maybe she'd been botoxed.

"Where is Sookie Stackhouse when I need her? We sure could use a mind-reader about now," I said.

"I'm the next best thing," Sheldon announced. "People will tell me anything if I glamour them."

"Isn't that unethical? You said so yourself."

"Not when you're hunting down the bad guys, only when you're using it for your own personal benefit."

Chapter Thirty-Four

The ad said, "The Morgue at Club Ozone in South Miami is one of the area's hottest clubs. This New Wave lounge features music such as combinations of electro-clash, dark wave, industrial, New Wave, synth pop, 80s retro, future pop, progressive hits and gothic sound. The DJ is Dracula's Daughter."

I had never heard of any of those musical genres but I was pleasantly surprised by a group called the Broken Dolls who sang a rather haunting number that I liked a lot. The music at The Morgue was loud, but thankfully, not deafening.

We didn't have any trouble getting in. The bouncer at the door was extremely friendly--he knew Hedwig. Everyone knew Hedwig. The club was dark, very dark, especially since just about everyone was wearing black with a smattering of folks in jeans and t-shirts. There were flashing laser lights so it was almost impossible to actually see anything clearly. Sheldon wasn't having any problem, though. He took my hand and I followed him around. Most of the girls had dead white faces with black lipstick and thick black eye makeup—and multiple piercings. I realized that if Mom and Miriam came here dressed in black with a lot of makeup no one would notice their age since it was so dark. Hedwig seemed to know a lot of the patrons—she circulated, hugging and chatting. I realized the club catered not only to Goths but to gays.

Sheldon and I started slow dancing, which felt wonderful. Sinking into his arms and being held was just what I needed after one of the most stressful days, and nights, of my life.

245

"Sheldon, I can't imagine my mother in a place like this. She hated rock and was horrified by kids with tattoos and piercings. She went nuts when I told her I was thinking of getting a tiny butterfly tattoo on my ankle."

"You know Jews think tattoos are desecrations of the body. The Hasids wouldn't bury anyone with a tattoo in their cemetery."

"I guess that's where her tattoo phobia came from. She might have been an atheist but she still had Jewish cultural roots."

"I wouldn't mind if you had that butterfly tattoo. It would be cute. You could even get one in a more intimate location, and I'd kiss it." Sheldon squeezed my butt.

"OK, after this is all over I'll get my butt tattooed to celebrate, but only if you get one too." I squeezed his butt.

"I can't get a tattoo, Rhoda, my body would reject the ink. It wants to stay the same as when I was made a vampire."

'"Why did Mom change so much when she became a vampire, Sheldon? You stayed the same, didn't you?"

"I did, but I was a young man, so I stayed young. Your mom was old and becoming a vampire enabled her to become young again, at least in some ways, so I think she went a bit wild. Remember Tess's story about being Disco Sally. I guess that's what happens—to some elder vampires."

"Elder vampires, eh? Sounds too politically correct to me. How about *alta cocker* vampires?"

"I like that better—but only for Jewish vampires, of course." Sheldon smiled.

We spun around some more as the music changed to the theme from *Phantom of the Opera* with an alternative rock spin. Who knew that Goths liked musicals, although if you thought about it Phantom is the ultimate Goth musical. That theme song always made me swoon when I heard it and tonight was no exception.

I had almost forgotten why were there, what with the three drinks I'd had, the dancing, the hypnotic laser lights, and my favorite theme song. But then Hedwig came over and gestured that we should follow her. There was a new band on the stage, so Dracula's Daughter wasn't DJ-ing. She was in the lobby waiting for us.

"This is Valerie Acosta." Hedwig introduced us. "Otherwise known as Dracula's Daughter." Valerie was a tall, gorgeous Latina with meticulously applied Goth makeup. She wore a skin-tight black leather sheath with a red velvet corset, lace overskirt and black boots with six-inch heels. If there were Goth models she definitely could have been one. "She knows something but she wanted to talk to Rhoda personally. She didn't want you to get the news second-hand from me."

"That sounds ominous." I was suddenly frightened. .

"I'm sorry, Honey," Valerie said, "but I did see your mom and her friend with Moses and Jesus last week. They're gay boys who sell meth, crack, ecstasy and every other drug you can imagine. They got thrown out of the club that night for dealing in the men's room."

"Gay boys, of course," I said to Hedwig. "They would see Mom and Miriam as trophies—as the ultimate fag hags—vampire fag hags."

"You got it, girl, sounds about right." Hedwig agreed.

"What's a fag hag?" Sheldon asked.

"A woman who likes to hang out with gay men," I said, reminding myself that Sheldon was still so nineteenth century. "Mom always did go for gay guys, and vice versa. She had a campy way about her. She probably had no idea these two were selling drugs. I doubt she knows what those drugs are."

"That's likely," Valerie said. "I hardly knew what half the stuff was. They were peddling a new designer drug every week."

"Where do we find these guys?" Sheldon asked.

"I don't know their last names or where they live," Valerie said with an apologetic shrug. "No one knows that kind of thing about the kids who hang out here. Let me ask the bartender for you, though. He knows a lot more than I do."

She walked back into the club while we waited in the lobby. I distracted myself by looking at the erotic Goth art on the wall, some of which was really good. I particularly liked an exquisitely detailed print of a fallen angel bending over her nude lover. There were a lot of depictions of bondage scenes involving leather and whips. I didn't realize the Goth lifestyle included S&M but of course that made perfect sense. I didn't even want to think what that meant for Mom.

Valerie came back. "The bartender actually had a threesome with those guys, so you're in luck. They ripped him off on the pot he bought from them so he's no friend of theirs. Seems they live in Little Havana, here's the address." The piece of paper also had an address on it and the last name of one of the boys, Moses Shapiro. He calls himself Mush. He didn't know the last name of the Cuban guy, Jesus. A Jewish drug dealer? I guessed it wasn't all that unusual in Miami, or anywhere else for that matter.

I went over to Valerie and hugged her. "Thank you thank you, dear. I am so grateful. I am desperate to find my mom."

She hugged me back and said, "Buena suerte, chica."

As we walked out Hedwig whistled, a rather loud masculine whistle. "This isn't going to be easy. I bet these guys are armed up the wazoo. I'm going to call in reinforcements before we visit them."

"Reinforcements?" I asked.

"The tranny police. We take care of our own. We might like to dress like women but we can be plenty macho when we have to. There's gay bashing down here like everywhere else, but they don't mess with us—they know the tranny police will whup their asses."

"I think I can handle them on my own," Sheldon asserted. "I'm a vampire after all."

"You may be a vampire but dealers down here have assault rifles that could blow even a vampire's head off, so we need all the help we can get," Hedwig said, sounding macho all of a sudden.

"OK, call in your troops. Where do we rendezvous?" Sheldon asked.

"There's a café called Versailles on 8th Street in the center of Little Havana. Meet us there in an hour."

Chapter Thirty-Five

Versailles was hard to miss. The huge sign said *Versailles, Cuban Cuisine*. The interior was a strange mix of institutional and kitch. There were cafeteria-type tables and chairs, but the walls were covered with illuminated mirrors, painted—or engraved—with elaborate designs that were supposed to be reminiscent of the Court at Versailles but looked more like they belonged in a Victorian bordello. The food, however, was terrific. I ordered a Cuban sandwich while we waited and gobbled it down with a café con leche. I hadn't realized how hungry I was. Sheldon sat there looking at me indulgently. I guess after a hundred years he didn't miss coffee. I couldn't survive without it.

"I can't imagine what these boys wanted with Mom and Miriam?" I said as I munched.

"I hate to tell you what I'm thinking," Sheldon said, knitting his eyebrows ominously.

I didn't ask. I knew he'd tell me more than I wanted to know.

"Think about it. They're at a Goth club where vampires are worshipped. They're criminals who come across a couple of real vampires. What do they want more than anything? To be vampires themselves of course. Ergo they want your mom and Miriam to turn them. I doubt either of the girls knows enough to accomplish that feat, but I suppose it's possible."

"I'm sorry I asked. Let's hope it hasn't happened. What about the bodies?"

"I suspect that was Mom and Miriam's work—sadly enough. At least the dead were bad guys who might have been killed anyway."

"Not much comfort in that."

I turned to see Hedwig and three very large friends of hers, two black and one white. They were dressed as women in the same flamboyant style that she flaunted, but they weren't women you'd want to run across in a dark alley if you'd just gay bashed someone they knew.

"Rhoda, Sheldon, this the tranny police: Divine, Eva Destruction, and Morticia DeVille." They all smiled broadly, Eva and Morticia showing a couple of gold teeth. Divine said hello with a gravelly basso profundo but Eva and Morticia, who looked like twins, had high-pitched, squeaky voices that didn't match their burly physiques.

"Wow, very creative names. I was a big fan of Divine," I said to Divine, who actually resembled her namesake, the star of some really gross campy films. She was over six feet and weighed at least 300 pounds. The other "girls" were equally hefty, though with bulging biceps.

"Let's get going," Hedwig said without sitting down. "The night isn't young anymore and Sheldon won't be either unless he gets his beauty sleep. We have a van outside that will fit us and the two ladies when we find them."

It was midnight but Little Havana was still rocking. Sounds of salsa and rumba came from all the stores, which were selling everything from café con leche to Santeria candles. The architecture was quirky, with buildings ranging from Art Deco to high-rise to crumbling old condo, most painted tropical colors. Old Cuban guys were playing dominoes in a park across the street from us, on a table with a bottle of rum in the middle of it. Hedwig led us to a battered old Chevy van around the corner, on a quiet street with no hubbub.

"Where'd you get this van, Hedwig?" I asked. "It's perfect, so anonymous looking."

"It's mine, Rhoda. All I can afford. I spend all my money on clothes," she laughed.

I hoped I hadn't insulted her, but Hedwig didn't look the least bit upset. We piled in and she drove in and out of a warren of little streets. She seemed to know where she was going—I would have gotten lost immediately without a GPS, which she certainly didn't have.

We wound up on a little street with shabby small one-family houses. There were no big condos or high rises here. Some houses were under construction and there were gaps where others had been torn down. I couldn't see a whole lot because the streetlights were dim and there weren't too many of them.

"This part of town got very run down after the last big hurricane," Hedwig explained. Then real estate values crashed and it's become a real dump—most of the properties that are left have been foreclosed on. The ones that are still occupied are either inhabited by dealers who rent, or just squat until the bank throws them out, or hold-out homeowners who have to get elaborate burglar alarms and arm themselves to survive. You wanna pick up a house cheap, this is the spot."

"I don't think so. Looks like a slum."

"For now," Divine chimed in. "But the Cubans are coming back to Little Havana. Trying to revitalize it. Someday this will be a good neighborhood.'

"This is the place, darlins." Hedwig turned to us. The house she pointed out needed a good paint job, the hurricane shutters were hanging down, and the porch was sagging. Despite its disrepair, there was a large, new car of some kind in the driveway, I thought it might be a Cadillac. My mom never would have been caught dead in such a place—when she was alive.

Hedwig parked in front of the house. "This van has its advantages. It's virtually invisible, especially in a neighborhood like this. We have to stake the place out for a while to see what's going on."

"How do we do that?" I asked.

"Sit here and watch I guess." Hedwig turned to Divine, who seemed to be the leader of the tranny police.

"You'll all sit here with Eva," Divine told Hedwig, "while Morticia and I go up to the house and ask to buy some crack or ecstasy or whatever they've got. If they want to know where we got the address we'll just say the bartender at The Morgue gave it to us. They won't be suspicious about that. He's a customer, and a good lay."

"What are they going to see from the door?" I asked.

"We are going in, sweetheart," Divine drawled. "We do not buy drugs that we don't sample first and we don't sample drugs on the street. No one suspects drag queens, Honey, we're so visible we're invisible. Outrageousness comes in handy sometimes."

Divine and Morticia jumped out of the van as if they were wearing sneakers not six-inch wedgies, pulled down their mini-skirts modestly as they exited, then strolled casually up to the house and rang the bell. I saw a man answer and after a few words, let them in. It was really lucky someone was home. But then someone had to be home to watch Mom and Miriam, if they were there.

We sat in the van for a half hour waiting for Divine and Morticia. I chewed my fingernails to the quick, a habit I thought I'd stopped long ago. Sheldon cadged a cigarette from Hedwig and lit up, which I'd never seen him do. Eva leaned against the window and snoozed. She was the calmest of us all.

After what seemed more like an hour the two drag queens came strolling back to the van, just as casually as they'd gone in.

"We smoked some damned good pot with those creeps," Morticia reported matter of factly as she climbed into the van, "but we didn't see anything suspicious. Wanna hit?" She passed a joint to Hedwig.

My heart started beating wildly and I had to force myself not to start shrieking. I was devastated.

"She's got to be in there. She just has to be."

"She is," Sheldon said, putting his arm around my shoulder. "I can feel it. We just need to go in and get her."

"How do you suggest we do that?" I asked him sarcastically, immediately regretting my tone. It wasn't his fault Mom had been kidnapped, or worse, by two drug dealers.

"Did they have any weapons?" Hedwig asked.

"Oh yes they did," Divine told her. "One of them was wearing a shoulder holster with an automatic, and the other had a gun stuck into his waistband. These characters weren't shy about carrying. I think they shoot first and ask questions later. Luckily they weren't threatened by us."

"I'm going to glamour them," Sheldon said a little too slowly. "I know I can do it."

"Why don't you sound more sure about that, Shel?" I asked.

"I haven't got any practice. I don't use the skill often. I told you, it's not ethical."

"I think it's our best shot," Hedwig said. "We are not packing automatic weapons, although we've all got small pistols in our purses, but even if we were, going in and shooting it out is going to bring the cops, not to speak of casualties."

"We need a strategy if it's going to work," Sheldon added. "There are two of them and I can't glamour them both at once. If I do it to one with the other one listening we're dead."

"I got an idea," Divine said. "One of them, I think it was Jesus, was really coming on to me. He was very hot after my big booty. I'll go back in alone and seduce Jesus--

hey that rhymes—pretend I just couldn't resist his charms so I ditched my girlfriend and came back. I'll get him into the bedroom and do him every which way—he will be flying—I am really good. I'll make sure he's naked, stoned, and his gun is stashed somewhere. Then in about a half hour Sheldon will come to the door and pretend to be my boyfriend who's jealous and looking for me. He'll glamour Moses and find out where Mom and Miriam are.

"What if Jesus hears the bell ring, or a conversation?" I asked.

"I'll make sure to include an instruction to tell him it was a customer if he hears anything," Sheldon said.

"Then what?" I asked.

"Sheldon comes back to the car and we strategize based on what he finds out."

"Well it is a plan," Hedwig said, raising her eyebrows doubtfully. "It better work or we're gunshot statistics tomorrow. "

"It will work," I said forcefully. "I have faith in Sheldon." Whether or not that was true, I wanted him to think I did.

Chapter Thirty-Six

Divine went in first, we waited a half hour as instructed, and then Sheldon rang the bell and was let in. He took his time glamouring Moses, while I sat in the van biting my cuticles because I'd run out of fingernails. My fingers were starting to look like they'd been through a shredder.

He came back with a big shit-eating grin on his face. "I did it, I actually glamoured the guy. I'm a real vampire, I can fly and I can glamour. What's next I wonder?"

"Maybe you can get a job on *True Blood*. They need a real vampire. I hear the pay is great." I was incredibly relieved that he'd come back in one piece.

"Can the repartee, dudes," Hedwig said. "We have a rescue mission to accomplish."

"What show is that from?" I turned to her

"Where are Fanny and Miriam, Sheldon? How do we get them out?" Hedwig asked.

"They're in there alright, in the back bedroom on the right down the hall, but I don't know how to get them out past that goon with his guns. I saw at least three firearms in plain sight. I made him forget that I was there and found out where they are, but he won't forget to shoot anyone who tries to get them."

"We have to case the joint," said Eva. "There's got to be a back entrance. All these Florida ranches have back doors, to patios."

"That sounds too easy," I said. "Wouldn't everything be locked?"

"We have a vampire here." Sheldon raised his hand. "Superior strength, can break down doors with a single kick."

"That's pretty noisy," Eva said. "We don't want Moses to start spraying us with his Uzi."

"Superior stealth," Sheldon added triumphantly. "Can open locks quietly with a single Swiss Army knife. Give me that little one you carry in your purse, Rhoda. I'll spring the lock."

"That is not a vampire talent," I said, handing him the knife. "Where did you learn it?"

"I've had to sneak into a lot of places in my day...and night. Don't ask!"

"Let's get going," Hedwig said. "This is the plan. Sheldon and Eva, you case out the back of the house, get in that way and get the ladies out. I will go to the front and tell Moses I'm looking for Divine. Then I'll make a lot of noise, screeching and carrying on about her sleeping with Jesus. I'll try to seduce Moses, or at least distract him while you two get the ladies out."

"How about me? What do I do?"

"You stay in the car," Hedwig told me. "You don't have super strength, super stealth or tranny police training. We don't want you getting shot at."

"But that's my mother in there. She needs to see me. I need to get her out."

"She'll see Sheldon. She knows him, he'll tell her you're waiting for her in the car."

"That won't work. She'll need to see me. I know her."

"Someone needs to stay in the car. I guess that's you then, Eva. Rhoda and Sheldon will get the ladies out. They're vampires after all, they won't need much help. Eva, you stay behind the wheel."

I didn't remind her that I wasn't a vampire.

Eva nodded. "I'm the best driver anyway. I once drove the Indy 500."

"How do we coordinate our exit?" I wanted to know. "There are two of you in the front of the house and four in the back, including Mom and Miriam."

"When you all get to the van with the ladies, call my cell," Hedwig said. "I'll have it in my pocket set to vibrate. I'll make sure Divine is out of there too. Once the ladies disappear they'll suspect her."

"Smart," I said. "Do you do this often?"

"More often than you want to know. I'm in the tranny police myself, we do a lot of search and rescue. In fact we've worked with Metro-Dade police on gay bashing cases."

"Someday you'll have to tell me all about that," I said. "But for now please get Mom."

Hedwig got out first and rang the front bell. I could hear her shrieking dramatically about Divine as soon as Moses answered. That piercing soprano would have covered the sound of a drive-by shooting.

Sheldon and I crept around to the back and he opened the back door in about a second. It was one of those doors with a simple push-button lock and he sprung it open easily. When we got in, we spotted the back bedroom immediately since it was the only bedroom in the back. This was not a big house. The door on that room wasn't locked, it opened easily, and there were Mom and Miriam sitting on a couch watching TV. They looked perfectly comfortable and relaxed, not the least bit kidnapped against their will. They were both wearing Goth costumes, however, which made them look pretty weird. I put my forefinger to my pursed lips, indicating they should keep quiet, but they didn't say a word at first. Mom didn't look startled at all. Miriam looked surprisingly calm as well.

"Where have you been, Rhoda?" Mom whispered sternly in her schoolteacher voice. "It certainly took you a long time to get here and rescue us."

I was stunned. How did she know we were coming? Or that we'd ever come?

"Let's get going mom, we'll talk about it later."

We all crept out the back and got into the van without alarming Moses or Jesus. Mom and Miriam were in the last row of seats, Sheldon and I in front of them, and the side door was open so Hedwig and Divine could jump quickly into the front row. Now, however, the difficult part was coming—getting Hedwig and Divine out of there without arousing suspicion. We didn't say a word in the van. I called Hedwig's cell and listened to it ring repeatedly. Then we waited, Eva at the wheel. I started picking my feet. This was a horrible habit I usually kept secret, but my fingers were picked clean.

After about ten minutes Divine and Hedwig strolled out, followed by Moses and Jesus. I heard Jesus ask, "Who the hell is in that van?" He turned to Moses and said, "Check on the old ladies."

Hedwig and Divine started running towards us. Unfortunately, the house was set back pretty far from the road so they had a ways to go, over a broken concrete walk. They were surprisingly fast and agile despite their high heels. I held my breath as they jumped into the van. Eva immediately hit the gas. It was an old wreck so it didn't get going very fast, but we did manage to pull out before Jesus appeared at the front of the house with a large automatic rifle. He started running after us and spraying the van with bullets. Mom and Miriam were in the most jeopardy since they were in the back. Sure enough the next second I heard Mom yell "Rhoda, I've been hit! I'm bleeding. Stop the car."

Eva did not stop, she sped up as fast as the van could go, and eventually the shots stopped.

I was terrified for Mom. I had no idea what to do, but Sheldon immediately reassured me, "Rhoda, she's a vampire. If she can yell, she's not mortally wounded. It's very hard to kill a vampire. She will heal very quickly."

"Mom, hang on," I shouted as I turned around. "We'll be out of here soon and we'll get your wounds tended to. You're a vampire, you'll be fine. "

Sheldon turned around too and reiterated what I'd said, talking to her in a calm, reassuring voice. I could see Mom holding her shoulder, which was bleeding profusely, and groaning in pain. I felt horrible. I wished it were me who'd been hit, even though I wasn't a vampire. My own mom—a gunshot victim. I felt guilty even though this time it really wasn't my fault. Well, it was my fault because I'd had her turned into a vampire.

Miriam was looking for something to staunch the wound. I handed back a package of antiseptic wipes, which was all I had, and Sheldon gallantly took off his shirt and gave it to Miriam.

I had no idea where to take Mom,. A hospital was out of the question. Who knew what they'd make of her? Century was much too far away. Sheldon called Tess, who was staying in Miami with Rachel, a Golden Grandma. Tess agreed that they would tend to Mom. The van dropped us off there. Before leaving I gave Hedwig a huge hug, mumbled something about being eternally grateful, and promised to call before we left for New York. She hugged me back. "I should thank *you*. Tonight was more fun than I've had in months."

Divine chimed in, "That Jesus was hot. Too bad he's a stone cold killer or I'd go back for more."

Chapter Thirty-Seven

By the time we got to Rachel's apartment, Mom was barely walking. Sheldon lifted her in his arms and walked up the one flight in the Miami condo on Collins Avenue. Rachel, a tall, slim Grandma in a chic linen dress opened the door, smiled and graciously ushered us in. I couldn't imagine her hanging out in Goth clubs. I noticed how stylishly decorated her place was—with a Southwestern theme--colorful couch pillows, burnt orange walls and Spanish tile flooring. There was none of the squishy pastel furniture or beige rugs you found in Century. That was just as well because Mom was bleeding on the floor. Tile would be easier to clean.

"Put her in here." Tess gestured to a dark bedroom. As we watched, she cleaned up the wound, put a bandage over it, and said, "Fanny, go to sleep now. It's almost dawn. By tomorrow night you will be healed. Don't worry about it. The pain will also subside very quickly if you just relax."

"What about the bullet? Don't we have to remove it?" I asked, trying to summon up whatever knowledge I had of emergency medicine from watching *Grey's Anatomy* for years.

"If it's still in there it will come out by itself," Tess said confidently. "Vampires automatically expel foreign matter and are not vulnerable to bacteria. There's only one problem. She's going to be ravenously hungry when she wakes up. Miriam probably is ravenous now, but she's too polite to say so. Luckily Hannah is on duty at Miami-Dade Memorial. I'll ask her to bring us some blood from the blood bank. We don't like to do it, because technically it's stealing, but this is an emergency."

I relaxed in relief. Tess, as usual, had everything under control.

"Sheldon, I need to rest myself. And it's bedtime for you too."

"Here's your bedroom, I prepared it beforehand." Rachel showed us to a bedroom with a huge king-size bed. I couldn't see much more because it was so dark. "The blackout curtains are drawn. Everything is ready for you," she said.

I tried to thank her but she shushed me. "If we Golden Grandmas don't stick together we're sunk. Do you know what happened to her and Miriam? How she wound up kidnapped by drug dealers?"

"I haven't had time to ask. I guess we'll have to wait until she wakes up."

As soon as Sheldon and I got into bed I wrapped myself around him and started crying.

"Oh baby, it'll be OK, Mom will be OK, I promise."

"It will never be OK. She's going to be a vampire forever and have to struggle with hunger and desires she never had before. She's looks old but feels young, that's a hell of a built-in dilemma. Mom is so headstrong, I'm afraid she'll keep on getting into trouble."

"We'll keep a closer eye on her from now on," Sheldon promised.

"How will we do that? I hardly ever see you when we're home."

"That's going to change too," Sheldon took my face and kissed me. "A lot of things will change when we get back. There are a lot of things I haven't told you. It's time for me to tell you the truth."

Suddenly I realized how much constant anxiety about our relationship had been plaguing me, how much misery I was in from never knowing what was going to happen from week to week, when he would show up, when he would disappear. The possibility that Sheldon was going to open up with me, be there for me, that things would change, lifted a burden from my heart, relieved an ache so persistent that I hadn't even known it was there. I'd somehow learned to live with that pain—to almost ignore it. Suddenly I felt for the first time in a long time that maybe we could be happy together.

"You mean that, Sheldon? Will you tell me what's been going on with you? What's been keeping you from making a commitment?"

"Yes, Rhoda, I'll tell you, but not now, not until we've got your mom sorted out and I figure out a few other things about my life in Crown Heights."

"I have stuff to tell you too, secrets I've been keeping."

Sheldon smiled at me and raised his eyebrows, "I'm sure you have. I can't be the only one with secrets."

"Let's make a pledge to stop keeping secrets from each other from now on."

"I wouldn't go that far, Rhoda. I'm a vampire. There are things about me you don't want to know, that I'll never tell you until ..."

"Until when?"

"Let's not talk about that now."

I knew he was referring to me becoming a vampire someday, something which we had never actually discussed. I knew it was something I wanted when I lost enough weight. I knew it was something he didn't want, both the weight loss and me changing into a vampire. But how would we deal with me getting old, or marriage, or any of that unless I became one. But if I did would he love me as much? He always said he loved my being human. And then there was another secret, one I'd never brought up with him and hardly ever admitted to myself. I wanted a child. Yes, I was forty-one but that wasn't too late, lots of women had babies after forty. Could vampires father children? Or would I have to have in vitro with a human sperm donor? Did he want a child? How could I become a vampire and be the mother of a human child? Was there such a thing as a half-vampire, half-human? A demi-demon perhaps? Bella had a baby with Edward, maybe I could have one with Sheldon. There were too many goddamned questions and no answers, at least not yet.

Chapter Thirty-Eight

Mom woke up the next night ravenous for blood, as predicted.

"I need the elixir of life!" she shouted from the bedroom. "I am parched. I feel like I am trudging across the desert seeking an oasis."

"Can the hyperbole, Mom," I shouted back. "Tess is getting you and Miriam some blood. You're both in the doghouse here so watch it. You almost got us all killed."

"I would never kill a doggie, so no dog house please. I'll take the pigpen. I know they're not kosher but who cares, they are tasty."

I walked into her bedroom and saw that she was sitting up looking very healthy. It occurred to me that she had fed recently—on human beings. I needed to get the details but I could wait.

"I see you haven't lost your sense of humor anyway."

"No, dear, although captivity was no fun." She hadn't looked all that upset when we found them, but I didn't bring that up.

Tess walked into the bedroom with one wineglass full of red liquid for Mom and one for me.

"I'll take the Merlot, give her the Type O."

Tess laughed, "I'll leave you two to catch up."

After Mom drank her fill I suggested a walk on the beach, just the two of us. I felt she would be more open if it was just me. Tess could question Miriam. Sheldon was still sleeping. He was totally beat.

We walked across the sand almost to the water's edge. There was still a tinge of orange sunset on the horizon, and a huge full moon in the night sky. The waves sparkled as they rolled into shore gently.

"I can see why someone wrote 'Moon Over Miami,'" I said to Mom. "This is quite a beautiful sight."

"I used to dance to the Ray Charles version with your dad. It was terribly romantic," she sniffled. "I wish he was around. I wish we'd done this together, then I wouldn't be so lonely." Mom gazed far into the distance.

I wished he was around too, then I wouldn't be so worried about her.

"I didn't know you were lonely, Mom," I murmured, trying to comfort her, putting my arm around her shoulder." You never used to be. You're always busy running around with the girls. Actually I thought I was the lonely one, at least until I met Sheldon."

"Since I became a vampire I've been feeling lonely. It's like my hormones are turned on, even though I know they're not. I miss being loved. I miss sex." She looked wistful.

"Too much information, at least the sex part. Is that why you went off with those boys, who were gay, by the way, in case you didn't realize it."

There were two couples tossing a volleyball in a big circle as we walked around them. The ball went wild traveling fast in our direction. Mom grabbed it right out of the air and tossed it back.

"You didn't know I used to play girls beach volleyball, did you? I was pretty damned good. And now I'm good again."

"I knew you were a tennis whiz, but I didn't know about beach volleyball."

"I looked good in a bathing suit too, but that's over. I hate feeling young, being able to do what I used to do, but looking old. I want it all I guess."

"So, were you hoping those boys would relieve your loneliness, Mom?"

"I knew they wouldn't, not really. But it was so flattering being fussed over by them. I knew they were gay, but I've always liked the gays and they like me."

"What happened? Tell me the entire story."

"I'll try. Some of it went by in a drugged haze. They gave us all kinds of stuff. We can't drink alcohol but we can smoke just about anything."

"Where did you meet them?"

"At that reggae club. Moses asked me to dance. I was flattered of course and we danced for hours."

"Did he know you were a vampire?"

"He figured something was strange about me. He asked, 'What's a nice old lady like you doing in a place like this?'" She giggled. "I said, 'I'm not so nice." He asked what I meant and I told him. He got really curious and asked all kinds of questions about what I ate, where I got blood, whether I'd ever attacked a human and drank their blood--ghoulish questions. I was already high on something he gave me, pot or maybe even crack, I have no idea, so I answered them. I was flattered by the attention."

"How did you wind up at The Morgue?"

"They both asked if we wanted to go there after the reggae club, and we said sure. They told us it was a Goth club. I'd never heard of Goth so they explained what it was, and said they'd love us over there. They were all kids pretending to be vampires and we were the real thing. That was how it started."

"How what started?" Mom talked so softly I had to ask her to raise her voice so I could hear her.

"We starting meeting them at the Morgue a couple of nights a week, we got hooked on whatever they gave us to smoke, and to drink."

"Drink?"

"This is the hard part. They were drug dealers. They had us killing rival drug dealers and drinking their blood. It was addictive. They used us to get into these dealers' places and surprise them. Then we'd pin them down and drink their blood. It was easy, I hate to say. The blood, well, it was the most delicious stuff I've tasted in my life. I couldn't stop."

"So they just kept you around to be their hit girls?"

"No, that's not all. They could have done their own killing, they wanted us to get hooked on the blood and turn them into vampires. That's what they really wanted from us."

"You didn't do it, I assume?"

"We couldn't. We really didn't know how. I know Sheldon turned me and Tess helped, but I couldn't have turned them. Too complicated. They'd need a coffin, a burial place and all the other mishegas. I didn't know how much blood I was supposed to take from them, we were afraid that if we started sucking their blood we couldn't stop. Then I had no idea how much of our blood to give them, or how to give it."

"Thank goodness for that."

"I guess." Mom did not sound anywhere near as relieved as I felt.

"What do you mean, you guess?"

"It was exciting. I miss the killing, the blood drinking. I know I was supposed to feel guilty but they were drug dealers, I couldn't work up too much sympathy for them. Good riddance to bad rubbish."

I was too shocked to respond. Here was my sweet little mom talking about how much she liked killing and drinking blood.

"I'm going to take a swim, Mom. Join me if you want."

Swimming was the only thing I could bear to do at the moment—it had always been my escape, my best anti-anxiety medication. I'd worn a bathing suit under my capris and t-shirt, just in case I needed a salt water fix. Tonight I hoped cutting through the surf would clear my head so I could think of what to do next. Unfortunately in New York there was nowhere I liked to swim, but here was a warm, inviting ocean. Plunging into it was irresistible. Maybe I could wash away my sins, and by extension, Mom's.

She did not join me. She found a stray broken beach chair that someone had abandoned and sat down with her head in her hands while I swam furiously until I was exhausted.

By the time I got out I'd realized one thing for sure, I couldn't deal with her alone.

Chapter Thirty-Nine

Tess and Sheldon were ready for us when we came back. They handed us brochures from the After Dark Rehab Center in Miami, which they had had been discussing with Miriam, who didn't look happy.

"Fanny, they say we have to go away to rehab, that we're too far gone to just go home," Miriam said glumly.

"What's rehab?"

"You go to a center for twenty-eight days as an inpatient to regain your sobriety."

"I'm sober," Mom said. "I haven't had a drink since I became a vampire."

"Mom," I said, stretching out the middle vowel, "sober, as in no human blood. You've had a lot of human blood lately, and you got it in the worst possible way."

"You need to be detoxed, Fanny," Sheldon chimed in. It won't be terrible, much easier than for alcoholics or drug addicts. You just have to be weaned from human blood and get used to animal blood again. While you're there you go to individual and group therapy to talk about your problems, whatever caused you to fall off the wagon in the first place."

"Problems? I haven't got any problems." Mom protested.

"You were just telling me about how lonely you feel, how you want what you can't have, Mom. That doesn't mean there's anything wrong with you, but these are problems in your lifestyle."

"Fanny, a lot of vampires go through extreme emotional as well as physical changes when they're turned. You, being older, have even more to face." Sheldon went over to her, took her hand, and looked sympathetically into her eyes. I noticed he diplomatically said "older" instead of old. Sheldon was such a sweetie.

"We can go together," Miriam said. "It won't be so bad."

Miriam, who had always had a calming effect on Mom, took her usual role as the voice of reason.

"When you get back to Century, you'll keep going to B.A. meetings," Tess added. "And from now on we're staying away from clubs and young men. We need to reduce temptation."

"That sounds dreary." Mom sounded disappointed. "I really loved going out dancing."

"If you were an alcoholic you wouldn't hang out in bars. This is the equivalent in B.A. terms, Fanny," Tess said.

"Have you been to the rehab?" Mom asked Tess plaintively. "Is it a nice place?"

"It's lovely, Fanny. Yes I've visited. I'm a B.A. counselor and have done some counseling there with vampires who have lost their abstinence. It's a farm, like our farm, with lots of yummy live animals, individual cabins with private baths and views overlooking the ocean."

"Can I go with her?" I was feeling anxious about sending Mom anywhere alone right now.

"No," Tess said. "This is just for vampires. You could visit for a family session, though. They do counsel families who may be enabling."

"Enabling? Am I enabling her?" I asked Tess.

"You worry too much about her. You feel responsible for her. You blame yourself if she gets in trouble. You're too quick to come to her rescue."

"What's wrong with that?"

271

"She has to be responsible for her own actions, and take the consequences without you constantly rescuing her."

"If I hadn't rescued her this time she would have killed half of Miami. Are you saying I shouldn't have done what I did?"

"Really, Rhoda, don't get insulted. I'm not saying anything. It would probably be helpful to you to attend Bal-Anon when you get back to New York. You'll learn how to deal with having a vampire in the family. There are a lot of issues you need support with.

"What's Bal-Anon?"

"Just like Al-Anon, Bal-Anon is a support group for humans who love vampires—you're involved with two vampires. You'll meet other humans who are in the same boat as you are, who are dealing with the same issues, such as should I or shouldn't I?"

"You mean should I or shouldn't I become one?"

"Yes. That's a huge issue for humans in your position."

She was right. It was a huge issue in my life, and I needed help from people in my boat—humans who loved vampires. Sheldon really couldn't help since he had too much at stake; he couldn't really understand.

"OK, I promise to go when I get back."

"Good, now we have to get Mom and Miriam to After Dark. It's not far from here. I'll take them. It's best if family doesn't come along—too emotional. You and Sheldon need to get back to your own lives."

"At least I'll know you're safe, Mom. That will be a huge relief."

"Can I make phone calls?" Mom asked Tess. "I want to call Rhoda and tell her how I'm doing."

"Sure, but not for a few days. They like the residents to settle in before they start calling out. Rhoda knows you're in good hands, so she won't worry. Am I right, Rhoda?"

She was right. "I feel so much better knowing that Mom's going to be taken care of by someone besides me—people who know about bloodaholism," I told her. "Mom, remember what you used to tell me when I was a teenager. 'If you can't be good be careful'? That goes double for you."

I went over to Mom and gave her a huge hug goodbye. She hugged me back a little too hard—she still didn't know her own strength.

Chapter Forty

Sheldon flew me back to Fort Lauderdale to Mom's condo that night to get some rest before going back to New York. It was the first night we'd had alone in what seemed like weeks. I was giddy with relief that the ordeal was over. This time I lay on his back and held onto his neck while flying, a somewhat more precarious position, but relaxing once I got the hang of it. Being caressed by balmy Florida breezes was a whole lot more fun than freezing in the sky over New York in winter. Sheldon carried me lazily over the ocean, where we were unlikely to be seen by passersby. The moon was still full; it seemed to hang on the horizon, reflecting a huge globe of light onto the waves. What a magical view. I didn't think I'd ever get over the thrill of being flown by Sheldon.

"How long can you do this, Shel? Could you fly us back to New York?"

"I'm only going about fifty miles an hour, Rhoda," he shouted up at me. "I doubt you'd want to go over a thousand miles at that speed. It's fine for a short trip—in nice weather—but what if it rains? Let's take Delta instead."

By the time we got back to Mom's condo I was ready to stand on solid ground. Flying was nice, but hanging on was strenuous. I kept being afraid I'd fall off. We fell into each other's arms before we even got inside—I was hungry for a meal, but even more ravenous for him. We hadn't made love in weeks, or it seemed like weeks. He was incredibly loving this time, caressing me, murmuring I love yous, going slow and easy. I felt like I was entering another dimension of pleasure. When we finally pulled apart after

274

what felt like hours, I realized I had carpet burn on my tush. We'd never made it to the bed.

We were suspended between our two lives. Mom was in rehab, Goldie and Hershel were in Brooklyn, my assignments were on hold. It was just me and Sheldon. But I still couldn't stop worrying about our future.

"Shel, what are you going to do about your mishpucha issues when we get back?"

"I wish I could forget about them," he said, with a wistful look. "I'm so tired of being responsible, of being a rabbi. I've had more fun down here than I've had in a hundred years of my boring undeath."

"Fun? You think rescuing Mom from drug dealers was fun?" I was horrified.

"It was exciting. I met Hedwig and the tranny police. I danced at a nightclub. I glamoured a bad guy and got away with it. I helped execute a daring rescue. I almost got my head shot off by an assault rifle. That's my idea of fun."

He was still a guy, I supposed, despite being a vampire sans testosterone. "Maybe you could work for the V.B.I. when we get back."

"Now that would be fun. Great idea! But that doesn't solve our relationship problems. What do we do about Goldie, and my *minyan*?"

"The only solution—if it is a solution—is a relationship counselor," I suggested. "But who would counsel us. Human or vampire? Jewish or goyish?"

"Reb Shmuley would counsel us," Sheldon said. "He's the Hasid who's on TV all the time giving relationship advice. He's a buddy of Michael Jackson, who looks more like a vampire than I do. They call him Dr. Ruth with a yarmulke. It would be a challenge for him."

"And he could even put us in his next book, or talk about us on his radio program or *The Today Show*," I added, thinking that he was the perfect choice. "I bet Shmuley would kill to be the first vampire-human relationship counselor."

"He's got an office in Crown Heights. I'll make an appointment for us," Sheldon said.

Chapter Forty-One

Reb Shmuley might have had an office in Crown Heights but he saw only film crews there—his wall of books looked very erudite in photos. Couples in need of advice met him for lunch at the Basil Pizza and Wine Bar, a trendy Crown Heights kosher restaurant that specialized in gourmet pizza made in a wood burning oven, arugula salads and avocado ice cream. It was a duplicate of similarly pricey non-kosher Manhattan eateries.

Everyone turned around when Shmuley walked in. He was a big, burly guy in a tailored black suit, with a patterned tie and neatly trimmed black beard, who looked very young despite his reputation as a *tzaddik*. The minute he opened his mouth, however, his booming voice, air of authority and undeniable charisma made it clear how he had become a TV star. We sat at a table in the corner that was somewhat private, but it seemed that every other patron knew Shmuley and greeted him loudly. Some came up to chat.

"Can we speak in confidence here?" Sheldon asked him nervously. "Won't we be overheard?"

"What's the big deal?" he replied. "Everyone knows everyone's business in this neighborhood. You live here. Everyone knows you."

"Shmuley," Sheldon whispered. "I'm a vampire and Rhoda isn't. That's what we're here to discuss. Everyone doesn't know that."

"You have your own building and your own *minyan* and everyone knows you're kind of weird—that you only come out at night. So what! You haven't eaten any Jews so you're OK by us."

"We only eat animals, just like you," Sheldon said. "Maybe not kosher because we drink blood but Jewish law says it's OK to eat non-kosher for survival."

"By me you're kosher." Shmuley smiled, waving at a couple in the corner who were dressed in the Ultra-Orthodox manner, the man in a black hat and long side curls and his wife in a wig and clothes that covered every bit of skin. "An observant Jew is kosher, no matter what he has for dinner."

"I helped those two," he said. "Taught them to have kosher sex—now they pretend they're a goy and a Jew having an adulterous affair. She may cover everything up on the outside, but under that long skirt, Victoria's Secret."

"TMI, Shmuley," I said.

"OK, OK, I'll shut up." Of course he knew that TMI means too much information. Shmuley was up to date on all the latest lingo.

"Speaking of food, how about a goat cheese pizza?"

"Sounds delicious," I said.

"Can you drink wine, Sheldon?" Shmuley asked. "I know you're not eating pizza."

"Well I can drink some, as long as it's red, preferably sweet. I love Manichevitz."

"Ugh, I like the kosher dry varietals from California, but I'll order a bottle of cough syrup for you." Shmuley called over the waitress and ordered a medium goat cheese pizza, cabernet for him and Concord Grape for Sheldon. I guess he figured I'd drink Manichevitz too. Actually I loved it, though I'd never admit it to my more sophisticated friends.

"So tell me about you two. What's the problem? I assume it's not boredom with your sex life?" He leered at Sheldon.

"The problem is my *minyan* and my *golem*." Sheldon got right to the point. "I can't leave Crown Heights and my *minyan* because there aren't any male vampires to replace me—I suppose they could do without my rabbinical services but not without a *minyan*. And Goldie, my golem, hates Rhoda because she's not Orthodox and not a vampire. She refuses to obey me anymore. She's out of control and I'm afraid she'll go on a rampage. You know those stories about golems. I can't get close enough to her to de-animate her."

"Goldie thinks she's his mother," I added, "And she acts like a typical Jewish mother—except worse."

"That's right," Sheldon said. "She's an expert guilt-pusher. And now she's started threatening me. She says she'll out me to the vampire hunters if I don't drop Rhoda."

"Plus we want to get married, but Sheldon doesn't want to make me into a vampire and I don't want to become one until I lose fifty pounds. You know what I mean?"

"I don't know why all Jewish women want to be skinny. We like a little zaftig,"

Shmuley said.

"Not this much zaftig." I said, pointing to my hips.

"Well maybe a little less zaftig," he agreed.

"I like her just the way she is, human and zaftig," Sheldon said, a little too loudly for my comfort. "In my day the most sexy women had a lot of meat on their bones, today they look like sticks."

"I have to think about these problems." He nodded sagely. "They're not what I'm used to counseling couples about. I mostly get the 'she or he doesn't want to have sex with me anymore' issues. Let's wait until we eat. I think better on a full stomach."

Luckily the pizza arrived at that moment, and we dug in. I thought better on a full stomach myself. Sheldon sipped at the Manichevitz, licking his lips happily. I know he loved the sweetness of it. Blood is salty.

Reb Shmuley ate most of the pizza and asked for another glass of wine before telling us he'd solved our problem.

"The *minyan* problem is the easiest to solve. Why does the tenth man have to be a vampire? Is there any reason?"

"Actually no," Sheldon said. "I just assumed …"

"I can get you a tenth man easily. I know every Hasid in Crown Heights. There are many Lubuvatchers who would be happy to pray with you at my request."

Sheldon's mouth dropped open. "I can't believe it would be that easy. I assumed we were outcasts in the Hasidic community."

"Times have changed," Shmuley reassured him. "We Lubuvatchers need all the Jews we can get, alive or dead. We want to bring Jews back into the fold, and that includes your *minyan*. If we send you a tenth man, you're one of us."

"You're sure about that? Won't he be frightened?"

"Hey, we Lubuvatchers have seen *Twilight.* I assume you don't sparkle."

"So, is that it? You all sorted out?" He turned away from us and waved to a friend who just walked in. "Hellooooo Dolly. Did you get on *The Today Show*? That's Dolly Bernstein, the famous matchmaker. All the singles are going to old-fashioned Jewish matchmakers these days even if they're not Orthodox. We work together sometimes. She makes the matches, I do the counseling."

"How about the human/vampire thing?" I asked him, trying to fit in a couple more questions before Regis walked in.

"I don't know anything about that," Shmuley said dismissively. "Not my department. You don't have to make a decision right away, do you? How long have you two been together?"

"Just a few months," I said.

"Give it a year and come back to me. Young people today are so impulsive."

"We're not young," Sheldon said. "I'm a hundred years old and Rhoda's forty-one."

"What's the rush. You're immortal and she's peri-menopausal. Do you want to have children?"

"We haven't discussed it," I said hastily. "I doubt it's possible."

"Where there's a will, etc." Shmuley nodded sagely. "I don't know about vampires but in vitro worked for a few of my clients."

Shmuley decided we were finished when yet another admirer shrieked, "Shmuley, Shmuley, you must come over here and meet my cousin who works for the *Times*, he's a fan of yours." He got up, grabbed his coat and was about to leave when Sheldon grabbed his arm. "Wait, wait. What do I do about Goldie? How do I de-animate her?"

"Rhoda has to do it."

"What?" I squealed. "That's impossible!"

He turned to Sheldon. "Only a human woman can de-animate a female golem who is out of control. Didn't you know that? She was only obeying you because she felt like it."

"How would I know that? My father made her, not me." Sheldon sounded as panicked as I felt.

"When a man makes a golem to be his servant he's asking for trouble, golems are very possessive," Shmuley said. "There is no free lunch."

"What do I do?" I was hysterical. "She's huge, she might hurt me."

"Not if you know what to say. Check my website. Click on the 'golem' link. I've got a surefire golem de-animation script."

He handed Sheldon the check, shook his hand and said, "Good luck. You're going to need it."

Chapter Forty-Two

The de-animation script on Shmuley's website was daunting. It confirmed that the person doing the de-animating had to be the same sex as the golem; it listed the Hebrew letters you had to recite, none of which I could understand, although I had to memorize them; it revealed the secret name of God that had to be used as well. Worst, it said the de-animation had to be done at daybreak when the golem was at her weakest for some reason. That meant Sheldon couldn't be there. I was on my own. Except for Charlene who had volunteered to back me up and recite the words with me. Bless her *goyishe* heart, she'd even agreed to learn a little Hebrew for a friend. As it turned out more than a little Hebrew was involved. Luckily Sheldon could coach us, even if he couldn't be there to help.

At least he felt bad about it. "I'm so sorry I can't be there, Rhoda, but Goldie could go nuts and decide to attack me while I sleep if she gets angry enough. I've seen her when she's really mad. She could hold me hostage."

"How reassuring. I've just confronted killer drug dealers and now I have to go mano a mano with a killer golem." I strolled over to the window and looked down at Second Avenue nostalgically, realizing that I might not see it again. I might not see Sheldon again for that matter.

"Now you're making me feel guilty," Sheldon said, smiling. "But don't worry. I'm used to it. I have total faith in you. Goldie is no match for my Rhoda." He must have been in denial because she was twice my size.

The process was ridiculously complicated, involving the "combination technique." I couldn't just erase the first letter from Goldie's forehead because she undoubtedly wouldn't let me near her. My journalism background came in handy because I was used to interviewing experts in various esoteric disciplines and explaining their theories in plain language.

It seems that each limb of the golem has a corresponding letter mentioned in the Sefer Yetzirah, a book of Kabbalah, and to create a golem this letter has to be combined with every other letter of the Hebrew alphabet to form pairs. Then a more general permutation is done (again for each limb separately) for each letter of the Hebrew alphabet with every other letter into letter pairs. This second, basic method of combination is called the "221 gates." Then each letter of the alphabet has to be combined with each vowel sound (apparently for each limb). That concludes the first stage, the formation of the golem's body. In the second stage you must combine each letter of the alphabet with each letter from the Tetragrammaton (YHVH), and pronounce each of the resulting letter pairs with every possible vowel sound. In this case the use of the Tetragrammaton, even though it is permutated, is the "activation word."

As if the above wasn't nonsensical enough, to destroy a golem you have to recite it all backwards, while circling the golem in a counterclockwise direction. The golem web pages noted that when done right, the process should be combined with meditative, paced breathing and pronunciation techniques. Some of these methods would have taken the Kabbalist thirty-six hours or more of uninterrupted meditation to complete!

I didn't understand a word, but Sheldon, in his rabbinical wisdom, boiled it down to a formula I could memorize. He wrote a transliteration of the Hebrew for me and Charlene. I would recite the words while circling Goldie, while Charlene read from the written version and coached me when I stumbled. Charlene, who had studied

Latin as part of her Catholic education was also good at memorizing esoteric languages.

This all took about a week, during which time Sheldon stayed at my apartment. After studying we got to make love for the rest of the night. It was heavenly. I definitely knew I could live with this man forever--that I wanted to live with him forever. I got so involved in my Hebrew studies that I almost forgot what I was studying for, but when I finally got it all down pat Sheldon reminded me that I actually had to confront Goldie.

At 5 a.m. on a cold February morning, Charlene and took a cab to Crown Heights. The sun was rising as we crossed the Brooklyn Bridge, which I would have found beautiful if I wasn't so scared. When the cabbie dropped us off in front of Sheldon's building, Charlene and I silently opened the outside door with the key we'd gotten from Sheldon, trudged into the vestibule, and up the three flights of stairs. When we got to his door I whispered to her, "Do you have the script ready? I hope I can remember my Hebrew alphabet...backwards. Actually I wouldn't know the difference either way."

"Let's get it over with, Rhoda. Open the goddamned door." Charlene was nervous as well. Goldie wasn't likely to spare her either if she went on a rampage before I could deactivate her.

When the door opened we both saw Goldie lying on the couch and snoring loudly. Who knew golems snored? One meaty arm was over her face and the other dropped to the floor. Her dress was hiked up, showing her huge thighs which looked like tree trunks, except smooth and gray. Her ratty underwear looked like it was left over from the Victorian era. She didn't look scary until she opened one eye and stared at us, her mouth curling down in an angry frown. She hopped up faster than I thought possible for a creature of her bulk, and glared at us.

"Is that Rhoda? Why are you here? Where's Sheldon? Who's this shiksa?" Did she have some kind of *shiksa* radar? How could she have known Charlene was a shiksa?

"Goldie, I'm really sorry but I'm here to deactivate you. You wouldn't let Sheldon do it so I have to. I promise Sheldon will reactivate you in a while, after we get married." I had no idea why I was telling her the truth, but I couldn't think of a story that would be the least bit convincing. We were so busy during the last week memorizing Hebrew that I forgot to come up with a cover story.

"Are you some kind of meshuganah? Goldie asked, looking bewildered. "Do you think I'd let a little *pisher* like you deactivate me. I'm twice your size. I could smash you against this wall until your brains leaked from your skull."

Goldie lurched towards me with her arms out, looking like the bride of Frankenstein. I wanted to start the deactivation process but there was no way I could walk around her while she was moving.

"Charlene, get behind her and try to slow her down."

Charlene obediently got behind Goldie but then stood there, looking bewildered. She obviously had no idea what to do.

"Grab her under the arms," I suggested.

"This thing is three times my size, Rhoda. She'll kill me."

Goldie lumbered around towards Charlene and growled, "You bet I will, *shiksa* whore."

At that point I grabbed Goldie's arms from the back and tried to subdue her. I don't know what I could have been thinking. She wheeled around again, picked me up with those huge arms if I were a squirming puppy, and carried me towards the window.

"I'm going to drop you out this window and squish you like a bug,"

Frantic, I started yelling for help. If I made enough noise, someone was bound to hear me.

"Shhh," she whispered to me. You don't want to wake the vampires."

"Yes I do!" I yelled. "Maybe one of them will help me."

"Why would they?" It was Goldie's turn to look bewildered. "You're not even Jewish."

"Yes I am," I insisted. "Look, I'm wearing a wig."

Goldie was strong, but she was also slow. Golems weren't known for agility. As she took one hand off me and grabbed my hair, trying to rip it off, I took the opportunity to elbow her in her iron gut, which knocked her off balance just enough so that I could get away from her. I scampered off and cowered in the corner, rubbing my head which was now missing a clump of hair, but at least I was temporarily out of her clutches.

"Bravo, Rhoda," Charlene cheered.

"Now I'm going to strangle you," she said, coming at me. "No one will hear you if you're choking."

"If you did that Sheldon would never forgive you"

She looked at me, stunned. That had obviously never occurred to her.

"He doesn't care about you, you're, you're …" She was at a loss for words. "You're just a *koorvah*," she flung the word at me as if I would crumple when I heard it.

"What's a *koorvah*? I never heard that expression."

Goldie had obviously lived with a rabbi long enough to know that answering a question superseded all other business.

"Whore, prostitute, bad woman," she said calmly as if she were instructing a class.

287

"Sheldon and I are getting married, Goldie, and there's not a thing you can do about it. Give up now and we'll reanimate you—sometime in the future."

At that Goldie came to an abrupt halt, put her head in her hands, and started wailing loudly. The sound was chilling. It didn't sound human, but like an enormous wind-up toy winding down.

"He can't marry you, I won't allow it." she wailed. "Sheldon is my baby. My little *boytshick*. You can't have him, you *nafka*." She started lurching again in my direction almost drunkenly

"I have no idea what a *nafka* is either, but I'm not one."

"You're a piece of *schmutz*, that's what you are," Goldie shouted.

"Rhoda, you have to get started," I heard Charlene say behind me. "She's not going gently into that good night."

I quickly started walking towards the bedroom to confuse her, since it happened to be in a counterclockwise direction, and chanted what I'd memorized in a low voice. I figured chanting was more authentic because that's how Hebrew prayers were recited.

"Nooooo," Goldie yowled, putting her hands over her ears, and turning her head away from me. "Not the Tetragrammaton, anything but the Tetragrammaton, that will kill me forever. You'll turn me into dust. Stoppp, please stoppp." She growled in a low voice, sounding like she was in excruciating pain.

I felt sorry for her but I didn't stop, I knew I had to keep going or all would be lost. Goldie reeled around the room holding her head and screaming. Then her hand went to her forehead and she scraped wildly at the letters, removing the *Aleph*. As soon as it was gone, she keeled over like a felled oak.

"Geez, Charlene. She committed suicide. I guess that was better than being turned to dust. Should we just leave her there?"

Charlene gazed down at her. "They say golems have no soul, but her devotion to Sheldon seemed pretty soulful. Yes, let's leave her there. She must weigh 300 pounds and I'm not about to throw my back out getting her up."

Chapter Forty-Three

I was shivering in the chilly fall night air, sitting on a tiny plastic folding chair that didn't support my entire rear end, under a huge tent at the Woodstock Jewish Congregation's High Holy Days Services. Sheldon was sitting next to me, not shivering, a beatific expression on his face. I realized he hadn't worshipped in a synagogue since the nineteenth century. I glanced around and noticed that everyone was wearing white, which is what you're supposed to wear on Yom Kippur, while I was wearing a peasant dress with a loud pattern. Why the hell couldn't I have worn something white, or at least beige? I mentally surveyed my closet and noticed some white garments I overlooked, upset about my sartorial faux pas. Sheldon was dressed in full Hasidic garb, with a long beard that he let grow for the holidays. He didn't exactly fit in among these hippie types, many of whom were wearing white jeans, but I noticed he was getting a lot of admiring stares. He looked remarkably handsome and imposing.

Over a thousand people were singing, swaying and praying, raising a storm of atonement although not much body heat. Rabbi Jonathan, a youthful folk singing incarnation of a charismatic rabbi along the lines of the Bal Shem Tov, led us in singing rounds, one section of the tent at a time. It was like a Jewish tent revival. We sang "Avinu Malkenu," and I started weeping. I decided I was crying for happiness because Sheldon and I were finally praying together, at a shul that couldn't care less about our inter-life relationship or religious choices. We got up and started singing with our arms around the people in our row. I had no idea who they were but felt grateful to them for accepting us.

290

The Woodstock Jewish Congregation had been Shmuley's suggestion. Sheldon had asked him where we could *davven* together. "We need a synagogue that will accept us. Rhoda is not going sit behind a *mehitza*."

"Have I got a shul for you," Shmuley had announced in his most authoritative voice. "This congregation takes everyone, from gays to Buddhists to transsexuals to Catholics—no questions asked. Vampires will be no big deal to them. Check out wjcshul.org. Their High Holy Day services are awesome."

He was certainly right about that.

After the service we went back to our room at the Inn on the Millstream, a lovely little bed and breakfast in Woodstock with a wide lawn, and comfy Adirondack chairs facing the rocky stream that runs through town. I got to eat two breakfasts, which wasn't good for my diet but the food was delicious. We'd rented a car to get up here since it was a bit too far to fly, and brought heavy curtains for the windows so Sheldon could sleep. He could only come to night services, which was a shame, but it was better than nothing—Erev Roshashana, Kol Nidre, and Neilah service after Yom Kippur were inspiring, especially Neilah, where we sang and swayed, lit aromatic herbs and wafted the smoke around, and listened to a multitude of shofars being blown.

"Sheldon, are you thinking what I'm thinking?" I asked him when we got back to our room

"You mean about what position we should do it in? Where we should do it? How about outside in the woods? We've never done that before."

"You have a one-track mind, like all men. Reb Shmuley would be proud of you. No that's not what I mean. I mean that we should move here. We'd have a synagogue that welcomes us, and we could buy a farm and keep animals for you and for visiting vampires. We're close enough to New York, so we could charge for feeding, plus you could get certified to declare the meat kosher and then we could sell it—just like they do in Florida. Might be a good business. We could be change facilitators too, providing a coffin and burial plot, and feeding after the change. All for a price, of course."

"Rhoda, I'm a diamond cutter not a butcher."

"We'll figure that out later. What do you think of moving? We could buy a house. No more tiny apartments."

"Wouldn't you miss Charlene? And your other friends?" he asked.

"She'll come to visit, and I'll make new friends. We both will. These old hippies will accept us for the odd couple we are."

"I'll think about it," Sheldon said. That was good enough for me at the moment. I'd learned from The Rules to leave well enough alone. He was not given to impulsive decisions like me—he had to think about things for a long time first. Of course, he was used to having a long time.

After seeing Shmuley we had started spending more time together, because now there was a tenth—human—man to make a *minyan*, but we still weren't living together. I had been going to his place and sometimes he came to mine. Sheldon was still the rabbi for his vampire *minyan* and he wanted to show up occasionally. Plus he felt terrible about Goldie, whom he had upended and put in her customary unanimated place in the corner. I insisted he turn her to the wall.

"She was such a good golem," he would intone solemnly every once in a while, with a gloomy expression.

I ignored him because I remembered how menacing she'd been to me. I wanted to be with Sheldon all the time but I didn't want to travel to Crown Heights so often, although we'd gotten into the habit of him flying to Manhattan to get me. Woodstock was a solution that might work for both of us.

"I heard from Mom yesterday, by the way," I told him while we were lying in bed at The Millstream. "She said she wants to come to visit but where is she going to stay? I don't have room for her and no way she'd stay in Crown Heights. She wants to do the town in Manhattan. Concerts, theatre, museums. Some museums have night hours now."

Since we'd rescued her, Mom was doing pretty well. She went to Fort Lauderdale B.A. regularly and Tess reported to us weekly about her progress. She was the star of vampire rehab because it involved a lot of group work and Mom knew how to work a room. In a social situation she was at her best—plus the younger vampires got a big kick out of her and Miriam. They became pets again, but in a good way. Mom still talked about finding a young boyfriend, though, and that was worrisome. I just put it out of my mind.

"Where will she stay if we move up here?" he asked.

That proved Sheldon was at least considering it. "We'd keep my apartment in the City. It's not that expensive. Well, it is that expensive but we can sublet it."

"Let's talk about this later. Take a walk with me by the stream."

It was a balmy night in early September so we strolled down to the water and sauntered along the rocks. There was a big flat rock right in the middle of the rushing waters and Sheldon jumped over to it. As soon as we got there he started pulling my jeans down and my t-shirt off.

"Sheldon, this is public. Someone could see us."

"It's midnight, it's Woodstock, no one will care. It's a moonless night."

It was incredibly exciting to be totally naked, both of us, in the middle of nature with water roaring around us. Sheldon lay me gently on the rock but made sure to hold my hips up as he entered me, managing to keep my whole body elevated a little so I wouldn't get battered on the hard surface. I was making love while floating. He kissed me deeply over and over, the sound of the water adding to the intensity of our lovemaking until after a while I felt like I was being carried downstream while being caressed all over. We made love on that rock for a long time, until I was exhausted. After it was over we both lay on our backs, holding hands, looking at the starry sky.

I was stunned when he leaned over me and said, "Darling, I will make you a vampire if it means you will be mine forever." Now I finally knew, without any reservations, that we were *beshert*, meant to be together.

About the author

Erica Manfred is a freelance journalist, humorous essayist, and author of two non-fiction self-help books, the most recent being *He's History You're Not; Surviving Divorce After Forty*, published by Globe Pequot Press in 2009. Her articles and essays have appeared in *Cosmopolitan, The New York Times Magazine, Ms, New Age Journal, New York Newsday, Village Voice, Woman's Day, SELF, Ladies Home Journal,* and many other publications. Erica lives in Woodstock, New York with her dog, Shadow. Brought up by Jewish parents who spoke Yiddish but avoided religion, she received her Jewish education at the Woodstock Jewish Congregation, which welcomes Jews from all backgrounds, from atheist to Orthodox. Visit her at
www.ericamanfred.com
Email her at askerica@gmail.com

www.ingramcontent.com/pod-product-compliance
Lightning Source LLC
Chambersburg PA
CBHW030029180626
46810CB00001B/276